Dornford Yates is the pseudo

into a middle-class Victorian family, his parents scraped together enough money to send him to Harrow. The son of a solicitor, he qualified for the Bar but gave up legal work in favour of his great passion for writing. As a consequence of education and experience, Yates' books feature the genteel life, a nostalgic glimpse at Edwardian decadence and a number of swindling solicitors. In his heyday and as a testament to the fine writing in his novels, Dornford Yates' work was placed in the bestseller list. Indeed, 'Berry' is one of the great comic creations of twentieth-century fiction, and 'Chandos' titles were successfully adapted for television.

Finding the English climate utterly unbearable, Yates chose to live in the French Pyrénées for eighteen years before moving on to Rhodesia where he died in 1960.

BY THE SAME AUTHOR
ALL PUBLISHED BY HOUSE OF STRATUS

Adèle and Co.
As Berry and I Were Saying
B-Berry and I Look Back
Berry and Co.
The Berry Scene
Blind Corner
Blood Royal
The Brother of Daphne
Cost Price
The Courts of Idleness
An Eye For a Tooth
Fire Below
Gale Warning
The House That Berry Built
Jonah and Co.
Ne'er Do Well
Perishable Goods
Red in the Morning
She Fell Among Thieves
She Painted Her Face

DORNFORD YATES

AND BERRY CAME TOO

HOUSE OF
STRATUS

This edition published in 2001 by House of Stratus, an imprint of Stratus Holdings plc, 24c Old Burlington Street, London, W1X 1RL, UK.

www.houseofstratus.com

Typeset, printed and bound by House of Stratus.

A catalogue record for this book is available from the British Library.

ISBN 1-84232-963-4

To JILL

I have an old patch-box – the flapjack of yesterday – on which is written VIRTUE IS THE FAIREST JEWEL THAT CAN ADORN THE FAIR. *As no one else that I know, you show forth these pretty words, for while you are lovely to look at, the steady light which belongs to your great, blue eyes would diminish any gem to be found in the Rue de la Paix.*

BERTRAM PLEYDELL
(of White Ladies, in the County of Hampshire)

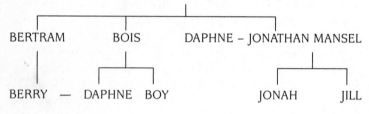

BERTRAM　　BOIS　　DAPHNE – JONATHAN MANSEL

BERRY — DAPHNE　BOY　　JONAH　JILL

Contents

NOTE

It is the duty of a tradesman to consult the convenience of his customers, though it be to his own derision. For that reason alone I make bold to say that, *mutatis mutandis*, the action of this book may be presumed to have taken place during the summer which followed the first chapter of BERRY AND CO. and preceded the second chapter of that book.

DORNFORD YATES.

1

How the Knave Set Out for Cock Feathers, and Berry Made an Acquaintance He Did Not Desire

Seated upon the terrace of the old grey house, I found myself wondering whether the precincts of White Ladies had ever seemed so fair.

The fantastic heat was over, the cool of the day was in, and a flawless sundown was having her gentle way. A flight of rooks freckled the painted sky; oak and elm and chestnut printed their fading effigies on grateful lawns; the air was breathless; sound, catching the magic, stole on the ear. The fragrance of a drenched flower bed rose from below the balustrade; the five green peacocks, new-washed, sparkled upon the low, yew wall from which they sprang; like some loudspeaker, the stately press of rhododendrons was dispensing a blackbird's song; and, beyond the sunk fence, a comfortable order of haycocks, redolent of Aesop and Virgil, remembered a golden world.

A slim shape passed between tree-trunks, and an instant later our two-year-old Alsatian, surnamed the Knave, moved gracefully upon the scene. Full in the open he stopped, to stand, like any statue, surveying the rolling meadows that made the park. So for a long moment, the beau-ideal of sentinels, all eyes and nose and ears, discharged his fealty: then the fine head came round and he glanced at the house. Steadily we regarded each other. Presently I lifted a hand… As though a wand had been waved, the statue leaped into life, flashed to the rhododendrons, plucked a ball from their fringe and cantered towards the terrace, sabre-tail at the carry and good-humoured eyes alight with confidence.

As I rose to meet him, my cousin's clear voice rang out.

"Boy, where are you? Boy!"

Before I could answer, my cousin sped out of the library on to the flags.

Jill has never grown up. Though she is more than twenty, she has the look and the way of a beautiful child. Her great, grey eyes and her golden hair are those of the fairy-tales. Who runs may read her nature – a lovely document.

Naturally forgetting all else, the Knave went bounding to meet her and touch her hand. She stooped to smile into his eyes. Then she lifted a troubled face.

"Oh, Boy," she cried, "do come and do what you can. Berry says he won't go tomorrow." She caught at my arm. "And he simply must. I mean, it's all been arranged – we've something on every day. And we can't throw everything up just because it's turned hot."

"I'll come," said I. "One moment."

I took her arm and turned again to the lawns and the pride of the spreading boughs and the sparkling yew. Then I pointed to the fabulous haycocks, each with his sugar-loaf shadow, rounding the scene.

"Were you calling me?" I said. "Or were you calling Boy Blue? He's lying under that big one. …And the Queen of Hearts has just gone. Lean over the balustrade and you'll smell her perfume. And a blackbird's been singing to the peacocks. It's only a matter of time – one day he'll sound the note that'll bring them to life. Some evening like this. And now can you blame Berry for hating to leave all this and go up to town?"

"I know, I know. I hate going. I can't bear leaving it all. But I do want to go to Ascot, and – and – any way, it's too late now. Everything's all arranged."

"All right, sweetheart," said I. "I'll do what I can."

"I don't believe you want to go."

"I don't," said I. "I'm a man. I don't want to have to dress up, and I'm much more comfortable here than I should be at any hotel. But I quite agree with you that it's too late now. I've got to start now, and so has Berry. I don't suppose he's serious."

"He is, Boy, really. I know by the look in his eyes."

"Come," said I, turning, "and let me see for myself." Followed by the Knave, we passed through the cool of the house, across the drive and on to the lawn beyond.

My sister was sitting upright in an easy chair: finger to beautiful lip, she regarded her husband gravely, as one who is uncertain how to retrieve a position which one false move will make irretrievable. Six feet away, Berry lay flat upon the turf: his eyes were shut, and but for the cigarette between his lips he might have been asleep; by his side was a tankard capable of containing an imperial quart.

As we came up –

"They say," said Berry, "that the hippopotamus – "

"Thank you," said his wife. "If it's anything like what you say they say about the rhinoceros – "

"I mean the rhinoceros," said Berry. "They say – "

Before the storm of protest the rumour was mercifully withheld.

"Disgusting beast," said Daphne. "Just because you don't want to move – "

"My object," said Berry, "was to divert your attention. Continued concentration upon the unattainable is bad for the brain."

I put in my oar.

"You can't back out now," I said bluntly.

Berry opened his eyes and rolled on to his side.

"And Satan came also," he said. "Never mind. Who's 'backing out' of what?"

"No one," said I. "It's too late. You know it as well as I."

My brother-in-law sat up.

"Look here," he said. "At great personal inconvenience I had arranged to accompany those I love upon a jaunt or junket to the metropolis. I now find that owing to the large anticyclone, unexpectedly stationary over Europe, my health will prove unequal to the projected sacrifice. Except that this discovery has caused me much pain, there's really no more to be said," and, with that, he shrugged his shoulders, picked up his tankard and drank deep and mournfully.

I took my seat upon the lawn.

"And what about me?" I said. "D'you think I'm going to enjoy it?"

"I've no idea," said Berry. "I've never considered the point." He glanced at his wrist. "Let's see. At this hour tomorrow you will have already dined and will be walking sharply in the direction of the car park." He raised his eyebrows. "I'm not sure you won't be running – if you're to be in time for the second act."

I set my teeth.

"You solemnly undertook to – "

"I know," said Berry. "I know. But this heat is an Act of God. In view of that, the contract is null and void."

"Rot," said I. "Supposing I said the same."

"If you had any sense, you would – all of you. But perhaps you can do without sleep. Unhappily, I can't. The last heat-wave in London shortened my life. Why? Because I rose in the mornings more dead than alive. And there's the rub. But for the nights, I'd do it. But for the nights, I'd strut and fret at Ascot, dine in broad daylight and stagger off to the play. But go without sleep I will not. Damn it, it can't be done. If you're to live like that – 'to grunt and sweat under a weary life,' *you – must – have – sleep*."

Here he drank again with great violence and then lay back upon the turf.

There was a little silence – which I employed in wondering how to attack a contention with which I entirely agreed. Then I caught Daphne's eye and turned again to the breach.

"That's so much wash," I said boldly.

"So much what?" said Berry.

"Wash," said I. "And you know it. I don't say Town will be pleasant, but that's not a good enough reason for chucking everything up. Besides, this heatwave will pass."

"Certain to," murmured Berry. "That's why they call them waves."

A step on the gravel behind us made me look round.

Then –

"Excuse me, sir," said the butler, "but the ice-machine has just failed. There's ice enough for tonight, sir, but I thought I should tell you at once."

"All right, Falcon," I said. "I'll be along…later on."

"Very good, sir."

As I lay back, my brother-in-law sat up.

"What are you waiting for?" he said. "As imitation electrician to this establishment – "

"What does it matter?" I murmured. "We're going away."

"And what about me?"

I shrugged my shoulders and stared at the reddening sky.

"I've no idea," said I. "I've never considered the point." My brother-in-law choked. "There is, however, a real electrician at Brooch. It's too late to telephone now: and tomorrow is Saturday; but he'll come on Monday all right, if you put in an SOS."

"On Monday?" screamed Berry. "*Monday?* Sixty hours of this weather without any ice!"

"If you put the butter – "

"Look here," said Berry shakily. "If you tell me where to put the butter, I shall suggest an even more appropriate depository for the pineapple chunks." He looked round wildly. "I suppose the idea is blackmail. 'Go to London, or stay here without any ice.' "

"Well, it serves you right," said Jill. "If..."

Berry rose to his feet, clasped his head in his hands and took a short walk. Plainly concerned at his demeanour, the Knave accompanied him.

As the two passed out of earshot –

"We've got him," breathed Daphne, excitedly. "Well done, Boy."

"Thank Fate and Falcon," said I. "They played clean into my hands."

Berry returned from his stroll, picked up his tankard and drank what was left of his beer. Then he turned to his wife.

"Do you subscribe to this treachery?"

"If it's going to get you to Town."

"I see. You'll allow that long-nosed leper to – "

"I will," said Daphne cheerfully.

With a manifest effort, her husband controlled his voice.

"My love," he said, "I beg you." He put out a beseeching hand. "Think of your health."

"My health?"

"Your blessed health," said Berry piously. "I had hoped by my withdrawal to dissuade you from putting in peril – "

"You wicked liar," said Jill.

"Remove that child," said Berry, excitedly. "Take her away and hear her catechism. Teach her how to spell 'reverently.' Just because I venture to hint that only a half-baked baboon who was bent upon self-destruction would choose this moment to – "

The sudden brush of tyres upon gravel cut the philippic short and switched our eyes to the drive.

A moment later Jonathan Mansel, Jill's brother, brought his Rolls to rest twenty paces away.

"Jonah?" cried Jill, and put a hand to her head. Her surprise was natural. Her brother lived in Town, and was to have dined with us the following day. And now he had come to us, when we should have gone to him.

We watched him leave the car and Carson, his servant, slip into the driver's seat.

As he reached the lawn, he nodded.

"Wrong way round," he said shortly.

"What's the matter?" said Daphne, rising.

"Plague broken out?" said Berry.

Jonah kissed his sister and then sat down on the sward. "No air in London," he said. "I've had no sleep for two nights."

There was an electric silence.

Then –

"Choose your drink," said Berry, brokenly. "Only say the word. I'll mix it myself – all of them. What about a spot of Moselle? And the glass washed out with curaçao, before it goes in?"

"Shandy-gaff, please," said Jonah. "About a third to two-thirds. You might bring a jug."

Shouting for Falcon, Berry ran to the house.

Hitherto speechless with horror, Daphne and Jill let out a wail of dismay.

"But, Jonah…"

"It's quite all right," said Jonah, producing a pipe. "I've rooms for us all at Cock Feathers. Used to be Amersham's place, but it's now an hotel. Fine old house, twenty minutes from Ascot and just about forty from Town."

I am prepared to wager that when the sixth Lord Amersham parted with his seat, Cock Feathers, it went to his heart to dispose of so lovely a thing. A sixteenth-century manor, in 'specimen' condition within and without, perfectly lighted and warmed and cunningly brought into line with the luxury mansion of today is not to be sneezed at: but add that its priceless ceilings have rung with the hearty laughter of Henry the Eighth, that Anne Boleyn has strolled in its formal garden and a baby Queen Elizabeth clambered up to its windows and played with her toys before its hearths – that these things are matters of fact and not of argument, and you will see that, standing in its broad meadows and squired by timber planted when it was built, Cock Feathers has that to offer which is not often for sale.

We had seen its glory by day: and now as we stole up the drive to find it sleeping beneath a peerless moon, I know that I blessed the foresight which Jonathan Mansel had shown. The peace about us was absolute, the air abundant and cool: the noisy pageant of London seemed stuff of another age. Yet thirty-five minutes ago we had been subscribing to the revelry of a stifling nightclub.

Berry alighted, to inspire luxuriously. Then he glanced about him, and a hand went up to his head.

"It's all coming back," he said visionally. "I knew it would. Directly I saw this place, I knew I'd been here before." He pointed a shaking finger. "Anne Boleyn was up at that window, laughing like blazes and clapping her pretty hands; and Henry the Eighth was down here, stamping holes in the flags. He'd just hit his head on the lintel, but she hadn't seen that bit and thought he was going gay. And then he looked up and saw her… It was an awful moment – I think we all feared the worst. And then Wolsey dropped his orange, and his mule kicked him well and truly while he was picking it up. I still think he did it on purpose. Any way, the situation was saved. They heard the King's laughter at Windsor – that's twelve miles off."

"And what did Wolsey do?" bubbled Jill.

"Rose to the occasion," said Berry. "I can see him now. He just looked round: then he pointed to the mule, whose name was Spongebag. '*Non* Spongebag, *sed* Shoelift,' he said."

Here the wicket-door was opened, and, Daphne and Jill alighting, Jonah drove off to the coach house to berth the Rolls beside his.

One by one, we entered – delicately. It was extremely easy to hit your head.

As I bowed to the presumptuous lintel –

"Captain Pleydell, sir?" said the night-porter.

"That's right," said I.

"I've a telephone message for you, sir." He turned to a pigeon-hole. "Come through about ten o'clock."

I glanced at the note. Then I called to the others and read the message aloud.

Very much regret to say the Knave cannot be found. Gave him his dinner myself at half past four, but has not been seen since. Respectfully suggest the dog may have gone off to find you.

Falcon.

When I say that the news shocked us, I am speaking no more than the truth. For one thing, we had no doubt that the butler's surmise was correct; never before had all of us left the Knave. For another, the roads were death traps: the Knave had never run free upon anything greater than a lane. Finally, we cherished the dog. On the day that he came to White Ladies, an unsteady scrap of a playmate that knew no gospel but that of faith and goodwill, he scrambled into our hearts, and now, after twenty-two months, his understanding and beauty, his devotion and handsome ways had made him as much one of us as a dog could be. He was 'lovely and pleasant in his life': and now, though he came direct, that life was to be imperilled for seventy treacherous miles.

After a dreadful silence –

"What do we do?" said Daphne. "My brain's a blank."

"We go to meet him," said I. "Not now, but tomorrow morning, as soon as it's light."

"That's right," said Berry. "We go to bed early tonight, and at dawn on Monday morning – "

"Monday?" screamed Jill. "You can't wait till – "

"I meant 'today'," said I. "We'd better tell the porter to call us at five."

"I see," said Berry, thoughtfully. "If we don't clean our teeth, that'll give us a good two hours." He laughed wildly. "What did I come here for? To be able to sleep. And now you suggest… Of course, you must be out of your mind. We shan't be able to see straight. As for looking about for dogs – why, you'll have your work cut out to keep the car on the road."

"We must drive by turns," I said stoutly. "It's got to be done. And the one who isn't driving must keep a look-out."

My brother-in-law swallowed desperately. Then –

"Someone," he said, "must stay here – in case the dog comes. I mean, cases have been known… Exactly. Very well. If we all go out, and he gets here to find us gone – I hardly like to say it, but our faithful, footsore friend will set off again."

"Oh, I can't bear it," said Daphne.

"I know," said Berry. "I know. Neither can I. And if I stay here in the drive – "

"That's Daphne's job," I said grimly. "Jill must go with Jonah, and you with me."

"Normally, yes," said Berry. "Normally, yes. But here we must have the best sight. And my eyes – "

"You can wear your glasses," said Jill.

"That's just what I can't do," said Berry. "I left them behind."

"I didn't," said his wife. "They're in my dressing-case."

Looking ready to burst –

"Splendid," said Berry, shakily. With starting eyes he regarded the dial of his watch. "And now I think I'll retire. I'm not tired really – I've only been on the job for nineteen hours. But as I've paid for the room – Oh, and who's going to ring up Falcon?"

"What for?" said Jill.

"What for?" snarled Berry. "Why, to know if the Knave's come back. I'm not going to get up at five and stagger about half-conscious, looking for a dog that's sprawling about in his basket, sleeping it off."

"I wish I could believe it," wailed Daphne. "I'd cheerfully get up at four, if – "

"All right. You do it," said Berry. "Ring up Falcon at four. If he says – "

"You can't do that," said his wife. "They'll all be asleep."

With an unearthly laugh, Berry lay back in his chair and drummed with his heels upon the floor. Then he leapt to his feet and looked round.

"Understand this," he said. "You can all please yourselves, but before I look for a needle in a bottle of hay I've got to be credibly informed that the needle is there. And that's my last word. If anyone rouses me and, having roused me, is unable to assure me that the Knave was not at White Ladies ten minutes ago, I'll commit an aggravated assault upon his person. I may do it any way. But without that information whoever does it is doomed."

With that, he stalked out of the hall just as Jonah came in.

After a hasty discussion, it was arranged that I should ring up Falcon at half past six and that, failing the news we hoped for, I should arouse the others without delay. Then, without more ado, we went heavily to bed.

For anxiety we had just cause. At large in the countryside, a stranger in a strange land, a swift Alsatian was in truth a needle in a bottle of hay. Between our home and Cock Feathers lay a very network of roads. And the Knave was unacquainted with traffic. And the roads on a handsome Sunday were sure to be crammed.

It was eight o'clock of that lovely mid-summer morning before we were on the road.

The order of our going was dreadful. I had not spoken with Falcon: more dead than alive, I had swayed for ten minutes by the switchboard, listening to the night porter wrangling with the unseen, only to learn that the telephone line to White Ladies was 'out of order.' For all we knew, therefore, the Knave had reappeared and was now asleep in his bed. This conception was distracting enough, but Berry's insistence upon it can be better imagined than described... Between us we had but one map, and our efforts to learn its lessons and then to agree and remember our several casts not only proved explosive but wasted valuable time. Finally it was determined that Jonah and Jill should drive direct to White Ladies by the way by which we had come, whilst Berry and I scoured the district, which, had he set out across country, the Knave might fairly have reached. As for communication, Jonah was to ring up the Granbys at twelve o'clock. The Granbys lived at Dewdrop, perhaps forty miles from Cock Feathers: we knew them well. Over all, the hopelessness of the venture hung like a thundercloud. For all that, there was only one Knave. If action was futile, inaction was not to be borne. The reflection that, if he were doomed, we should, at least, have made what efforts we could, spurred even Berry up to the starting gate.

It was shortly before ten o'clock that the incident occurred.

Some thirty-five miles from Cock Feathers, Berry and I were moving in country we did not know, and proving a web of by-roads that sprawled between two highways. I was driving and watching the road itself, while Berry was up on his feet, looking over the quickset hedges and scanning the woods and meadows on either side.

For the hundredth time –

"The point is this," said my brother-in-law. "If I knew that the Knave was in trouble and somebody told me where, I'd run five miles in my socks to help him out of his grief. He's been a good dog to me, and I like his ways. But the game that we're playing now would make a congenital idiot burst into tears. I mean, be honest. What sort of…"

I heard the words die on his lips.

As I glanced up –

"*My God, there he is,*" screamed Berry, pointing a shaking hand. "*Stop the car, Boy. Stop. He's making for – KNAVE!*"

As Berry shouted, the horn of some car behind us demanded way. No human voice could compete with so deafening a blast: but, what was worse, because of the bend ahead, whoever was driving continued to hold his horn-button down.

Raving incoherence I could not hear, Berry flung out of the Rolls, tore to a gate we had passed, and hurled himself over into the meadows it kept.

Then the oncoming car went by, like some hag-ridden squall, and I stood up in the Rolls to see Berry running like a madman towards a billowing wood. The Knave was not to be seen. Unable to hear Berry's voice, because of the horn, he had, no doubt, left the meadows and entered the wood.

For a moment I wondered whether to follow Berry or to drive on past the wood before leaving the car. Then my brother-in-law settled my doubts by frantically waving me forward and making encircling gestures which none could have failed to read.

Trembling with excitement, I took the seat I had left. The incredible had happened. If Berry was right and it was the Knave he had seen, we had achieved such a feat as no patrol had ever achieved before. With seventy miles of blind country in which to fail, we had actually intercepted…

As I set a foot on the clutch, I heard a car coming behind, and since I was at rest, I waited, to let it go by.

It did so – with squealing brakes.

As it stopped, twenty paces ahead, the police on its running-boards left it, to dash to my side.

The sergeant blared in my ear.

"Follow that car jus' gone by – with the 'ighpitched 'orn."

"Yes, but – "

"Name o' the Law," snapped the sergeant, and swung himself on to the step.

Mechanically I let in the clutch…

As the Rolls moved forward, I sought to protest again.

"Why can't you – "

"Sorry, sir," said the sergeant. "Step on it, please." He jerked his head at the car from which he had come. "Can't do it with that: it's only a fifteen-'orse."

There was nothing to be done. Knave or no Knave, the police had to be obeyed. Reflecting rather dismally that the sooner I caught the car, the sooner I should be released, I let the Rolls go…

As we flashed round the bend ahead –

"What's he done?" said I.

"Who knows?" said the sergeant, darkly. "As like as not, they're jool-thieves. A packet o' jools was taken an hour ago. Anyway it's a stolen car."

Neither the police nor I will ever forget that drive. The narrow, tortuous ways were forbidding high speed: crossroads gaped upon us with their mouths: blind corners frowned and threatened, and scores of road signs warned us – to no avail. Flirting with sudden death, we flouted the lot. Hereabouts, as luck would have it, the traffic was slight: such as there was we outraged, cutting in, thrusting and squeezing, as a man that elbows his way. That shouts and yells should pursue us was natural enough. Our withers were unwrung. 'In the name of the Law'…

Clinging to the nearside door, a sad-faced constable presently opened his mouth.

"There's their 'orn," he said grimly.

The man was right.

As we flashed up a rise, I heard the ear-splitting note, and as we swooped over the crest, I saw the car we were chasing turn off to the left.

The two police-whistles rang out…

I had to slow for the corner, but though, by the time we were round, the other was not to be seen, I knew very well she was less than a furlong away. So did the police.

"We'll have 'em yet," said the sergeant. " 'Ow many was there, Dane?"

"I only see one," said Dane. "But there may 'ave been others there as was bendin' down."

"What d'you want me to do?" said I.

"Pass him, sir, an' then block him. We'll do the rest."

My question was premature. Though the Rolls was the swifter car, there were breakers ahead.

I rounded a bend at sixty, to see the car we wanted with another on either side. For an instant the three seemed coherent: then the car on the right left the road and took to the ditch, while its ruthless oppressor went on to make good his escape.

"There you are," said the sergeant. "Wot did I say? No one don't drive like that who hasn't got more in his sleeve than a stolen car. I'll lay they've got the stuff on them. Put her along, sir, please. If he's on the road much longer, there'll be bloody murder done."

I did my best to obey, but the traffic was heavier now, and though I continued to take every sort of risk, I could hardly compel a third party to take such a course as might very well break his neck. Then, again, the sins of the thief were visited on my head, and drivers whom he had jostled declined to be jostled again. Wherever the road was open we went up, hand over fist, but the checks were our undoing and stole our winnings away. Do what I would, the fellow was keeping his distance: when another five minutes had passed, he was still a furlong ahead.

From the dance he led us, I judge that he knew the roads, for, while he turned and doubled like any hare, he never once led us into a village street. As for me, I was utterly lost. I knew neither where I was nor the way I had come, for the pace at which we were moving demanded a concentration which left me aware of nothing but a winding black and brown ribbon, all edged with green.

All of a sudden the luck of the road became ours. The traffic grew sensibly lighter, and gaps which the thief had to force seemed to open for us. And a hill rose up to help us – we took it with the rush of a lift. …As the Rolls flew over the crest, I saw the stolen car not seventy paces ahead.

"Got 'im now," breathed the sergeant.

I began to think how I should pass…

We were fifty paces behind when I sighted the furniture-van. This was going our way and was travelling fast. Its breadth of beam was hideous. The mammoth was using three-fourths of the narrow road. Had this been one foot less wide, neither the thief nor I could have made our way past: as it was, if the van gave way, a possible passage would open – a gauntlet for fools to run.

" 'E's done," said the sergeant. " 'E's blocked. If 'e tries to go by at that pace – "

"He can do it," said I. "We'll both be glad to be through, but it can be done."

"Gawd 'elp," said Dane, and tightened his grip on the door.

In the course of the chase we had taken far graver risks; but, while we had taken the others before there was time to think, this risk could be weighed and measured, the chances of success could be pondered and the consequences of failure not so much pictured as perceived. In a word, to be honest, the risk was less grave than it seemed, for the swaying bulk of the van diminished the width of the road.

An instant later the ear-splitting horn rang out…

The van never slackened its speed but it lurched to its left, thereby for the first time disclosing what lay ahead. A fork in the road was coming: in another ten seconds the road was to split into two. And the right-hand prong of the fork – the only one I could see – was no more than a lane.

As the stolen car squeezed by, I sounded my horn: but all the answer I got was an outstretched hand.

As I clapped on my brakes, the van swung across my bows…

And then we were all in the lane – stolen car, van and Rolls…but the car was in front of the van, while the Rolls was behind.

That the race was as good as over was painfully clear. The lane accepted the van with perhaps six inches to spare. At certain points a bicycle might have gone by: but nothing larger.

The next seven minutes were crowded.

I, of course, could do nothing but follow the van, whose pace had now fallen to ten or twelve miles an hour; Dane tried, without success, to make his way past its bulk to the driver's cab; and the sergeant described heavy traffic "wot didn't ought to be on the roads at all" with a compelling savagery of metaphor which did my heart good. As for the van itself, the banks of the lane being high and the gradient steep, the stench of oil and the scream of labouring metal will stay with me till I die.

Then at last the nightmare was over, the van was a thing of the past and we were upon a fair road, smooth and straight and empty – a perfect place for the capture which we had hoped to make.

There was a pregnant silence. Then –

" 'Eart breakin'," said the sergeant. "That's wot it is."

"Well, that's that," said I, and wiped the sweat from my face. "Have you any idea where we are?"

"No idea," said the sergeant shortly.

"Well, I must get back," said I. "I left my brother-in-law where you picked me up. D'you know where that was at all?"

"Well, it was this side of Basing, but…"

"It mayn't be now," said Dane, miserably.

"I must get back," I said firmly. "And I'd better take you along. Between us we ought to be able to find the way."

With that, I increased my speed, proposing to turn the car round at the first side-road. A moment later I saw the mouth of a road sixty paces away…

It was as I came abreast of the mouth that the sergeant let out a yell.

"Look there, sir," he raved. "Look at that."

Twenty paces from the mouth of the road the car which we had been chasing was leaning against a paling with two of its wheels in the ditch.

What had happened was clear as day. For once the thief had taken a corner too fast.

Dane was the first to get there. From the jerk of his head I knew that our quarry was gone. The sergeant fell upon two cyclists who were standing, saucer-eyed, in the midst of the way.

"What d'yer know?" he barked. "Did yer see the smash?"

I could not hear the answer, but after one or two passes had been exchanged I saw the cyclists point to a pleasant beechwood which rose, as a cliff from deep water, out of the blowing meadows that lapped the road.

A moment later the police had climbed the fence and were lumbering over the grass.

I like to think that they did not expect me to wait. Be that as it may, I had turned the Rolls round and was moving before they had reached the trees…

The burden of the hour that followed was of a kind which I should be glad to forget. My object was, of course, to return by the way I had come: but to recognize something which you have never seen requires, I suppose, an instinct with which I am not endowed. Thanks to the finger-posts, I soon found out where I was, and I knew to within five miles where Berry and I had parted and the Rolls had been commandeered. But I was without a map, and so surely as some road seemed familiar it led me away from the district for which I believed I should make. I was not so much lost as bewildered, and I turned and backed and wandered until I was sick of life. What was worst of all, I knew nothing. It might not have been the Knave that Berry had seen. If it was, I presumed he had caught him. The thought that he had failed where I might well have succeeded was scarcely bearable.

For eighty blazing minutes I sought my brother-in-law. Then at last I threw in my hand and drove all out for Dewdrop, to keep my appointment with Jonah and give him my wretched news. I need hardly say that I ought to have started before: but I know no fascination like that of the hope forlorn. The glaring fact remains that I entered the Granbys' lodge gates exactly half an hour late for the call which I was to have taken at twelve o'clock.

As I brought the car to rest in front of the creeper-clad house, a girl I had never set eyes on appeared at the head of the steps. To say she was attractive means nothing. Had her figure been all her fortune, she would have been rich: but the light in her gay, brown eyes and the curve of her small, red mouth were unforgettable.

As I took off my hat, she nodded.

"Good morning," she said. "Have you any news of the Knave?"

Feeling rather dazed –

"Berry's got him," I said.

"He hasn't!"

"I believe he has," said I. "The whole thing's rather mixed up."

"I should think it was," said the girl. "You wait till you hear the message I took from your cousin just now. But how on earth did you find him?"

Shortly I told my tale. When I had finished, my lady raised her eyes.

"And they told me England was sleepy. Never mind. Come and see what I know."

I left the car and followed her into a hall. This was cool and dim, making a blessed contrast to the heat and the glare without.

My companion touched my arm and pointed to a well-furnished tray.

"That's meant to be used," she said. "Your cousin said you liked beer."

As she moved to a writing table –

"I should like," I said, "to remember you in my prayers. Of course I can refer to you as Hebe, the darling of the gods. But – "

"Try Perdita Boyte, Captain Pleydell. My mother's renting this house. And when your cousin rang up, neither of us saw any reason why I shouldn't bear a hand. I've a Sealyham away in Boston that I wouldn't care to lose."

"It's perfectly clear," said I, "that you are as sweet as you look," and with that I poured the liquor and drank her very good health.

Miss Perdita Boyte inclined her beautiful head. Then she took up a sheet of paper and held it out.

"This is what your cousin dictated – for you to read. Look it through, Captain Pleydell, and see if you feel the same."

I took the sheet curiously.

Falcon never sent the message we got last night. It never came from White Ladies. It couldn't have come, for the telephone wire was cut. All the same, that message was true. The Knave is not here. THAT MESSAGE IS JUST THE MESSAGE WHICH FALCON PROPOSED TO SEND LAST NIGHT AT ELEVEN O'CLOCK: BUT WHEN HE PICKED UP THE RECEIVER HE FOUND THAT THE LINE WAS DEAD.

Make what you can of this. I'm inclined to think that the Knave was decoyed away by the fellow who cut the wire. You know. Prospective burglary. But all is all right at While

Ladies, and nobody seems to have tried to get into the house. And why the telephone message?

Get your wits to work, for I'm fairly beat. Any way I'm seeing the police. Any news to The Fountain *at Brooch up to half past one.*

"Why the telephone message?"

I looked up sharply, and things about me took shape.

"Exactly," said I. "That's, so to speak, the keyhole. Find the key that fits it, and we shall unlock the truth," and, with that, I emptied my tankard, sat down upon a sofa that offered, and re-read my cousin's dispatch with a hand to my head.

When I looked up again, Miss Boyte had taken her seat on the arm of a mighty chair. As my eyes met hers, she shook her head gravely enough.

"It's not fair, is it?" she said.

"You're very understanding," said I. "That's just how I feel. Things like this can't happen: so when they do, it upsets you. One's armed to cope with Life – not with *Alice in Wonderland*. I mean, messages may go astray; but I never heard of one fetching up which had never been sent."

Miss Boyte frowned.

"Don't make it too hard," she said. "The message must have been sent."

I fingered my chin.

"That I'll admit," said I. "I received the message, so the message must have been sent. But it didn't come from White Ladies. And only the staff at White Ladies could have known what message to send."

There was a little silence.

At length –

"You spoke of a keyhole," said Miss Boyte. She hesitated. Then: "Whilst I've been waiting for you, I've been trying…various keys."

I looked at her very hard. Delicate eyebrows raised, the girl was regarding the palm of an exquisite hand. But that was a pose. Voice and fingers declared the excitement she felt.

At once I caught the infection and got to my feet. "Go on," I cried. "Go on. What keys have you tried?"

My lady frowned.

"I may be quite wrong," she said. "And I don't want to make things worse by – "

"If I think you're wrong, I'll say so. Please say what you think."

Miss Boyte looked up.

"First, tell me this," she said. "If thieves broke into White Ladies, what would they get?"

"Silver," said I. "Nothing else. My sister's got her jewels with her. And so has Jill."

"Quite so," said Perdita Boyte. "Well, here's the key that I fancy – I may be wrong. The word 'decoyed' made me think. Supposing *you've* been decoyed. You and your cousin and Berry – I don't know his other name. Decoyed away from Cock Feathers, in search of the Knave."

"Good God," said I, staring upon her, as well I might.

"Listen," said the girl. "Assume that a gang is after your sister's jewels. They know your movements, of course: and they see that your stay at Cock Feathers is going to give them their chance. But they must get you out of the way. *That's 'why the telephone message,'* saying the dog you worshipped had disappeared. In fact it was true. But how could the thieves know that? So they cut the wire – to prevent your ringing up Falcon and learning that the message was false."

For a moment my brain zigzagged, and I was aware of nothing but the glowing face before me and the light in the big, brown eyes. The pose I had noticed was gone, – and, with it, the smart young lady, called Perdita Boyte. A child was leaning forward – an eager, beautiful child, natural and sweet as the breath of her parted lips.

"And – and the car I chased?" I stammered.

"I'll bet that was them," said the child. "It all fits in."

I fell on the telephone like a man possessed. "Cock Feathers," I cried. "Near Amble. I think it's Amble 29."

"Amble 29," replied a dispassionate voice…

Waiting for the call to come through, I covered my eyes and went over the ground again.

Daphne and Jill had worn their jewels last night: they had returned too late to have them put into the safe: the news of the Knave's disappearance not only had filled our minds but had brought us all abroad before the office was open and we could deposit the gems – for my sister had risen with us and had proved the gardens and meadows before we had left… If Perdita Boyte was right and a gang was after those jewels, we had as good as given them into their hands. As for the car I had chased, if the jewels were not at Cock Feathers, it seemed extremely likely that they had been in that car. Time and distance allowed it. The thought that, but for that mammoth blocking my way – The stammer of the telephone-bell blew my reflections to bits.

Miss Boyte had the spare receiver almost before I could speak.

"Is that Cock Feathers? I want Mrs Pleydell at once."

After a maddening delay –

"At last," wailed my sister's voice. "Oh, Boy, I'm beside myself. I've been trying to get you or Jonah since half past nine. All our jewels have been stolen, and a message has just come through that Berry's under arrest."

"Berry under arrest?" I screamed. "But what has he done?"

"I've no idea," wailed Daphne. "I thought you'd know. They say he's at Basingstoke. And everything's gone, Boy. Jill's pearls and my bracelets and all. Have you found the Knave?"

"I think so. At least, I don't know. I thought Berry had."

"I don't understand," cried Daphne. "If you were with him – "

"I wasn't. I – I had to go on. When I saw him last he was running after the Knave. At least, he said he was, but he may have been wrong."

Miss Boyte began to shake with laughter.

"May have been wrong?" shrieked Daphne. "D'you mean he's out of his mind?"

"Of course not," said I. "But I couldn't see any dog. He simply said 'There he is,' and ran off to a wood."

"Ran after a wood? But you said – Besides, who ever heard – "

"*Off to*," I yelled. "*Off to*. But I tell you, I never saw him. It may have been a goat, or something."

"A what?" screamed my sister.

"A *goat*," I roared. "A thing with horns. G for Godfrey."

Miss Boyte shut her eyes and clapped a hand to her mouth.

"Well, what about it? Whose goat?"

"Nobody's goat. I only said – "

"Where's Jonah?" said Daphne, faintly. "I can't go on talking to you. And I'm not in the least surprised that Berry is under arrest. But what's to be done about it? Will you go and bail him out or whatever one does?"

"I will. And you ring up Jonah. You'll get him at *The Fountain* at Brooch. Tell him – "

"I'll tell him all right," snapped my sister. "Meanwhile that poor, blessed dog – "

"Is at Basingstoke," said I. "Basingstoke for a monkey. If Berry was right when he – "

My sister rang off…

I addressed myself to Miss Boyte, who was wiping the tears from her eyes.

"Overwrought," I said shortly. "That's what's the matter with her. And of course, I'm not at my best. But you can't compress a social upheaval into a three-minute call. And when you don't get the right questions…

"Yes, I noticed that," said Miss Boyte. "Never mind." She picked up a hat. "May I come to Basingstoke with you? I – I'd like to be in at the death."

As she moved to a looking glass –

"My dear," said I, "the idea of going without you had not occurred to me. Twenty minutes ago you were a luxury: now you have become a necessary. Besides, I have a feeling there's more to come. When Fate puts on her Cap of Coincidence – "

" 'Is Saul also among the prophets?' "

From the mirror a brown eye mocked mine.

"I beg your pardon," said I. "There is no goddess but Beauty, and Perdita is her prophetess. I imagine that the prison gates of Basingstoke will fly open at your approach. And if you'd come on to Cock Feathers, I'm sure you'd make Daphne well. Besides, I want to be seen with you. Anyone would."

A child had hold of my arm.

"Did you think I meant to rebuke you? I didn't, indeed. I meant – oh, it doesn't matter. I'll love to do all you say."

I took the pointed fingers and put them up to my lips. "A little more," I said, "and I shall go down on my knees."

An hour and a quarter later we ran into Basingstoke.

As I was handing Perdita out of the Rolls –

"I think," she said, "there's somebody trying to catch your eye."

I turned to see Constable Dane descending the police station steps.

As a hand went up to his helmet –

"Hullo, Dane," said I. "Did you get him?"

Dane permitted himself the ghost of a smile.

"Got them both, sir," he said. "And every bit of the stuff."

"Not the emerald bracelets?" I cried.

The constable started and stared.

"There was two bracelets," he said cautiously.

I threw my hat in the air.

"And a diamond necklace," I said, "and a beautiful rope of pearls."

Dane put a hand to his head.

"An' three good rings," he said. "But – excuse me, sir, but 'ow on earth do you know?"

"It's easy enough," said I. "It's my sister's stuff. The moment I heard she'd been robbed, I wondered if I'd been helping to chase the thief."

Dane blinked from Perdita to me.

"Well, there's a go," he said slowly. "It's like one o' them story-tales. An' another thing. 'Ow could you 'ave come here to identify stolen jools wot you didn't know 'ad been found?"

"I haven't," said I. "I came here to bail a man out."

My words might have been a spell.

Open-mouthed, wide-eyed, the constable seemed to recoil. Then –

"B-bail a man out?" he stammered. "Not a – not a man wot's got an Alsachun an'…"

His voice tailed off.

I was doing a double-shuffle and Perdita was laughing to glory and hanging on to my arm.

"The Knave!" I shouted. "He's got him! Two o'clock of a glorious sunshiny day, *and all's well!*"

"Hush," bubbled Perdita, "hush. You'll be under arrest yourself if you don't look out."

I pulled myself together and turned to the station steps. But these were empty. Constable Dane was gone.

I returned to Perdita.

"Come along, my dear," I said. "Come along and be in at the death."

One minute later we entered a sultry charge room, to find the 'Inspector on duty' frowning upon his own writing and wiping the sweat from his face.

As we came in, he looked round. Then he got to his feet.

"Yes, sir?" he said abruptly.

"I've come," I said, "to bail out my brother-in-law. There's some mistake, of course. I mean – "

"What's his name, please?"

"Major Pleydell."

The inspector raised his eyebrows.

"D'you know what he's charged with?" he said.

"I can't imagine," said I. "When I – "

"Felony," said the inspector. "*Having in his possession stolen goods.*"

"I shan't be the same," said Berry. "No man born of woman could stand what I've stood today and be the same. I rather think I died more than once. There are, so to speak, hiatus in my recollection. I am unable to recall those circumstances immediately subsequent to the more brutal of the shocks which I received. I submit that on such occasions I was without my ghost. Bludgeoned beyond endurance, the spirit had fled… I mean, take the opening of the masque. There was the Knave *within earshot*. He couldn't have failed to hear me, but for that horn – that *vox humana* of Hell. I shouldn't even have had to get out of the car. But a foul and malignant Fate selected that vital moment to drown my voice, and I had the unspeakable anguish of seeing a miracle happen and then the fruits of that miracle run out like a basin of water because I couldn't shove in the plug. Well, that's the sort of thing that uproots the soul. I don't remember leaving the Rolls or how I got into the field. The first thing I do remember was falling down. Blear-eyed with emotion, I failed to perceive, until too late, that the meadow had been recently tenanted by cows which I have every reason to believe not only were magnificent specimens but enjoyed the best of health. The havoc I wrought was too awful. Had I been desired to obliterate all traces of their tenancy, I couldn't have done so more thoroughly. When I got up you could hardly see where they'd been.

"Well, I passed on into the trees, alternately lamenting the Vandalism and trying to whistle for the Knave. I regret to say that I did more damage, by falling, to what was an excellent grove. Finally I emerged, hoarse and torn and bleeding, plastered with new-laid dung and sweating with a freedom which verged upon the obscene – to see a speck in the distance lope into a second wood...

"I must have proceeded – somehow. Somehow I must have traversed the largest expanse of meadow I ever saw and somehow I must have savaged that second wood, for the next thing I knew was that twenty-five paces away a brook was flowing through pastures and the Knave was standing knee-deep in one of its pools. Very wisely, no doubt, he had stopped for a wash and brush up. Be that as it may, there he was, not only as large as life, but as fresh as paint. And I didn't have to call him. I fancy he heard my breathing before I was clear of the trees...

"Well, you know his idea of a welcome. If you've been away half an hour, it's grievous bodily harm. I've a notion I tried to run, but of course I hadn't a chance. I just went down before him, as corn goes down before the blade. When I came to, he'd damned near licked my face off and was rolling upon my body for all he was worth. Exactly. My condition appealed to him. I was, in his eyes, wearing a wedding garment.

"When it was all over, I managed to crawl to the brook. There I made the sort of toilet one tries to forget: and then we lay down together to take some rest. He seemed to like the idea, which was just as well: myself, I was past speaking. The wave of reaction alone would have submerged a sage.

"How long I slept I don't know. I should think for about six minutes – it may have been more. The fact remains that when I awoke and sat up, *the Knave was gone*.

"You may say what you like, but a brain must be seated in rubber to weather a shock like that. And the physical effects were frightful. Without the slightest warning, the whole of my contents gave way. How far they fell I don't know, but I rose from that sunlit sward, the shell of a man. My very screams rang hollow. My lights had failed.

"When I couldn't shout any more, I crossed the stream by wading and stumbled towards a beechwood, a drive and a chip away, reviling myself like a madman for not having tied the dog up. Not that he had a collar – he must have lost that by the way – but mine would have done him nicely, and my tie would have made him a lead. This would have entailed no sacrifice. All that my raiment was fit for was household use. I retained it for decency's sake, but a tramp would have had to be paid to take it away.

"And then I heard the Knave bark – from the midst of the wood...

"He heard me that time all right – it's astounding the noise you can make when the hounds of Hell have got you by the nape of the neck – and he bounded out of the wood as I came to the trees. For a moment we mixed it, as usual; and then, before I could get him, he'd gone again.

"I give you my word, I thought the dog was bewitched. And then, as I started to run, the scales of misunderstanding fell from my eyes. *I'd forgotten my instructions to Boy – to take the Rolls on and try to encircle the wood. But Boy had carried them out, and now the Knave had found him and was doing liaison between us as best he could.* I mean, the thing was too obvious...

"After that, I took it easy.

"Sure enough the Knave returned, committed a hasty assault and then flicked back out of sight by the way he had come. At my own pace I followed.

"My theory was perfectly sound, except for the basic fact that *it was not Boy*. Liaison had been maintained with a man I had never set eyes on in all my life. There he was, with his back to a beech, and the Knave was leaping about him, nosing his clothes and pretending to bite his dispatch case and barking with an abandon that makes you feel that something may snap.

"Well, of course I called the dog off and I said the usual things. I confess I felt my position. As you may have gathered, I wasn't looking my best, and I hate being made a fool of at any time.

"The stranger went straight to the point.

" 'Can't you stop him barking?' he said.

" 'More,' said I. 'If I can only get him, I'll take him away.'

" 'That's all right,' said the other. 'You keep him here. I want to get on, I do.'

"Well, I collared the dog somehow, and the fellow went off through the wood by the way I had come. And now believe me or not, but if I hadn't held him tight the Knave would have run by his side. An utter stranger, mark you. And a tough-looking cove, at that. And there he was whining and trembling as though his dearest friend was walking out of his life.

"I tried not to lose my temper, because that dog's a good dog; but, considering what it had cost me to get to his side, the sudden fancy he'd taken stuck in my throat. Fancy? Infatuation – for a bounder he'd never dreamed of ten minutes before.

"I got my collar on him and made my tie into a leash, but the moment he started straining I knew it was bound to go. And so it did – before I had time to think. I dived for his tail, of course. I might as well have dived for a passing swift. As for issuing any order, before I could open my mouth he was out of sight.

"Well, at least I knew where he'd gone. There wasn't much doubt about that. By the time I was clear of the wood, there he was on the farther side of the water, fawning upon his darling, wagging his tail like a mad thing and barking to beat the band. His addresses were furiously rejected. Before my eyes his darling aimed a blow at the dog. But the Knave only thought he was playing and whipped in and out of range and nibbled his heels. Over-ripe for violence, I started off in pursuit…

"Approaching the idyll, I don't think I ever felt such a blasted fool.

"As I called the Knave to order –

" 'What's the matter with that dog?' said the stranger.

"I told him I wished I knew.

" 'Well, I've got to get on,' said the fellow. 'I'm late as it is.'

" 'I'm extremely sorry,' said I. 'If I can only catch him – '

" 'You stop him barking,' said the other. 'It's enough to drive a man mad.'

"Well, for reasons which must be obvious, the Knave wouldn't come to me: however, he stood quite still, with his ears on the back of his neck, so I started to go to him, mouthing treachery about 'good dogs' and that sort of tripe. How he lapped it up, I don't know: but I was within one foot when that fool of a fellow moved…

"We passed up the rise together – the Knave like a ram upon the mountains bounding about his beloved, the stranger describing all dogs with a wealth and variety of imagery which no one could have failed to admire, and myself conjuring the Knave in accents which might have been heard five furlongs away.

"As we came to the second wood the stranger looked back.

" 'Put a sock in it, can't you?' he spat. 'You're as bad as the dog.'

"That was, of course, the last straw. The back of my forbearance was broken – *yet what could I do?* The hellish answer was *Nothing*. I couldn't protest: I couldn't even withdraw. The Knave was pestering the fellow. This, as the dog's master, it was my duty to stop. But I was unable to stop it, because the dog declined to do as I said. Add to this that I had to stick to the dog… The desire to lie down and scream was almost irresistible. Rage and mortification possessed my soul. Indeed, but for the fact that my nose began to bleed I believe I should have had a seizure. At least, I like to look at it that way. It makes the remembrance less grievous.

"In hatred, malice and all uncharitableness, we made our way into that wood – the stranger spouting imprecations and seething with wrath, the Knave curvetting about him, a witless

Bacchant wooing his surly god, and myself, five paces in rear, chewing the cud of degradation and wiping my nose on the collar which should have been round the Knave's neck.

"We were in the heart of the wood when the stranger, goaded to frenzy, launched his attack. Using his dispatch case as a sort of morning star, he went for that dog with a concentrated fury which would have made a jaguar think. But the Knave, like Gallio, cared for none of these things. Avoiding the onslaught with the grace of a toreador, he danced in and out of range in manifest ecstasy, only waiting for the other to fall, as he presently did, before seizing the case in his jaws and doing his best to wrest it out of his hand. With a thousand dogs out of a thousand, that would have been my chance, but either the devil was in him or the Knave was the thousand and first. Still, if I missed him, at least I made him let go: for all that, the honours were his, for he took a scrap of silk with him which there seemed no doubt he had torn from some garment within the case. I suppose it had been protruding, for the case had seen better days. Any way there it was in his jaws, a delicate rose-coloured trophy – believe me, he flaunted the thing, mouthing it in obvious derision a short six paces away.

"The stranger sat up and wiped the sweat from his face.

" 'How long,' he snarled, 'is this comic cuts going on?'

" 'I'm damned if I know,' said I, and sat down on a rotting stump. 'Have you far to go?'

"The man made a choking noise.

" 'You can see for yourself,' I continued, 'it isn't my fault. I've run three miles across country – '

" 'You oughtn't to have a dog what you can't control.'

" 'Look here,' said I, 'it's no good playing with words. In the ordinary way that dog's an obedient dog. But he has found something about you he can't resist. You've some fatal attraction for him – I don't know what.'

" 'Attraction be — ,' said the fellow. 'It's blasted persecution – that's what it is. Biting me heels and tearing stuff out of my case. That's my wife's nightdress, that is – what he's got in his mouth.'

" 'I'm extremely sorry,' said I. 'If you'll give me your name and address, I'll have another one sent to – er – Mrs – er – '

"The stranger leaped to his feet.

" 'I don't want another one sent. I want to get on. Why can't you lay 'old of the swine and let me go?'

" 'I'm sorry,' said I, 'but you know the answer to that.' I rose from my stump. 'If you want to get on – we'll go with you. That's all I can say.'

"The fellow pushed back his hat and threw a hunted look round. Then he squatted down and tried to allure that dog. His first attempt was abortive, for the Knave misconstrued his efforts and thought he was out to play. And when the Knave plays, he barks. Now no one knows better than I how distracting a dog's bark can be, but I really thought that that man would go out of his mind. Squinting with emotion and clasping his head in his hands, he writhed like a soul in torment, calling upon me to 'stop him' as though the dog was not barking but passing sentence of death. I managed to stop him – of course by shouting him down; but so far from being grateful, the look that that fellow gave me would have poisoned a sewage farm.

" 'You and your dog,' he hissed. 'I guess I'll remember you: but not in my prayers.'

" 'I don't know that I blame you,' I said, 'but that's neither here nor there. If you want to catch that dog, I shouldn't bend down.'

"The advice, which he took, was sound. In fact his second attempt would have been a success. After some hesitation, the Knave began to approach, mouthing the silk like a plaything which he was disposed to share. He was less than four feet away and still coming on when all of a sudden he stiffened and dropped the silk. He was looking past the stranger and of course I knew in a flash that we were no longer alone. As I turned to follow his gaze, a couple of uniformed police stepped out from behind a couple of burly trees.

" 'Good morning, gents,' said the sergeant. 'It's a lovely day to take the dog for a stroll. And now might I see the contents of that dispatch case? I daresay it's only sponge cakes, but I'd like to be sure.'

"Well, here we have another hiatus. All I can tell you is that I realized certain things. I understood why the stranger had been so mad to get on and why he had shown such a violent objection to noise. The Knave's infatuation had cooked his goose. The dog had delayed and betrayed an escaping thief. And something else I perceived. And that was that *I was involved.* Already the police had assumed that the stranger and I were colleagues: my presence there was suspicious: I was plainly on terms with the thief: my appearance was dead against me: the truth was too fantastic to be believed, and the Knave was without the collar that bore my name and address: what was a thousand times worse, the dog's demeanour was insisting that the stranger and I were close friends – we might have been his joint-owners... And there I met the thief's eyes – and read my doom. The glare of Vengeance was sliding into a grin. My dog and I had ruined his chance of escape. Here and now was his chance of paying me back.

" 'Well, George,' he said slowly, 'I guess we'll be wise to go quiet. And perhaps another time, you'll do as I say. If we'd stuck to that road...'

"I called him a blasted liar and turned to the police. I can't remember how I had meant to begin, but I know that the words I had chosen died on my lips. The sergeant had opened the dispatch case, and out of Jill's nightdress he was withdrawing Jill's pearls.

" 'Good God,' I said. 'They're my cousin's.'

"Then three things happened – all together.

"First, the police were shaken. I'd spoken straight from the heart, and I saw the doubt in their eyes. Secondly, I saw that the Knave was a super-dog – that he bore no love to the stranger, but had scented and meant to stick to his mistress' clothes. You ought to have seen him licking that sergeant's face. Thirdly, I made a movement – I clapped my hands to my coat…one to each breast-pocket…TO SEE IF DAPHNE'S BRACELETS WERE SAFE.

"I'd forgotten all about them. I picked them up this morning, just as I was leaving our room. They were on the dressing-table, and I thought it was madness to leave them for any odd thief to pick up. She was out in the garden then, and I meant to give them to her before I went off in the car.

"Yes, the constable saw my movement, and before I knew where I was he had hold of my wrists. And the sergeant abstracted the bracelets with bulging eyes…

"Well, there you are. I maintain that I died at that moment. I suggest that upon that buffet my ghost withdrew. Life was a shade too pregnant – too big with frightfulness.

"When I rose again, I found myself cuffed to the stranger and staggering over the sward. The sergeant was walking in front and the Knave was trotting beside me, licking my hand. But I was past consolation. What happened then and thereafter is pardonably and mercifully blurred. The one thing that does stand out was the stare of respect and admiration inhabiting the eyes of the thief. You see, I'd left him standing – Greek had met Greek. He'd lain for those bracelets for weeks, and I'd got in before him and whipped them from under his nose."

Five hours and more had gone by, and Basingstoke and the police were things of the past. Sick, I suppose, of life, 'the stranger' had betrayed his accomplice – a footman whom we had engaged some six weeks before: my brother-in-law and the Knave had been borne to and received at Cock Feathers as though they were demigods – a triumph which, to my mind, they most justly deserved; and Perdita and I were strolling the formal garden upon flagstones which had been tapped by Queen Elizabeth's heels. This, in silence. My companion may or may not have had ears to hear: that she had eyes to see was most apparent: her full appreciation of the manor had been immediate, and her quiet recognition of beauties which I had missed had shown me that I should do better to hold my peace.

"I think that should be the nursery." A slim hand pointed to a casement which was lighting a corner room on the second floor. "Do you think we might go up and see?"

"I don't see why not," said I. "If somebody's dressing there, we can always withdraw. But how do you tell a nursery? I mean, how – "

"From the ceiling. If it's still the original ceiling, we'll know at once. There'll be animals there – in plaster. We do the same today when we paper a nursery's walls."

Feeling extremely humble, I followed her into the mansion and up the lovely staircase which led to the room she sought. Happily, this was empty…

The low-pitched ceiling was squared with a moulding of plaster from wall to wall: in each corner of every square was a plaster beast – elephants, bears and peacocks, to gladden a baby's eyes.

As soon as I could speak –

"Have you been here before?" said I.

Perdita shook her head.

"All the same, if you look over there, you'll find my name on one of the window panes. My grandmother's home was Cock Feathers and she used to play in this room. She's told me all about it so many times. When she was only a scrap, she fell off a chair one day and hurt her head: and just at that moment her father, the fourth Lord Amersham, opened the door. And to stop her crying, he took off a ring he was wearing and with the diamond he cut her name on the pane."

Together we moved to the casement.

The straggling copper-plate writing was easy enough to read.

Perdita 1844.

After a long look I straightened my back.

"My dear," I said, "words fail me – and that's the truth."

Perdita the Second smiled.

"It only shows that Saul was among the prophets. If you remember, you said there was more to come."

"The Knave, the diamonds…and the Queen."

" 'The Lost Lady' – that's what *Perdita* means."

"I picked up a Queen," I said firmly. "The Knave found the diamonds, and Berry found the Knave: but I found the Queen that was missing for ninety years."

Her chin on her shoulder, a child looked up to my face. All the sweet of her nature looked out of her glorious eyes.

"Do I seem to belong here, Boy?"

I glanced round the nursery, gay with the precious issue of evening sun.

"Yes, sweetheart," I said, stooping. "And always will."

2

How Berry Perceived the Obvious, and Daphne and I Put Spokes in Each Other's Wheels

Berry pushed back his plate and lighted a cigarette.

"I suppose," he said, "that if I were to venture to protest, I should be subjected to insult."

"That," said I, "is more than probable – because your idea of protesting is to compare unfavourably and most offensively those with whom you happen to disagree."

"Permit me to observe," said Berry, "that that is a venomous lie. Because, under great provocation I may have gone so far as to suggest that my views would receive more consideration from the humbler denizens of the jungle than from my own flesh and blood – "

" 'A bunch of blue-bottomed baboons,' " said Daphne. "That was your elegant phrase."

" 'Blue-based,' " said her husband. " 'Blue-based.' Never mind. As I was saying, I confess that upon occasion I have hinted that I should value the ruling of mammals more simple-minded than ourselves. Frankly, I should value it now."

"There you are," said Daphne. "What did Boy say?"

Berry expired.

"What is there offensive," he demanded, "in saying that I should like to submit the point at issue to one or more baboons – blue-based, if possible?"

"Nothing at all," said Jonah, "provided you don't aver that their considered opinion would be of more value than ours."

"Oh, I shouldn't do that," said Berry. "I should never do more than suggest that, if they were so consulted, the baboons would agree with me." He sighed. "I suggest as much now."

"Well, what if they would?" said Jill. "Baboons don't count. They're simply idiotic."

"Worse," said Berry, mournfully. "Baboons – particularly the B-B B's – are actively imbecile. Not only is their outlook, if any, beneath contempt, but their utter inability to concentrate is aggravated by a distracting irrelevance which is sometimes, I grieve to say, characterized by vulgarity." He sighed again. "That, of course, is inexcusable."

"Then why," began Jill…

"Don't," said Daphne. "You'll only play into his hands. I admit I can't see the catch, but I know it's there."

"There's no deception," said Berry. "I can't put it more plainly than I have."

A pregnant silence succeeded these highly equivocal words. We looked from one to the other, each of us seeking guidance and finding none. The deadly insult had not been levelled at us. Of course, if we chose to appropriate it… As though awaiting our decision, the author of our vexation gazed at the chandelier with the artless, dreaming air of a little child. To corroborate this conceit, he began to illustrate the alphabet.

"A is for Argument – battle of wits,
B for Baboon who is blue where he sits,
C is for Character, noble and wise,
D for Deception which far from us flies…"

His delivery was so faithful to the traditions of childhood that I surveyed my surroundings – rather than catch Jill's eye.

The dining-room was pleasantly cool and quick with the lively splendour of indirect sun. This swelled in through the windows after the manner of music, organ-made. Without, the world was blazing: the turf was brilliant: flowers glowed like jewels in their beds: the very foliage glanced, and already the haze of heat was masking the face of Distance with a shimmer that teased the sight.

I found myself hoping very hard that weather like this would smile upon Perdita Boyte. The latter was due at White Ladies in four days' time.

My sister returned to the charge.

"Why," she demanded, "why shouldn't we go to the sale?"

"Because we've no money to spend, but already more furniture than we can conveniently house."

"But I don't want to buy anything."

"I know," said Berry. "I know. This is where the baboons come in. You don't want to buy anything: yet you want to rush fifty miles across country to go to a sale. Now if those two facts were communicated to our parti-coloured friends, what gesture do you think they would make?"

There was another silence.

Only the night before I had happened to read in *The Times* that the contents of Hammercloth Hall were being sold. The announcement was common enough: had we not stayed at the house, it might not have caught my eye: as it was, we were more than interested. We knew 'the contents,' and when we saw them described as 'one of the finest private collections of Jacobean furniture,' we knew that the description was just.

Grey-eyed Jill pushed back her chair.

"Of course we must go," she said. "If that table's not too expensive..."

"Ah," said Berry, quietly – and left it there.

The lovely refectory table had stood in our hearts for three years. Massive, yet elegant; perfectly proportioned and preserved; laid with a gorgeous patina which Time had taken three hundred years to spread, it was one of the most glorious survivals that we had ever known. More. The moment you saw it, it called up the spirit of its age: the men that had made it and used it rose up about its oak: it was as though something of their natures had entered into the wood. Imagination, if you will: but the table inspired imagination, presenting, to eyes that could see, the manners of vanished days. But that was not all. *It might have been made for White Ladies, our Hampshire home.* Panelling, sideboard and chairs – we had the rest: but for us there was only one table, and that was at Hammercloth Hall, some fifty miles off. For all that, we had never dared hope that the object of our desire would ever be sold. Its owner, Geoffrey Majoribanks, was very rich and clearly enjoyed the collection which he and his father had made. But now, for some reason or other, his heart was changed.

In a way, our chance was at hand…

My sister threw down the mask.

"It may go for nothing," she said.

Her husband wrinkled his brow.

"It may," he said. "I don't quite see why it should, but you never know. At the critical moment those present might lose the power of speech. And movement. But unless they do, it should make six hundred pounds. Or more."

"At least, we can go and – "

"No, we can't," said Berry. "I'll tell you why. Once we set eyes on that table, the awful lust for possession will take command. We shall simply have to have it…at any price. The result will be what an auctioneer calls 'a fight,' and whether we win or lose, we shall purchase the brand of trouble which comes to stay. If we win, we shall beggar ourselves: if we lose, we shall be for ever tormented by the thought that we might have won, if only we'd kept our nerve and sprung another ten pounds."

Jonathan Mansel looked up.

"May be all over," he said. "The sale began yesterday."

I shook my head.

"Yesterday, household stuff: furniture, today and tomorrow: silver on Thursday."

Here a pressure upon my left thigh remembered the Knave, and I turned to regard the Alsatian we all adored. For a moment his brown eyes held mine, then he lifted his lovely head to stare at the toast. All the time, his great tail was swaying...

Such address was that of a courtly, forgotten age.

"Sir, It will give me great pleasure if you can see your way to oblige, Your most obedient servant."

As I stretched out my hand to the rack, I touched my breakfast-cup with the cuff of my coat...

Upon such incidents do the fates of nations depend. Together, Jill and I proceeded to deal with the mess in the time-honoured way – by lifting the edge of the cloth and thrusting a plate between the stain and the wood. This simple operation exposed the table itself – the nice-looking board which had served us for twenty years.

My cousin ran her slim fingers along the edge of the oak. Then she looked up.

"What should we do with this one? We couldn't possibly sell it. It's part of our home."

"I agree," said Daphne. "The old fellow's done us too well. He'd go very well in the hall where the coffer is now."

"That's right," said I. "And the coffer at the head of the stairs."

"With the Kneller above it," said Jonah. "Then we can put the tallboy where the Kneller is now and hang the Morland where it always ought to have hung."

"That's an idea," cried Daphne...

So we entered the broad, smooth road that was leading to Hammercloth Hall and the sale-by-auction of a table which we could not afford to buy. Our descent of this pleasant way was easy enough. We perceived a whole chain of improvements which our purchase of the piece would begin: reviewing these charming effects, we saw that upon its acquisition was depending the condition of our home: we began to style it 'a godsend': an eager anticipation subdued the qualms of conscience in unfair fight; and we hugged our guilty intention with the ardour which only mischief can ever inspire.

I am bound to say, in his favour, that Berry hung back, but at length he threw in his hand and joined in the rout.

"But for God's sake," he said, "don't let's make fools of ourselves."

"We're doing that by going," said Jonah.

"I know," said Berry. "I know. The baboons wouldn't go. Not even the B-B B's. But it's too late now. We've visualized possession: we've eaten the apples of desire. But don't let's magnify our folly. If the dealers go after that table, we've got to withdraw."

"Let's be clear about this," said Daphne. "How far d'you think we can go?"

"My conscience," replied her husband, "suggests about twelve and six. But I'm not going to listen to that. If Jonah and Boy will come in, I'll let my tailor wait and scratch up a hundred pounds."

"Three hundred, then?" said Jonah.

After a painful calculation, I nodded assent.

"Of course that's hopeless," said Daphne. "Three hundred pounds!"

"Well, sell your sables," said Berry, "and call it three hundred and ten."

"Don't be a fool," said his wife. "You said yourself it would fetch six hundred or more."

"So it will," said Berry.

"Then, what's the good of our going?"

"No good at all," said Berry. "It's about the most futile thing that we've ever done. I tell you, the baboons wouldn't go. They may be feeble-minded, but they wouldn't drive fifty miles to pick up a stomach-ache."

A master of the art of provocation, my brother-in-law's delight is to sow the wind. As the whirlwind subsided –

"The point is this," said Jonah. "The saleroom is full of surprises. Sales are not governed by the law of supply and demand. The bids are ruled by private calculations which no one on earth can divine. That table might go for two hundred – just because, for private reasons, nobody present considered it worth his while to pay any more." He glanced at his watch. "If I am to drive, I must have an hour and a half. And the sale begins at midday. If we start in a quarter of an hour, we ought to get there on time."

As we fled from table –

"But what about lunch?" screamed Berry. "I'm not going to…

Ten minutes later we pushed him into the Rolls.

The way to Hammercloth ran through the lively pageant which only an English June can ever present. It had rained the night before, and now the grateful sunshine was clothing a world refreshed in a magic of green and silver that filled the eye. The pale-blue sky was cloudless, the cool, still air was charged with the lovely odour of English earth, and the brown roads were printed with shadows of the lovely creations which another summer had designed for the wayside trees.

As we ran through the village of Broomstick, the church clock told us the hour – eleven o'clock. With twenty miles behind us, we had a bare thirty to go.

I was sitting with Jonah, and Berry was seated behind, between Daphne and Jill. At their feet the Knave lay couched, as a good dog should.

My sister addressed her husband.

"Have you got your chequebook?" she said.

"A good moment to ask," said Berry. "We're very near half-way there. If you'd asked me as we were leaving – "

"Well, I've only just thought of it."

"That's my point," said Berry. "Now If I had forgotten the thing, I should be abused and reviled till I couldn't think straight. Yet you yourself have let twenty-one miles go by before – "

"Have you got it?" demanded Daphne.

"I decline to answer," said Berry, "until you admit your fault. What about the tickets last week? Nobody gave them a thought till we got to the theatre steps – but I had to stand the racket. Talk about execration… I might have been Titus Oates."

"Oh, be a sport," purred Daphne. "Just for my peace of mind."

"Confess your fault," said her husband.

"All right. I confess. I ought to have asked you before."

"Then we're both to blame," said Berry, "because I've left it behind."

The explosion of dismay which greeted this shocking announcement may be better imagined than set down. Daphne and Jill recoiled from the delinquent – two lovely Furies, bristling with horror and wrath: voicing his indignation, my cousin set a foot on the brake: I flung round in my seat, fiercely demanding confirmation of a fact which I could not accept; and the Knave, from whom nothing was hid, leaped from his place to plant his forepaws upon Berry and bark like a fiend possessed.

As the storm died down –

"If we go back," said Jonah, "we shall not get to the sale before a quarter to one. That may not matter at all. The table may not come up till this afternoon. But of course it may come up at a quarter past twelve."

"We'd better go on," said I. "They'll probably waive the deposit if we can give them a card."

"Have you got a card?" said Daphne.

"No," said Berry, "I haven't. I've three pounds ten in notes and a snapshot of you at Biarritz in '94. Perhaps if we showed them that – "

"Who's got a card?" – violently.

There was a painful silence – nobody had a card.

"I did get it out," murmured Berry. "It's on the library table, south of the blotting pad. I can see it now." He turned to his wife. "I can't think how we forgot it," he added reproachfully.

Before Daphne could find her tongue –

"Who's doing the sale?" said Jonah. "If it's a firm that knows us – "

"That's an idea," said Berry. "What luck if it's Bamptons. We owe them two hundred pounds."

As luck would have it, I had the day's *Times* by my side. With no time to read it at home, I had brought it along.

Together my cousin and I examined its sheets…

For a while the announcement escaped us, and the others, including the Knave, stood up in the car and added their eyes to the quest.

Then Jill's pink finger stabbed at the foot of a page.

"Hammercloth – there it is, Boy."

As I followed her indication, a cry of anguish from Berry rang in my ear.

"Who said it began at midday?"

With his words I found the legend:

Today, Tuesday, June 16th, precisely at half past ten…

There was a ghastly silence. Then –

"Deposit be damned," said Jonah, and let in the clutch.

It was five and twenty to twelve when we sighted the chimneys of Hammercloth, rosy against the blue. Two minutes later we swept past the waiting cars and up to the front of the house.

Doors and windows were open; the broad, white steps bore the print of many feet; but nobody was to be seen. The only sign of life was the clear-cut voice of a man – floating out of a latticed casement, perhaps ten paces away.

"*Two hundred and forty-five pounds. Two hundred and forty-five pounds. Any advance on two hundred and forty-five pounds? A poor bid, gentlemen, for such a magnificent lot. Worth treble that, and you know it. Two hundred and forty-five pounds…*"

For an instant we sat paralysed. Then we all made to leave the Rolls, as though the car was afire.

I was the first to alight.

As I tore to the open window, I heard the relentless voice.

"*For the last time any advance on two hundred and forty-five pounds?*"

I thrust my head into the room.

"Fifty," I cried.

The hammer which had been lifted sank to the desk: some seventy heads came round and I found myself the cynosure of every eye in the room.

The auctioneer smiled and nodded.

"*Two hundred and fifty, thank you. Two hundred and fifty pounds. Any advance on…*"

There was no advance.

As I entered the hall, Jonah met me to say that I had become the owner of six Jacobean chairs.

When I explained that I had neither chequebook nor card, the auctioneer's clerk declared that that did not matter at all.

"You can pay on delivery, sir. We'll send them over to you whenever you like."

The table had not been sold. It seemed clear that it would not be reached before half past two.

The village of Hammercloth had but one decent inn, and since this was sure to be crowded with dealers attending the sale, we drove to the neighbouring hamlet of Shepherd's Pipe. Here the staff of *The Woolpack* received us with open arms, for Shepherd's Pipe is retired, and strangers, except upon Sundays, are seldom seen: the garden was put at our disposal, a coach-house at that of the Rolls, and, before we had time to ask, our amiable host had proposed that our lunch should be served on the lawn in the shade of an oak. We assented gratefully...

Berry removed his coat, hung this on the back of a chair, commanded a quart of ale and laid himself down on the grass.

"You may have observed," he said, addressing his wife, "that since your dear brother's *coup*, I have not opened my mouth. Now, however, I feel disposed to inquire why we are lunching here, instead of at home."

"You can't blame Boy," said Jill, who was sitting down with the Knave. "Supposing it had been the table."

"I decline to suppose," said Berry. "The facts are pregnant enough. Against my will I've been rushed some fifty odd miles in the heat of the day for the privilege of hearing an entirely unauthorized person spend eighty-three pounds six shillings and eightpence of my money on the purchase of some worm-eaten chairs. I may be peculiar, but a little of that sort of excitement lasts me a very long time. I feel that I want to go home – and get under the spare-room bed. I mean, I'm mentally sick. Anyone would be."

"I acted for the best," said I. "I know I took a chance in a million, but no one's more sorry than I that it didn't come off."

"Don't think I blame you," said Berry. "I blame myself. If I like to go about with a maniac, I must expect to be involved in transactions like this. But that doesn't mean I enjoy them." He sat up and looked about him. "I suppose it is real, isn't it? It isn't a hideous dream? Or haven't we been to Hammercloth?"

"In and out," said Jonah. "We got out of the car for two minutes and then got back."

My brother-in-law shuddered.

"We must try," he said hoarsely, "and keep it from the baboons. I mean, they'd laugh themselves sick. We risk our lives for that table by doing a mile a minute for half an hour upon highly dangerous roads: we arrive with three hours to spare, but before we've been there ten seconds, we sink five-sixths of our money on something we do not want and have never seen. I mean, can you beat it?"

"I shall always maintain," said Daphne, "that Boy did right. If it had been the table and he hadn't bid as he did, we'd have lost it for good and all."

"But we've lost it now," screamed her husband. He pointed at me. "That Napoleon's spent our money…on a filthy set of roach-backed stools that – "

"Rot," said Daphne. "They mayn't be what we wanted, but they're very good-looking chairs."

"As you please," said Berry. "I'm not going to argue the point. The unsavoury fact remains that, wisely or unwisely, we have expended the money we never had. In these – to me, repugnant circumstances, I repeat my desire to be informed why we are lunching here instead of at home."

"Because of the table," said Jill. "We've still got fifty pounds left."

Berry closed his eyes and put a hand to his head. "Oh, give me strength," he said brokenly. Then he turned to the Knave. "They're going back," he said wildly. "Back to the shambles, old fellow. Back to the lucky dip. I wonder what they'll get this time." He laughed idiotically. "Perhaps it'll be a what-not."

Pleased with his confidence, the Knave rolled on to his back and put his paws in the air.

"I entirely agree," said Berry. "I give them up," and, with that, he covered his face and once more lay back upon the sward.

"We must bid for the table," said Daphne, "exactly as we arranged. We've still got three hundred pounds, for we've only to sell the chairs. As a matter of fact, we've got more. I quite expect that in London they'd go for double the price."

"We can't risk that," said Jonah. "We must dispose of the chairs before the table comes up. It's simple enough. We find the runner-up – the fellow that Boy outbid. He'll take them off us all right – at two hundred and forty-five pounds. Two hundred and fifty perhaps, and glad of the chance."

My sister fingered her lip.

"It does seem a pity," she said. "I'm sure if we sold them in London, they'd fetch much more."

"I'm inclined to agree," said Jonah. "I believe Boy's done a good deal. But, as I say, we can't risk it. If we are to go for that table, we must first get rid of those chairs."

There was a little silence – devoted to speculation of a fantastic sort. If the chairs were worth five hundred and the table was going to go to four hundred and ninety pounds...

"May I speak?" said Berry. "I mean would it be in order for me to refer to the projected disposal of my property and the laying out of the proceeds on something else?"

"If," said Daphne, "you've anything useful to say."

"That's a moot point," said her husband. "Some might think it uncalled-for. Others might rank it above the drippings of wisdom with which we have just been regaled. But I leave it to you to judge. I gather that you wish to exchange the six chairs we now possess for the table we set out to buy. Unless I am permitted to attempt this operation without any sort of interference from any of you, don't count on a farthing from me, either towards the chairs or towards any other commitment which you may presently make."

The ultimatum took us aback.

"This is blackmail," said Daphne.

"It isn't really," said Berry, "but I think I know what you mean. I am putting upon you a pressure before which, placed as you are, you are practically bound to give way."

"But that isn't fair."

"Possibly not," was the answer, "from your point of view. From mine, it's a measure of what is called self-preservation. I don't want what happened this morning to happen again. I do not want to be ruined, because somebody else has an urge to 'act for the best.' Myself, I think it's natural – I may be wrong."

"I think it's most natural," said I, "and I agree to your terms. If ever there was one, this is a one-man job, and you can't do worse than I have, whatever you do."

"That," said my brother-in-law, "remains to be seen. But pray forget any strictures which I may have passed on your deal and accept one of my cigarettes – which are still in the car. I don't suggest you should get them. There's no reason why you should."

The Knave went with me...

I had entered and left the coach-house, recrossed the sunlit forecourt and re-entered the cool of the hall, when I heard the brush of a tire on the gravel outside. As I turned, a magnificent car came slowly to rest some three or four paces away from the door of the inn. Faintly surprised, curious to see its contents, and well aware that, because of the glare without, I could not be seen, I stood where I was, waiting.

At once there emerged from the car as unpleasant-looking a being as ever I saw. His appearance was so startling and repulsive that I put down a hand to the Knave for fear that the dog, so confronted, would launch an attack. As I did so, I heard him growl, and, as I sought for his collar, I found the hackles risen along his chine. The dog may be forgiven. The creature that he was regarding suggested a clothed baboon.

I heard him address his chauffeur.

"You will go straight to Hammercloth – that is the village to come. Mr Aaron is there – at the Hall. But you will not drive up to the house nor go near the inn. Turn back when you see the big gates and wait for Mr Aaron a little way off. When he has arrived, bring him here."

As I left the house for the garden, I heard the car leave the forecourt and then its master's voice demanding a private room.

Berry was where I had left him, but the others had strolled away and were not to be seen. I took my seat by his side and made him free of my news. He listened carefully.

"A baboon," he said. "What a most remarkable thing. I wonder if he's blue-based... Never mind. The sale, of course... He's after that table or something. But he daren't show up himself, so Aaron is taking his place. And Aaron is coming to report, as soon as they rise for lunch."

"Why daren't he show up?" said I.

"Because he is too well known to get anything cheap. The moment he shows his mug the dealers sit up: and if he begins to bid, they know that they're on a winner and take him up." He fingered his chin. "I wonder what time they'll rise. I'd like to see Mr Aaron, and I'd like very much indeed to hear his report."

Though all this was pure speculation, it might have been a statement of fact. My brother-in-law had been speaking not so much with conviction as though he were repeating some information received, and though my reason told me that he might be entirely wrong, his quiet recital went far to compel belief.

As though he could read my thoughts –

"I know I'm right," said Berry. "The moment you said 'baboon,' I knew we were off. Fate's always pointing her finger, but we're too blind to see it until too late. Very, very rarely man is permitted to perceive the obvious in time. Once before, it happened to me. And now for the second time... Didn't I say this morning that *I should value the ruling of a baboon?* Well, here we are. Here's the baboon I spoke of...*whose ruling is of such value that he dare not show up at the sale...*" He broke off, to gaze at the distance with narrowed eyes. "What I cannot see is how his ruling will help us. To know that he's after that table won't help us at all. It's money, not ruling we need... Get hold of Jonah, will you? We must know when Aaron arrives, and we'll have to take it in turns to picket that hall."

The spin of a coin had decided that my second turn of duty should start at a quarter past one. It was then that I relieved Jonah, who had spent his time in the coach house, ready to cross the forecourt the moment he heard the big car. Myself, I thought it better to stay in the hall, for Aaron had only to see me to know me at once for the man who had bid from the window an hour or so back. And that would put him on his guard. But the hall was dim, and the staircase, passage and garden offered three lines of retreat. It was, of course, still more important that Aaron's repulsive master should entertain no suspicion that Aaron was being awaited by anyone else.

The man had been given a room whose windows gave to the forecourt, whose door to the hall. So much Berry had discovered. With my eyes on that door, I hovered between my three exits. Mercifully, the staff was still busy about our lunch.

A third of my duty was past when I saw the door handle move. In a flash I had gained the stairs which rose in two flights. Out of view, on the second flight, I stood like some escaped convict, straining my ears.

For a moment I heard no sound: and then the man was moving – moving very softly, as though he did not wish to be heard.

I fell to my hands and knees and peered between the staves of the balustrade.

More simian in appearance than ever, the fellow was treading a-tiptoe, poking his head and listening with every step. What on earth had aroused his suspicions, I cannot conceive; but something – some horrid instinct had suggested that I was at hand: he was out to prove this suggestion… Failure would discredit his instinct and send him back to his room with an easy mind: success would ruin such plans as Berry had laid and would so humiliate me as to shorten my life.

I watched him survey the passage and steal to the garden-door. As he leaned into the garden, I climbed the remaining stairs and took my stand on the landing, back to the wall. So for perhaps thirty seconds. Then I heard the rap of a stair rod against its eye…

I threw one frantic look round – and read my doom. Though the landing was none too big, it gave to a promising passage which would, I am sure, have offered some way of escape. But I could not gain the passage, unless I crossed the head of the stairs. As it was, I was in a blind alley some twelve feet square, in which were two doors and a window, all three of them shut.

For an instant, I hesitated. Then I slid to the nearest door, opened it noiselessly and glided within the room. In a flash I had shut the door and was standing with my ear to the frame. As I held my breath, I heard a board creak upon the landing…

And then and there, I think, the fellow's suspicions were laid, for he let out a satisfied grunt and a moment later I heard him descending the stairs.

As I wiped the sweat from my face –

"Won't you sit down?" said a voice. "Your sigh of relief suggests that the danger is past."

As in a dream, I was gazing at Perdita Boyte, who was looking extremely lovely and lying at ease in a bed, with three or four pillows behind her and a novel, face down, on her lap.

"Perdita?" I breathed, staring. "Whatever are you doing here?"

"The same to you," said Perdita. "This is my room."

Quietly I told her my tale.

"But I shan't say I'm sorry," I concluded, "because I'm an honest man. I'm much too glad to see you. The pity is I'm not Herrick. *To Julia, abed*, would have been a sonnet worth reading. Oh, and who says Fate doesn't know best? First, she brings us here and then she fairly hounds me into your room."

"It does look like it," said Perdita. "Mother and I were *en route* and I ricked my back. Yesterday evening, that was, and this was the nearest inn. The silly part is that she's gone to call upon you, to ask you to do what you've done. Visit the sick, I mean. The doctor says I'll be here for another two days. But all that can wait for the moment. If you really want the ruling of your baboon, I should stay where you are: they asked me if, as mother was out, the fellow could lunch in our room: and I said 'yes.' Well, that room's directly below us, and the ceiling is very thin. If he and Aaron speak up, you'll hear every word."

"Good lord," said I. "What a chance! All the same, I don't like eavesdropping. I mean – "

"Don't be a fool," said Perdita. "Quite apart from anything else, you may bet your happy days that a man who is so suspicious is up to no good."

With her words came the sound of a car, and a moment later the crunch of tires upon gravel declared that the curtain was up.

The baboon was out in the forecourt before I had reached the window commanding the scene.

Oozing servility, a willowy, pale-faced youth emerged from the limousine – to be met with a glare which would have made a lion tamer think.

"What does this mean? Where's Aaron?" Hat in hand, the unfortunate creature blenched. "I'm very sorry, Mr Stench, but Mr Aaron is ill – with stomachic pain. So he gave me your catalogue and – "

With a working face, his master turned right about and blundered into the inn. The other followed delicately, goggle-eyed...

I tiptoed to Perdita's side.

As I opened my mouth, she laid a hand on my arm.

"Stay with me, please. I – "

From below, the voice of a brute cut her sentence in two.

"Have you got the things?"

"Every lot but one, Mr Stench, so far. And all well below your figures. If I may say so, I think we've done – "

"Which one did you lose?"

"The set of chairs, Mr – "

A howl of anguish rang out.

"All but the chairs? That's what you came for, you blockhead – to buy those chairs."

"I'm sure I'm very sorry, Mr Stench, but it wasn't my fault. I went to the figure you'd written down in the margin, and just as I thought – "

"What did they go for?"

"Two hundred and fifty pounds."

For a moment there was dead silence. Then came a hideous sound – a gobbling noise...

As I turned to meet the horror in Perdita's eyes, Aaron's unfortunate deputy voiced his dismay.

"Don't, Mr Stench," he whimpered. "What have I done?"

His master spoke through his teeth.

"Look at that, you blundering idiot."

"What about it, Mr Stench? Two hundred and – Oh, my God, Mr Stench, that isn't a 'one'?"

"That is a 'one.' One before two makes twelve. *One thousand* two hundred and fifty is what I wrote. I've as good as sold those chairs for two thousand pounds, and you've let some country counterjumper..."

I think that was all I heard: at least, I remember no more – except the blaze of excitement in Perdita's glorious eyes.

"Go and buy your table," she breathed. "And – and then, if you please, come back and revisit the sick. The sick will be very grateful. I don't know that they can promise to make your fortune again, but – "

"The light in your eyes is my fortune, you pretty maid."

"I'm afraid that's not legal tender. Goodbye, Herrick."

"There's plenty of time," said I, and picked up her fingertips. "Gather ye rosebuds while ye may."

"Business first," said my lady, and whipped her fingers away. "You've got to be clear of this house before the deputy Aaron comes out of that room."

"I don't believe *Julia* would have – "

"If you don't go," said Perdita, "I shall call Mr Stench."

It was nearly a quarter to four before the table came up: but though the seats in the saleroom were painfully hard, our discomfort of body was salved by our peace of mind. The chairs I had bought had passed – and I had a note of hand for one thousand pounds.

As was only to be expected, Mr Stench's man had approached me the moment he saw my face and had offered to purchase my 'bargain' for 'a five-pound note.' Such impudence steeled my heart and I had but little compunction in making him climb the steps which I knew as well as he he was ready to tread.

Imperceptibly the room had grown full. From where I was sitting with Berry, I could no longer set eyes upon Daphne and Jill. They were, I knew, close to the door, because of the Knave – who had found the fall of the hammer matter for wrath. Jonah, who had been beside us, had left his seat for a moment to lose it for good. When I saw him next, he was standing some ten feet away on the edge of the press.

Not to be defeated by distance, he sent me a little note.

We're in for a fight all right. At least five London dealers are now in the room.

I passed it to Berry and took another look round.

On the farther side of the table a thick-set Jew was making his neighbour free of spurts of confidential information which the other steadfastly ignored. A comfortable lady in black alternately toyed with her pencil and set her chin on her shoulder to speak with a hatchet-faced man who was stooping behind. A nice-looking fellow in grey, directly facing the rostrum, bid from time to time with a whimsical smile. The picture of despair, a Jew of some seventy summers, continually looked about him, as though he were caged and were seeking some way of escape. Occasionally he bid – agonizedly. Seated almost below the rostrum, a jolly-faced man in blue maintained a cheerful conversation with some crony behind his chair, only interrupting this communion to nod to the auctioneer – a curious contrast to his neighbour, who tiny, bespectacled, bird-like, stared with an air of indignation on all he saw.

"*Lot four hundred and six,*" said the auctioneer.

A ripple of preparation ran through the room.

Throats were cleared, lips moistened, feet moved: glasses were adjusted: men settled themselves on their chairs, and those that were standing strove to improve their view.

Silence followed. Even the man in blue suspended his flow of soul.

"*A fine oak table. May I say – Three hundred, thank you. I'm bid three hundred pounds.*"

"Whose bid?" whispered Berry.

"I don't know. I couldn't see."

"*And ten… Twenty… Thirty… Forty…*"

The auctioneer's head was flicking from side to side. In vain I endeavoured to see from whom the bids came.

"*Three hundred and ninety pounds.*"

"Four hundred," said a man in pince-nez, with his hat on the back of his head.

"That fellow there," I whispered, "with his catalogue up to his nose."

"*Four hundred, thank you. And ten… Twenty… Thirty…*"

"Who's bidding against him?" breathed Berry.

In vain I tried to follow the eye of the auctioneer.

"Can't you see who's against him?" – irritably.

"I tell you I can't," I breathed. "I'm doing my best."

"*Five hundred pounds. And ten…*"

My sister's face appeared – between two bowler hats on the edge of the press. Her eyes flung some frantic question of which, of course, I took no notice at all. At the moment the slightest gesture would have been read as a bid. When I ventured to look again, she had disappeared.

The bidding continued to rise.

At seven hundred and fifty the man with the pince-nez dropped out.

"*Eight hundred pounds... Eight hundred... Eight hundred pounds.*"

My brother-in-law glanced at the rostrum.

"*And ten, thank you. Twenty... Thirty...*"

"Who's against me?" hissed Berry. "You must be able to see."

Subduing an impulse to scream, I sought for some tell-tale gesture, and sought in vain.

A note was thrust into my hand.

Stench's man is not bidding – J.

When I offered the note to Berry, he pushed it away.

"Can't you see who's taking me up?"

"It isn't Stench."

"That," said Berry, "is what I wanted to know."

"*Nine hundred pounds.*"

The auctioneer was looking at Berry.

As the latter lifted his chin –

"*And ten... Twenty.*"

"Damn the fellow," breathed Berry, and nodded again.

"*Thirty... Forty.*"

An oppressive silence followed. Then Berry inclined his head.

"*Fifty... Sixty.*"

Berry raised his eyebrows – and lifted his chin.

"*Seventy... Eighty.*"

"Make it a thousand," said Berry.

"*One thousand pounds, thank you.*"

A sudden buzz of excitement rose and fell. As it died down –

"*And ten,*" said the auctioneer.

To my amazement, Berry sat back in his chair.

"Well, that's that," he murmured.

I could hardly believe my ears.

"You're not going to stop?"

"Of course I am," said Berry. "Our limit is reached."

"*One thousand and ten pounds.*"

"But we've still got three – "

"That's all washed out. I'm not going to blue our own money on something that Stench won't touch."

"*One thousand and ten pounds.*"

Looking up, I met Daphne's gaze. Her agonized look of inquiry showed that she did not know whether the last of the bids was Berry's or not. Her doubts were rudely dispersed.

"*It's against you, sir.*"

My brother-in-law shook his head.

The auctioneer raised his hammer.

"*For the last time, one thousand and ten pounds.*"

As the hammer was falling, I nodded my head.

"*Twenty, thank you. Thirty... Forty... Fifty.*"

"Are you doing this?" said Berry.

"Some of it," said I, and nodded again.

"*Sixty... Seventy... Eighty...*"

"You're out of your mind," breathed Berry. "No table on earth is worth it. Besides, if – "

"*Eleven hundred... And ten...*"

"I won't come in," said Berry. "I warn you, I won't come in. You've had the straightest of tips and you're flying bung in its face."

"So did you," I retorted, and nodded again. "You knew that Stench – "

"We had a thousand to play with. If we chose to – "

"*Twelve hundred pounds.*"

The auctioneer was looking at me.

Once again I nodded.

"*Twelve hundred and ten... Twenty...*"

As I nodded again, I saw Berry start and stare – at the end of the room. Then he turned and caught at my arm.

"Perhaps this'll stop you," he hissed. "It's Daphne that's bidding against you. I saw her nod."

"Good God," said I, weakly.

"*Twelve hundred and forty pounds.*"

"Can you beat it?" said Berry grimly. "Baboon eating baboon."

"*Twelve hundred and forty pounds.*"

I got to my feet.

"How long – "

"Who knows?" said Berry, rising. "She probably took me up."

"*It's against you, sir.*"

I shook my head...

As the hammer fell, I made my way out of the press.

Standing at the back of the room, my sister and I regarded one another.

"I suppose," said I, "you came in when Berry stopped."

"As you did," said Daphne. "It's really all his fault for not going on."

"It's a mercy he saw you," said I. "I tremble to think – "

"Don't talk about it," said Daphne. "When Jonah came and told me, I nearly died."

I slid my arm through hers.

"Well, come and claim it, my darling. At least, you had the last word."

My sister frowned.

"Twelve forty, he said."

"I know. I bid twelve thirty, and you put me up."

"But I didn't," cried Daphne. "The moment Jonah told me, I turned away."

"Yes, but that was after twelve forty."

"I bid twelve twenty," said Daphne, "and then Jonah caught my arm. Twelve twenty or thirty. I can't be sure which it was."

"You've got it wrong, my darling. I bid twelve thirty. I must have."

The auctioneer's clerk put us straight.

"I'm afraid it's neither of yours, sir. When the lady dropped out, we took up the bidding again. We were bidding for one of our clients who isn't here. I'm very sorry, sir – more sorry than I can say. If you'd bid once more, you'd have had it. We had instructions to go to twelve hundred and fifty pounds."

I pass over the next three days, the burden of which was as bitter as they were long. Daphne and Jill were inconsolable, and the comfort which Berry offered sent half out of their minds. The latter made no secret of his relief.

"It's a case of divine intervention. You flouted the lead Stench gave us, and a merciful Fate preserved us against your will. In the very nick of time she shoved a spoke in your wheel – both wheels. When I think... Oh, and that thousand pounds isn't ours. If we'd spent it at Hammercloth, we might have tried to pretend that we'd handed it back. As it is, we are spared that effort. It belongs to Geoffrey Majoribanks, and I'm going to send him a cheque."

While we all accepted this ruling, the other argument salted our gaping wounds. We rent and were rent in turn, and when Jonah announced his conversion to Berry's faith, our house was indeed divided against itself.

So, as I say, for three days. On the fourth came Miss Perdita Boyte.

In fact, I fetched her myself – from *The Woolpack* of Shepherd's Pipe.

The afternoon was lively. Clouds, like full-rigged galleons, sailed in a flawless sky, and a harlequin breeze was abroad in the countryside. Cornfields rippled like pools, old elms nodded their heads and every shadow was dancing to the humour of wind and sun.

As we floated into the festival –

"There is no health in us," I said. "The loss of that table has fairly ripped the balloon."

Perdita raised two eyebrows which Joshua Reynolds would have been happy to limn.

"Why didn't you stick to that thousand? If you hadn't put in your oar, those chairs would have gone to Stench for two hundred and forty-five pounds."

"I know. But, you see, we know Geoffrey Majoribanks. You can't make a profit like that out of one of your friends."

"But if you'd bought the table, you would have. Twist it about as you please – you would have paid for that table with money which you contend was morally his. I don't agree with your contention. I think the thousand was yours. And I don't believe that he will accept your cheque. But that is beside the point. Feeling as you do, every time you sat down at that table your conscience would have recited the debt that you owed your friend."

"I wonder," said I, thoughtfully.

"I don't," said Perdita. "I know. It's as plain as the nose on your face. If you could focus, you'd see it as clearly as I. But your mind's eye is out of focus – thanks to the punch which you got from the auctioneer's clerk. Of course, that man is a fool. To tell you you'd lost by one bid was a brutal act. And now, while that medicine's working, let's talk about something else."

"There was once a physician," said I, "with eyebrows like Helen of Troy's and a star in each of her eyes. Her mouth was made of red magic and had to be seen to be believed: and her hands were so small and so lovely that they were almost unfair. As for her legs – "

"The first duty of a driver," said Perdita, "is to keep his eyes on the road."

I sighed.

"You've no right to be so distracting. On the way here I felt quite monkish."

"After all, Herrick took orders," said Perdita Boyte. "Monkish," I said severely. "A word that Robert Herrick couldn't have spelt. I perceived the consolations of an ascetic life... charity in the sunshine and honesty in the breeze – "

"*Il penseroso*," murmured Perdita.

" – the countryside a blowing benediction... But now that's changed. The breeze is flirting, the sunshine is debonair, the countryside is enchanted – and you're to blame."

"I?"

"You," I shouted. "You with your eager air and the flash of your smile. You with your rosy – "

"Hush," bubbled Perdita, "hush." She laid a slim hand on my sleeve. "I'm sure those people heard you. I saw them – "

"I'm better already," I said, and glanced at her hand. "If we could stay like this for the rest of the way..."

An hour and a quarter later we saw White Ladies aglow in the evening sun...

As I brought the Rolls to rest, Berry burst out of the house with the Knave at his heels.

"Read that," he commanded, "and then get out of the car and go down on your knees."

'That' was an open letter.

Miss Boyte and I read it together – with bated breath.

My dear Berry,

I return herewith the cheque for one thousand pounds which it was just like you to send. I've made a heap out of the sale and am only too delighted that you should be up on your deal. Thank God you missed that table. You needn't spread it abroad, but that table was made to my order in 1912. And it cost me thirty-five pounds. I still have the receipt.

Yours ever,
GEOFFREY MAJORIBANKS.

"Stench knew," said Berry quietly. "And what of the sage who commended the ruling of a baboon?"

3

How Berry Prophesied Evil, and the Knave Purged His Contempt

"If you ask me," said Berry, "we're doomed," and, with that, he drank up his cocktail and lighted a cigarette.

"When," said I, "do you put the date of our, er, dissolution?"

"Any moment now," said Berry, cheerfully. " 'Thus far and no further,' says Nature, and we're well over the line."

"Don't be absurd," said Daphne.

"My dear," said her husband, "we can't go on like this. Nobody can. The whole world's luxury-mad. Besides, History repeats itself."

"You mean," said Perdita, "we're over-civilized?"

"Highly," said Berry. "Just as the Romans were. And as they went, we shall go. You see."

"How did they go?" said Jill.

"I can't remember," said Berry. "I think they were overrun."

Jonah looked up.

"No reincarnations just then?"

"Unhappily, no," said Berry. "I was a proconsul in the time of Caligula, and the last thing that I remember was lying on a bed of Turkish sponges in a hot, rose-water bath full of lily-buds, eating olives stuffed with caviare, while a Grecian artist was painting a fable of Aesop on each of my fingernails. That was the fashion just then. My next reincarnation was very brief. When I recovered consciousness, I was wearing a pig-skin loin-cloth and standing on a frozen swamp, trying to explain to Attila. That was as far as anyone ever got with Attila – a most impatient man. After that, I became a giantess at Barcelona."

"From what you say," bubbled Perdita, "it seems that we shall survive."

"Indubitably," said Berry. "But we'll never be so comfortable again. At least not for thousands of years. After the crash one goes back to the primitive state. Think of eating stewed eagle in a cave, listening to the wolves outside and arguing as to who ought to have brought the baby in."

"I wish you'd be quiet," said Daphne uneasily. "I can't think where you get these disgusting ideas."

The comparison was certainly odious.

The glorious voluntary of sundown had sped to its rest another magnificent day, and we were at ease upon the terrace, bathed and changed and right-minded, waiting to be summoned to a dinner which we proposed to enjoy. Before us, the old-world garden rested the eye: behind us, the comfortable mansion assured an immediate future of peace and luxury: we breathed the air of contentment – as well we might.

"And another thing," said Berry. "We're growing Babelish. And if that isn't asking for trouble, I don't know what is."

"What's Babelish?"

"Building Towers of Babel," said Berry. "Playing the fool with science. Swimming baths in liners and wireless in cars. Paying a film-star child ten times as much a year as a High Court Judge. Well, that sort of thing's offensive."

"I entirely agree," said Jonah. "But what d'you suggest we should do?"

"Live for today," said Berry. "There's nothing else to be done. One sucking-pig couldn't stop the Gadarene swine. When I was a Vestal Virgin – "

"That's more than enough," said Daphne. "First, you spoil our appetites and then – "

"On the contrary," said her husband. "I was a very Dorcas in a naughty world. They used to call me Nesta the Nonsuch: and after my death a cesspool was sunk in my memory, close to the Appian Way."

"Thank you very much," said Daphne, shakily. "And now, if you've quite finished, supposing we talk about tomorrow – on the chance that it comes. I simply must go to Velvet, to see Aunt Elise. Jonah is going to take me, so count us out. And Perdita says she's no wishes. So – "

"May I take that back?" said Perdita.

"Of course," said everyone.

My lady regarded her elegant fingertips.

"I knew there was something," she said, "but when you asked me just now, I couldn't think what it was. And then Berry reminded me – by something he said… I want to see a survival – a living, moving picture, made in the Middle Ages, and showing at Salisbury last week. Mother and I heard the trumpets, whilst we were deep in a shop. Later we asked the chauffeur what the fanfare had meant. And he said The Red Judge had gone by in his fine glass coach, with his coachman wearing a wig and his footmen standing on the tail-board. He was going from the Court to his Lodging in the Cathedral Close… You probably know it so well that it's nothing to you: but since then I've read it up, and I'd love to see the pageant that Cromwell was petitioned to stop."

"So you shall," cried Berry, and smacked the arm of his chair. "There's nothing doing tomorrow, because it's Sunday, but on Monday, at Brooch, the Summer Assize will be opened by Peppery Joe – one of the strongest Judges that ever sat up on a Bench. Mr Justice Scarlet, to give him his proper name. It was he you just missed at Salisbury. His temper's said to be short, but he knows how to try a case, and he has the finest presence I ever saw."

"Shall you ever forget," said Jonah, "his sending down 'Silver' Gilt?"

"Never," said Berry. "I wouldn't have missed it for worlds."

"What happened?" said Jill.

Berry sat back in his chair.

"They'd been after Gilt for ages, and they got him at last for robbery under arms. That must be twelve years ago. He stood his trial at Brooch, and Peppery Joe was the Judge. Gilt was most brilliantly defended and I think he would have got off – with a weaker Judge. But Peppery Joe had his measure, and Peppery Joe was determined to send him down. His summing-up was deadly, and the case was as good as over before the jury retired.

"Now, when a man's found guilty, before the Judge passes sentence, the prisoner is always asked if he has anything to say. When the usual question was put, 'Silver' Gilt looked at the Judge.

" 'I'll give you a tip,' he said slowly. 'The longer you make my sentence, the longer you'll have to live.'

"The threat was ugly enough, but the look in his eyes as he made it – I give you my word, it made my blood run cold. But Peppery Joe never blinked.

" 'So be it,' he said quietly. 'Let's both have fifteen years.' "

"Then he isn't out yet?" said Jill.

Berry shrugged his shoulders.

"He should be soon. If he behaves himself, they'll let him off two or three years. But in fact that kind of threat is never redeemed. After a while the iron in the soul grows cold."

There was a little silence, and a great owl swooped from a cedar across the breadth of the lawn.

"He's early tonight," said Jonah. "It's usually just after dinner he makes that move."

"Well, Brooch on Monday," said I, "to see The Red Judge. What do we do tomorrow?"

"Nothing," said Perdita swiftly. "It's lovely here. In the afternoon, perhaps, if anyone wants a drive..."

"We'll take our tea," said Jill, "and show her The Long Lane."

"That has no turning?" said Perdita.

"Not so much as a bend," said I, "for nearly three statute miles. Hence its name."

"Oh, I don't believe you," said Perdita.

"Strange as it may seem," said Berry, "for once he is telling the truth. It's a bit of a Roman road – a bit that was bypassed hundreds of years ago. It's linked up now, of course, but it serves no particular place, so it's little used. One day the char-à-bancs will find it, and the glory which departed with the legions will come again – in the shape of concertinas and paper bags and all the other emblems of social majesty. But at present it's dull, and birds presume to sing there, and I have seen a horse go by with a man on his back."

"Oh, come," said Perdita, smiling. "Half the England I've seen is still like that. And your byroads always lead to the scene of some Nursery Rhyme."

My brother-in-law bowed.

"Fine ladies' luck," he said simply. "They shall have music wherever they go."

"Perdita," said Jill, "look there."

We followed her gaze.

At the foot of the terrace steps the Knave was standing a-tiptoe, looking at us. His eyes were alight with mischief: his ears were pricked: in his mouth was a little silk slipper, taken from Perdita's room.

To every dog the way of his heart. Friendly and gentle to all, the Alsatian reserved this honour for those he loved.

"You see," breathed Jill, "to take away a slipper of yours is his idea of a compliment. He's on his way to the garden, to bury it there. But he thinks you might be inconvenienced, so he's come round this way to show you what he's about. If you were to say 'All right,' he'd be gone in a flash: but if you say 'Oh, Knave,' he'll bring it to you."

"Isn't it beautiful?" said Berry. "In fact there's only one snag – if you shouldn't happen to see him, he, er, hopes for the best. I'd a new pair of evening shoes… They cost me seven pounds ten, and I'd only worn them once… I still have one: I might lose a leg or something – you never know."

"You don't know that he took it," said Jill.

"If you mean that I didn't see him, I've been at some pains to point out that that's perfectly true. I also admit that on being desired to find it, he appeared incapable of complying with the request." He covered his eyes. "Snowing like hell, it was, and there we were with two gardeners and half the house, crawling about all under the rhododendrons and rooting about like so many hungry hogs… And all that dog did was to wait till we began scratching and then start in. Hole after hole he dug: and we stood round and watched him: and when he'd finished, the gardeners would fill it in. Talk about being made fools of… Look out. He's tired of waiting."

"Oh, Knave," said Perdita, quickly.

At once the Alsatian stopped: then his fine head came round, as though in surprise.

"Oh, Knave."

The silky ears fell back and the great tail began to sway. Then very slowly the Knave ascended the steps and, moving to Perdita's side, laid in her lap a trophy which I should have liked myself.

As the applause died down –

"It's asking for trouble," said Berry. "You can call it 'his pretty way' or dress it up as you please. In fact it's larceny. He stole and took and carried that slipper away, and if Jill hadn't happened to see him, it would have shared – with one of the best-looking shoes I ever put on – some sodden mausoleum to which he alone has the key."

"Our dog is a good dog," purred Daphne, caressing the velvety muzzle the Knave had laid on her knee.

"That's right," said her husband. "Play the false prophet. Slobber over iniquity."

"I'm not," indignantly. "How dare you say such a thing? Just because once you couldn't find one of your shoes – "

"Oh, give me strength," said Berry.

" – you want to jump on his very humble endeavour to show goodwill. It's very clumsy, of course: but when he was only a scrap, he thought of it all himself, and – "

"Oh, I can't bear it," said Berry. "Come here, old fellow." The Knave was at his side in a flash. "You know that I wouldn't hurt you for anything in the world."

The Knave gave a whimper of pleasure and licked his face.

"And now you have done it," said Jonah. "He knows you've withdrawn the protest he heard you make."

My brother-in-law swallowed.

"After all," he said, "so long as he always brings the footwear to us..."

I turned to see the butler by Daphne's side.

"Dinner is served, madam."

Twenty shining hours had gone by, and Berry's forebodings had melted as mists before the smile of the sun.

We had proved the pleasant borders of The Long Lane: we had left the Rolls and had strolled on the dead-straight switchback, as others had strolled upon it for nearly two thousand years: finally we had entered a meadow, to break our fast in the shade of a monster oak. The spot was peaceful and ministered to the mind. We had to ourselves a fold of the countryside, the natural beauty of which had been adorned by years of husbandry. Our meadow sloped to the lane, where a five-barred gate of grey oak maintained its privacy: before us, a poppied cornfield was kept by the finest hedgerows I ever saw; and the ridge behind us was clothed with a stretch of woodland, rich and clean and sturdy, to temper the wind to the georgic that lay below.

The afternoon was lazy and very still: stretched on the turf, we fleeted it carelessly, murmuring conversation, or musing, or fast asleep: body and soul relaxed: we were out of the world.

Berry slumbered faithfully: flat on my back, I considered the ceiling of oak leaves directly above – and found it a hanging garden, fit for the use of dreams: their voices subdued, Perdita and Jill were talking steadily…

I cannot tell what it was that made me, all of a sudden, remember the Knave. We had all forgotten the dog. He had, no doubt, wandered away, and out of sight, out of mind. It must have been half an hour since I had seen him nosing the meadow for savoury scents.

With a shock I sat up – to see him standing before me, *with his eyes alight with mischief and a good-looking shoe in his mouth.*

If my exclamation was natural, it put an end to our peace. Perdita and Jill cried out and Berry started out of his slumber as though he had been suddenly stung.

"What on earth's the matter?" he demanded.

"This," said I, and took a man's left shoe from the jaws of the Knave. He suffered me gently, if reluctantly.

Yet heavy with sleep, my brother-in-law stared upon his footwear and then upon mine. Then he looked dazedly about him.

"Where's Jonah?" he said.

The position was explained to him excitedly.

"It belongs to some stranger," I concluded. "How or where he obtained it, I can't conceive. But – "

"What did I say?" said Berry, whose senses had now returned. "Only last night I said you were playing with fire."

"Well, what if you did?" said I. "I never taught him to do the blasted trick."

"You encouraged him," said Berry. "You led that dumb animal to think – "

"And what about you?" cried Jill. "You said he oughtn't to do it and then you withdrew what you said. Jonah said at the time – "

"We're dealing with a dog," said Berry. "Not a recording angel with outsize ears. I suppose you'll say in a minute I set him on."

"I wouldn't say that," said I, "but the fact remains he's never done this before. The last thing you said was this – 'So long as he always brings the footwear to us.' Well, he's brought it to us, hasn't he? Of course, it may be a coincidence, but – "

"Of course if you talk like that," said Berry, "you'll be afflicted. Some judgment will come upon you… Here am I, the only one of us all who has ever protested against a course the folly of which would put a swine off its food, and you turn round and say I'm responsible." He took a deep breath. "You know, that's an obscene libel."

"It's no good bluffing," said Jill. "You know the Knave understands every word that we say. And last night you gave him leave to do what he's done."

"Leave me out for a moment and answer me this. Whenever that dog's done his trick, have you or have you not applauded him?"

"Yes," said Jill, "we have. But – "

"Then," said Berry, "why don't you applaud him now? I think he's done rather well to find a shoe like this in the countryside."

There was an uneasy silence. After a little, I got to my feet and looked about me.

"Exactly," said Berry, grimly. "There isn't a private house for at least four miles, and who leaves a shoe like that in the woods or fields? You can see it's practically new: and it's just as good as I've ever had made for me."

"I can't believe," said Jill, "he'd go into a private house."

"More," said I. "Who can he like about here? He'd never take the shoe of someone he didn't like."

"Oh, that's fantastic," said Berry. "There's nobody here he knows. But the shoe must have come from somewhere where shoes are kept. And shoes like that are kept in a private house."

"What about a tent?" said Perdita.

"Well done," said everyone.

We had no doubt that her reading of the riddle was good. Camping out in fine weather was all the rage. Some tent, no doubt, had been pitched somewhere near at hand, and the Knave had come upon it, while its owners were taking the air.

"The Knave shall guide us," said Berry, and got to his feet. "Give him the shoe again and tell him to take it back. You'll have to go and see that he does it, but – "

"You do it," said I, and put the shoe into his hand...

Berry was painfully explicit, but the Knave has fixed ideas upon the uses of gifts. For the next five minutes he cantered about the meadow, with Berry, panting invective, in close pursuit, while Perdita, Jill and I abandoned ourselves to a laughter which left us weak. At last the performers lay down – some six feet apart. After another five minutes, Jill and I, between us, recovered the shoe. Then we began, all five, to look for the tent...

The hour that followed, did much to reduce our weight, for the heat of the day was not over and the duty we tried to do was that of a mounted patrol. The country, of course, was against us. As I have hinted, the hedgerows were most efficient, while the woods, as a bulwark, left nothing to be desired. I cannot say that we used the Knave as a guide, but his zeal to lead the way would have disconcerted a mind that was made of brass. Hideously mistrustful of his motives, again and again we proved his shocking excursions, fighting our way to join him in some inaccessible place, for the dog could pass where we could not – except at the price of a disorder which sent us half out of our minds. And always his leadership failed us – as we had known it would. Again and again we deposed him from the role which he had assumed and helped one another back to take up a line of our own, but the Knave would be back before us, waiting to make some point which we dared not ignore.

"Yes, I see him," said Berry, licking the blood from his wrist. "But some other fool can buy it. That dog's a wicked liar."

"You can't be sure," said Jill, tremulously. "There might be a tent behind there."

Berry regarded the bullfinch with starting eyes.

"There might," he said. "There might be a circus behind it for all I know. But I'm going to assume there isn't. And I'll tell you another thing. If I can walk so far, I'm going back to the car. It's been a delicious ramble, but I've had enough of playing at Paradise Lost." He shambled up to a chestnut and set his back to its trunk. "If you want my private opinion, the dog's possessed. Some wandering evil spirit was jealous of our content, so he entered into the Knave and possessed him to steal that shoe: he knew we should try to restore it – anyone would: and for more than an hour he's done nothing but twist our tails. Well, mine's come off now..." For the fiftieth time he wiped the sweat from his throat. "We're not meant to find this camp. We never were meant to find it. We were meant to exchange an existence which was almost too good to be true for one which could be relied on not only to ravage the body, but to distort the soul." He broke off and looked about him. "Where's he now? I don't want any more of his conjuring tricks."

"There he is," said Perdita, "digging a hole."

"To bury his spoil in," – grimly. "Well, I'm not sure he isn't right."

"We can't do that," said I, regarding the shoe. "We'd better take it to a police station."

"Not if I know it," said Berry. "Whoever that shoe belongs to is going to go raving mad. I know what I'm saying – I've had some. To steal one shoe suggests malice... I've had enough trouble today and I'm not going out of my way to buy any more. After all, we've tried to return it: and if people like to be careless and leave their belongings about – "

"But we can't leave it here," said Jill.

"We are going to leave it," said Berry, "beneath this tree. I'm not going to have any truck with stolen goods. And that shoe may well have been stolen before the Knave put in his oar. We've found no tent, have we? But we may have missed a tramp who didn't want to be seen – because he had with him the goods he had stolen the day before."

The suggestion was more than enough.

I hurriedly laid the shoe at the foot of the trunk, and we made our way back across country as well as we could.

Twenty minutes later we clambered into the Rolls...

We had covered perhaps half a mile when we floated over a hillock to see a man's figure ahead. His back was towards us and he was moving slowly and going dead lame.

"He's hurt himself," said I. "We must give him a lift."

Perdita caught at my arm.

"Wouldn't he walk like that if he'd cast a shoe?"

There was an electric silence, and, without thinking what I did, I set a foot on the brake.

"My God, she's right," cried Berry. "I can see the grey of his sock."

"We must go and get it," breathed Jill. "We must – "

"Not so fast," said Berry. "We've got to restore it, of course: but this is a case for finesse. You can lay he's ripe for murder, and somehow or other we've got to keep out of the wet. We shall have to bluff him somehow. He's probably feeble-minded – going out for a stroll and losing one of his shoes."

Here the stranger glanced over his shoulder and, seeing the Rolls approaching, immediately turned towards us and put up a stick.

"Well, you've got to do it," said I. "My brain's a blank."

"That's all right," said Berry. "First we smooth him down and then we say we think, if he's very good, we – "

"Don't keep saying 'we'," said Jill. "I'm not going to open my mouth."

As we drew near to our victim I saw he was a fine-looking man, some sixty years old. His gaze was bent upon the ground, but though he leaned on his stick and lifted his foot, the dignity of his demeanour was unmistakable.

"Slow as you dare," said Berry. "What about this? We saw some children playing a little way back. They were playing 'Hunt the slipper': and now that we come to think..."

Perdita began to shake with laughter.

"He doesn't look," said I, "as if he'd eat out of your hand."

"That's because he's ruffled," said Berry. "Once we've smoothed him down..."

And then and there the stranger raised a magnificent head.

For a moment there was dead silence.

Then –

"Gongs of Gehenna," breathed Berry. "*It's Peppery Joe.*"

As I brought the Rolls to rest, Mr Justice Scarlet lifted his hat.

"May I ask you to give me a lift for one or two miles? A car should be waiting for me upon the main road."

"Er, of course," mouthed Berry, rising. "We hope – I mean, I fear you must have met with an accident."

The Judge glanced down at his foot.

"If," he said, "to be the victim of a pleasantry commonly supposed to be the prerogative of apes is to meet with an accident, then your surmise is correct."

"How – how very shocking," said Berry. With bulging eyes, he descended into the road. "Did they, er – I mean, I do trust they didn't use violence."

"Who?" said the Judge, frowning.

"Why, the apes," said Berry. "I mean the per-perpetrators – the ones who did it on you."

"Did it on me?"

"Victimized you," said Berry. "That's the word – victimized."

The Judge shook his head.

"The facts," he said, "are simple. I know this country well and was taking a ten-mile walk – for the good of my health. By the time I had covered five miles, my shoes, which were fairly new, had begun to trouble my feet. After another two miles, I sat myself down in a meadow and took them off, proposing, when my feet were relieved, to finish in comfort a walk I had much enjoyed. Whilst I was waiting, I slept. When I awoke, one of my shoes had been taken, the other left."

"Taken?" said Berry. "What a – what a most extraordinary thing."

"The shoe," said the Judge, "was gone. Now to take one shoe is not the way of a thief – nor, I should have supposed, the way of a decent man." His grey eyes glowed in his head and he smote with his stick upon the ground. "Some mind diseased – some distorted sense of humour decided otherwise."

"Oh, no," said Berry. "Not that. I mean, are you sure?"

"Sure?" snapped the Judge. "Who can be sure of what happens when he is asleep? But I'm not a fool, sir. I don't believe in witchcraft and I never yet heard of a shoe that walked by itself."

"Out of the question," said Berry, and wiped the sweat from his face.

"Very well, then. My shoe was taken... This evening some 'bright young thing' will relate to his grinning peers the enterprise with which he discomfited a stranger who lay asleep."

With that, he entered the Rolls and, bowing politely to Jill, took his seat by her side. As he did so, the Knave rose up, laid his head on the Judge's knee and gazed with apparent devotion into his victim's face. As the latter made to caress him, the dog put his paws on his shoulders and licked his chin.

"Down, Knave, down," said Jill quickly.

"It's quite all right," said the Judge. "I expect he knows that I've a weakness for dogs."

I saw Berry moisten his lips.

"I, er, can't get over it," he faltered.

"Over what?" said the Judge.

"Why the – the outrage," said Berry. "The taking away of your shoe. I mean, it seems so wanton."

"Many epithets," said the Judge, "have occurred to me and that among them. But pray don't dwell on the matter. With your arrival my embarrassment disappeared. As for the shoe, that's gone."

"It can't be far," said Perdita.

"Why do you say that?" said the Judge.

"Because, if you're right, it's not theft, but a practical joke. Well, a practical joker would never take it away. He'd pitch it over a hedgerow or something like that."

"I quite agree," said the Judge. "But I sought it high and low for nearly an hour."

"Why not let our dog try?", said Perdita. "I wouldn't suggest such a thing, only, as it happens, he's awfully clever like that. It's not just ordinary seeking: he seems to be able somehow to track a thing down...to trace it away from its owner – I don't know how to explain."

"It's like a bloodhound," said Berry, "only the other way round. I mean, we've had many examples. Only last week he found a wife for my bag – I mean a bag for my wife."

The Judge regarded him straitly.

"Are you being serious?" he said.

"We are indeed," said Perdita. "I think it must be instinct. It can't be scent."

"Half and half," said Berry. "He has to know the person who's lost the thing."

"And what he's to look for," said Perdita.

"That's essential," said Berry, and mopped his face. "Jill, my darling, show him Sir Joseph's shoe."

Mr Justice Scarlet looked at him very hard.

"Have we met before?"

"I'm a magistrate, sir," said Berry. "I've seen you in Court," and, with that, he gave him our names and we made our bows.

Jill was addressing the Knave.

"Good boy, Knave, look at that. Now you've got to find its fellow. You understand?" The Knave let out a bark and took the shoe in his mouth. "No, no. Not that one. The fellow. Will you be a good dog and find it?" She patted the Judge's arm. "It's his shoe, you see, and he's lost it..."

Again the Knave pawed Sir Joseph and nosed his face.

Pleasedly the latter caressed him.

"He certainly seems," he said, "to understand what you say."

"He does indeed," said Jill. "We honestly have to be careful what we say in front of this dog."

"Careful?" cried the Judge. "You're not going to tell me he talks."

"Not quite," said Jill. "But he heard us discussing an aunt who was coming to stay. We were saying what she was fit for. And an hour before she arrived, he went and was sick in her room."

As the laughter died down – "That's more than understanding," said his lordship. "That's *savoir faire*."

"I'll go with him," said I, and got out of the car. "If you'll tell me the meadow, sir..."

The Judge pointed over his shoulder.

"Five minutes' walk," he said, "when you're properly shod. The second gate on your left. I rested at the top of the meadow, close to the wood."

Perdita was down in the road.

"I'll come with you," she said. "I'd like a walk. But I think he should have something of Sir Joseph's, just to keep his mind on the job."

"What about this?" said the Judge, and held up a well-worn pouch.

The Knave took it out of his hand and leaped out of the car.

Once over the crest of the hillock and so out of sight of the Rolls, I turned to Miss Perdita Boyte and fell on my knees.

" 'Holy, fair and wise is she,

'The heaven such grace did lend her.' "

"Don't be a fool," said Perdita.

"I'm not a fool," said I, "I'm a thankful man. By your wit you've delivered us out of the lion's mouth. When our bones were turned to water, you – "

"I'll give you twenty minutes to get the shoe and come back."

I got to my feet.

"I heard you say," said I, "that you wanted a walk."

"That was *suggestio falsi*. I wanted the Judge to infer that we hadn't been out of the car. Still, if you'll undertake to behave..."

"I reserve the right," said I, "to admire you and all your works."

The Knave preceded us gaily, pouch in mouth.

"If only we'd known that he had a weakness for dogs."

"Ah," said I. "Then we could have told him the truth."

"Exactly," said Perdita, nodding. "However, there's no harm done. He knows we didn't take it, but he knows we know where it is."

"Oh, hell," said I. "D'you think so?"

"I'm sure, He's terribly shrewd. He can't make out how we know or why we won't tell him the truth. But he knows that there's no ill will, so he's very wisely content to allow us to play the hand. But, honestly, Boy, can you beat it? Last night I express a desire to see The Red Judge. Today I'm given a close-up – of the very finest figure I ever saw."

"He's equally lucky," said I. "He probably dreamed last night of a witch with a mouth like Psyche's and a couple of stars in her eyes."

"Who tried to deceive him. I wish we'd told him the truth."

"You needn't fret," said I. "There's something more precious than stars in your pretty brown eyes."

A child slid her arm through mine.

"I like you," she said. "You don't always tell the truth, but you always say the right thing."

The restoration was over.

If the Judge suspected collusion, he covered it up very well, and the fuss which he made of the Knave, if more restrained, was as handsome as that which the Knave made of him. Finally, we all stood invited to tea at The Judge's Lodgings the following day.

As we floated home in the Rolls –

"Now, why did this happen?" said Berry. "Did the Knave overhear us last night and act upon what he had heard? Or did he just pinch that shoe because he had taken a liking to a very remarkable man? And why should he fall for a stranger who wasn't aware of his presence because he was fast asleep?"

"Try reincarnation," said Perdita. "Perhaps in some other existence the Knave was his dog."

"That won't do," said Berry. "You don't remember the past."

"I beg your pardon," said I. "I seem to have heard you remember – "

"Vaguely," said Berry, "vaguely. I sometimes think that when I was the Queen of Sheba, you were my favourite skunk. You've a way of wiping your nose... But I can't be sure."

Before I could counter this insult –

"I believe," said Jill, "that the Knave's got a curious power that we haven't got. It's not second sight, exactly. But if ever he does something funny, you know, if we wait a little, we find that he's perfectly right."

"I see," said Berry, thoughtfully. "It's rather a daring theory, isn't it? 'There's *an Alsatian* that shapes our ends, Rough-hew them how *he* will.' Well, you may be right, but if Peppery Joe knew the truth, I hardly think he'd subscribe to that point of view."

"You like the Judge, don't you?" said I.

"I like him immensely," said Berry. "And that's impertinent. The man is worshipful."

"So the Knave found him," said I. "He looked upon him and loved him – and then, by way of homage, made off with his shoe."

"What sewage," said Berry " – to use a ladylike word. I don't believe he ever fell for the Judge. The fuss which he made was simply reflected affection – the mother embracing the stranger who's saved her child. The Knave made much of Sir Joseph, because some instinct told him that he was the very being whom we were desirous to see. And he took his shoe to bring that consummation about."

"Tripe," said I. "And then I'm being polite. But in trying to read this riddle we're wasting our time. We're flattening our noses against that pane of glass through which we can only see darkly. Some dogs, and the Knave among them, obey a faculty which our intelligence is unable to comprehend."

"But what a gem," said Berry. "You ought to write a pamphlet – *Things I have Rubbed my Nose in*, by *Nauseous*."

"No, he oughtn't," shrieked Jill. "He's right. You'd have said it yourself, if you could have put it so well."

"Hush," said Berry. "That little mouth was never made to utter blasphemy. And now let's hear Perdita's view. Her little finger is thicker than most of our loins."

My lady spoke over her shoulder.

"I have no view, but one thing I do observe. 'Second sight,' 'instinct,' 'faculty' – you're all of you flirting with one and the same idea. And I don't see how you can help it, for he does understand what we say and he must have heard us last night – I saw him below the terrace before he came to the steps. If, however, he took to the Judge on sight, I think we must come down to earth and admit that it's nothing but chance. And as to that, I should let the Knave speak for himself. He's been asked to tea tomorrow. I think he'll be more than polite if he really cares."

"I know," piped Jill. "We'll take him with us in the morning, to see Sir Joseph go by. Then if he gets excited – "

"Better still," said Berry. "We'll wash the morning out and go in the afternoon. We've been asked to tea at five. That means he's not going to rise before half past four. If we go over early and wait in the Close, we shall see the coach drive up and his lordship get out. Perdita will have her pageant, with a very much finer setting than the busy streets can provide, and the Knave will have a fair chance of recognizing his man."

"And 'his man,' " said I, "will look very different just then. His wig and his robes of scarlet will make a most effective disguise. But personality will out. If the Knave really fell for Sir Joseph, he'll fall for The Red Judge."

Some cathedrals have more than one close, and Brooch among them. The Judge's Lodging stands in the lesser close – as fair a court as ever a temple had. The spot is sanctuary – a place of lawns and flagstones and whispering elms, of distant murmurs and the flutter of pigeons' wings, of solitary footfalls and the quiet chime of bells. Sometimes the crunch of wheels declares that a car is stealing over its gravelled drive, and sometimes a slant of music – the organ framing the voice – tells such a tale as transfigures its fine old face: but these things are but the fishes that leap from time to time from the depths of some silver pool, for the life of the close is that of untroubled water, sweet and deep and reflective, and running so very slowly that it seems to be standing still.

At one end a grey old gate house admits the world: at the other a pride of buttresses springs from the emerald turf and, above them, a great wheel-window is serving an echoing transept of the cathedral church: on either side are mansions, standing well back, each with its garden or forecourt and all of them long and low. Their styles are different, but every one is lovely because it was built by a master and has been arrayed by Time. The sunshine has painted their faces, and wind and weather have laboured to tire their heads, and the tale of those they have sheltered lives in the stone of their thresholds – one and all worn to a curve by the passage of many feet.

The Judge's Lodging stands at the end of the close, under the shadow of the cathedral's wall. Between the two lies a gap which leads to the cloister-garth, but vehicles may not pass there, because it is holy ground. As is fitting, the house has a sober mien, and its fine, flagged forecourt is sunk, so that, leaving the door, you go down and then go up to the close by a flight of steps. The entry might have been planned with an eye to the stately procession which passes every morning over its flags – the High Sheriff in blue and silver, wand of office in hand; then the Judge's chaplain in gown and hood, and, last of all, His Majesty's Justice in Eyre. But this we were not to see, for when the Court has risen, his lordship returns alone.

"If we stand about here," said Berry, "we'll see the whole of the show – the coach coming under the archway and driving the length of the close. When it's passed us, we turn to follow. By the time it's pulled up at the Lodging we'll be about ten paces off. If he sees us, it doesn't matter – he'll go straight into the house: but the Knave will see him crossing the pavement – it's good and wide."

Perdita gazed about her and put up a hand to her head.

"It seems unreal," she said. "It's like a scene in some play. Not a human being in sight – to tell us we haven't stepped back four hundred years."

Here a man strolled into our view from the way to the cloister-garth.

"Oh, you shouldn't have said it," cried Jill.

"He's too late," said Perdita, swiftly. "The perfect impression's been taken – I've got it here, in my heart. Besides, he'll be gone in a minute."

Had he been bound for the gate house, this would have been true but, as though to deny our wishes, after some twenty paces, he turned on his heel and strolled back.

"As I feared, when I saw him," said Berry. "You'll have to accept his presence. He's a plain-clothes man who's been put in charge of the Judge. You saw him looking at us. Well, if we went and stood by the entrance he'd move us on."

Perdita laughed.

"He'd have his work cut out, if the truth were known. If the guide-books printed the picture we're going to see – well, you'd have to shut the gates of the close. Don't tell me they're still shut at sundown, just as they used to be."

"From time immemorial," said I, "when the great bell strikes seventeen, at five minutes past nine. One stroke for every Crusader that lies in the church below."

Perdita closed her eyes.

"I ask a question," she said, "and you, by way of answer, just pick me some lovely flower. I'll have such a precious nosegay to take away when I sail."

"And what shall we have?" said Jill.

"The perfume," said I, "which she lent to the flowers she left."

"Eyes on the gate house," said Berry. "It's nearly a quarter to five."

"It's all right. I'm watching," said Jill...

A gentle-faced prelate came out of a garden beside us to cross the close, and a nursemaid appeared with a child on the opposite side. And then they, too, were gone, and the place was still.

As in a play, I heard the ring of hoofs on the cobbled street. An instant later, the coach swung under the archway and clattered out of the shadow into the sun.

The picture was most arresting, but not, I think, so arresting as the look upon Perdita's face. All the romance of her nature was welling out of her heart and flooding her lively beauty with a radiance I cannot describe. It is written, Your young men shall see visions. Be that as it may, I know that her cup was full.

So I never saw the pageant, until it had passed us by – a blaze of gold and crimson and flashing glass, wigs and white silk stockings, hammercloth, body and tail-board moving against a background which was before coaches were.

We had turned as Berry had counselled and were moving towards The Lodging before the coach came to rest. That the Knave was excited was nothing, for he must have felt our interest in what was afoot. We saw the men leave the tail-board and one of them open the door and let down the steps. And still the setting was perfect – the stage was clear. The burly detective was mercifully not to be seen. We saw The Red Judge descend and begin to cross the pavement, which must have been twelve feet wide.

"Look, Knave," breathed Jill, beside me…

I glanced at the dog, but an exclamation from Berry made me look back.

The Judge had stopped – on the pavement, and the plain-clothes man had appeared. He was standing just clear of the entrance, facing the Judge.

I think we were all of us staring, when Berry spoke with a voice I should like to forget.

"God Almighty," he croaked. "*It's 'Silver' Gilt.*"

The horror of that instant will stay with me while I live. For a quarter of an hour we had shared the close with Murder: and now her mask was off, and she was standing before us, about to lay her hand on the man we knew. And nothing on earth could stop her…

Too late we flung ourselves forward – the convict's hand was moving, and we were ten paces away.

Something spurted into my vision – a flash of brown and silver, seeming to skim the pavement, *ventre à terre*.

As the shot was fired, the Knave landed – where the throat runs into the neck, and Gilt went flying as a skittle that is floored by a full-pitched ball…

Sir Joseph was answering Berry.

"Through my cuff, I think. Yes, there's the hole. His aim was true, but he fired just an instant too late."

Berry turned to me.

"Get the girls away and wait for me in the car."

As I went, I glanced over my shoulder.

The Judge's butler and Berry were deep in excited talk. 'Silver' Gilt, looking very shaken, was arm in arm with the footmen – but not in a friendly way. Behind him was standing the coachman, with a splinter-bar clubbed in his hands. And The Red Judge was down on one knee, with an arm about the Knave's shoulders, looking into his eyes. But the Knave was looking past me...

I turned to see Jill very white, with a hand to her head. I was just in time to catch her, before she fell. As I picked her up in my arms, the Knave was leaping beside me, to lick her face.

Three days later we took our tea with the Judge.

The affair of Monday was not mentioned. This was as well, for at home, for the last three days, we had spoken of little else. I will only say that Jill's contention was honoured – that the Knave had a 'sight' which we had not, and the will and the wit to act upon what he 'saw.'

Tea was served in what was the inner hall, in the bay of an oriel-window, commanding the garden below. No one could have been more charming than was our distinguished host, and his Marshal, who did the honours, showed us throughout a respect which we did not deserve. Proposing to stay for an hour, we stayed for twice that time, while Sir Joseph remembered for us the high and mighty burden of other days.

As at last we rose –

"And you were his Marshal?" said Perdita.

"I was," said the Judge. "When he went circuit, he always rode on horseback the whole of the way." He glanced at the open windows. "We rode into Brooch one evening as lovely as this. We were very tired and thirsty, and he threw himself down on those cushions and called for beer. When the beer came it was sour and he'd pitched it out of that window before I could think. A quart of sour beer... And a maid was standing below in a brand-new gown... I had to say I'd done it – that's what the Marshal's for. And he had the girl up and he dressed me down before her – he never did things by halves."

And there I saw his face change. For a moment he appeared to consider: then a look of understanding entered his eyes, the smile on his lips seemed to tremble, and a hand went up as though to conceal his mirth.

And then I saw Berry's face...and followed his gaze.

His eyes alight with mischief, the Knave was looking at us from the foot of the stairs: in his mouth was a buckled slipper, such as Sir Joseph was wearing three days before.

4

How Daphne was Given a Present, and Jonah Took off His Coat

Dusk had come into the panelled dining-room, and the radiance the candles lent to the tablecloth made bold, as the bark of a puppy, to speed the parting day. And something else it did. It showed to great advantage the beauty that graced our board. On my left, my sister, Daphne, recalled the dark perfection of Reynolds' days: on my right, my golden-haired cousin remembered those pretty princesses that live in the fairy-tales: on the other side of the table, the natural and lively sweetness of Perdita Boyte suggested a hamadryad acquainted with Vanity Fair. One other thing held the eye – and that was the pink champagne. The table was jewelled with six little rose-coloured pools, that caught the sober light and made it dance and sparkle with infinite mirth.

"I'm all disappointed," said Perdita. "White Ladies ought to have a ghost. I mean, if ever there was a house…"

"That," said Berry, "is what I have always said. This place would be stiff with ghosts – if there were such things."

"But there are," said his wife. "Just because you don't happen to have seen one – "

"Neither have you," said Berry. "None of us have."

"I know people who have," said I.

"Who say they have," said Berry. "But they're always short of a witness to bear them out."

"There's Abbess' Oak," said Jill.

"A legend," said Berry, "that no one on earth can confirm."

"I dare you," said I, "to stand alone under that tree for a quarter of an hour on end on a winter's night."

My brother-in-law frowned.

"Certainly not," he said. "I don't believe in apparitions, but I do believe in a presence you cannot see. And that can be most disconcerting."

"Then you do believe the legend," said Jonah.

"No, I don't," said Berry, "but I'm not going to take any risks. If by chance it was true, the lady would resent my intrusion, and I don't want any spirits biting my neck."

"Bigot," said Daphne. "You value your unbelief."

"He's none to value," said I. "You ought to have been at Cockcrow, when they wanted to put him to sleep in the haunted room."

Berry addressed Miss Boyte.

"Happily," he said, "I am proof against the darts of the ungodly. This I attribute entirely to meekness of soul – a quality more apparent to the lower animals than to certain blasphemous lepers who defile the faculty of speech. Besides, the room was hung with black arras."

Perdita shuddered.

"That was unfair – even to a heretic. Please may I hear the legend of Abbess' Oak?"

I emptied my glass.

"Once upon a time," said I, "an abbey stood here – an abbey of nuns. It had the reputation of being immensely rich. It was, as were many others, suppressed by Henry the Eighth: but, in this particular case, the abbey was burned to the ground – and five years later this house was built on the site. That is all matter of fact: and now for the legend. The Abbess was warned that the King's men were on their way, so, before they came, she got all the treasure away and sent it down to the coast and over to France. Robbed of their spoil, the King's men went mad with rage: and they not only burned the abbey but they hanged the Abbess herself from a bough of the oak that stands by the mouth of the drive. And ever since then her ghost has walked of nights where the crime was done."

Perdita took a deep breath.

"Was nothing left of the Abbey?"

"Only the cellars," said Berry. He lifted his glass. "This wine came out of them. They're simply gigantic. In fact, unless the nuns entertained a good deal, one is forced to the conclusion that the abbey was justly suppressed."

"I'd love to see them."

"Tomorrow morning," said I.

"The dowser," said Daphne, "is coming tomorrow morning."

"For a fee of ten guineas," said Berry. "You know, you make me tired."

"You won't be tired if he finds us another spring."

With a manifest effort, Berry controlled his voice.

"There are moments," he said, "when I could bark with emotion. Bark... To hear you talk, nobody would dream we'd ever had a dowser before – and dropped two hundred quid because we believed what he said."

There was an uneasy silence.

The remembrance was more than grievous. At the place which the wizard selected, we had dug an expensive well. At forty-two feet we found water, and at forty-three we found rock – exactly one foot of water, forty feet down. And when we had pumped it dry, the well took twelve hours to refill...

"Well, we must do something," said Daphne. "The garden – "

"We must have water brought," said Berry. "Conveyed by road."

"Hopeless," said Jonah. "We'd need six carts a day for the lawns alone."

"Then," said Berry, "we must deepen the wells we have."

"Out of the question," said Jonah. "If we are to have more water, we've got to find a new spring. And that is where the water diviner comes in. I don't like taking his word: but we'll prove him right or wrong for a matter of thirty pounds."

"It isn't the money," said Berry. "It's the knowledge that we'll have been done – *for the second time*...in the crudest possible way. You wouldn't have a child on twice, and we're not infants-in-arms."

"*Force majeure*," said I. "There's nothing else to be done."

"I'll tell you what," said Jill. "We can watch the Knave. He'll know if the dowser's honest. And if the Knave doesn't like him, we needn't dig."

"Better still," said Berry. "We bury a bottle of whisky before he comes, and while he's walking about we watch his nose. If this begins to go red, we write home and warn his wife. And when he's gone, with his cheque – "

"I know," said Perdita. "Couldn't you lay a trap? Hide one of the wells, and see if he finds it out?"

There was an electric silence. Then –

"The stable well," said Jonah. "Ground sheet over the flap and a flower bed on top. You know. Like they make them for shows. Old Thorn will love to do it, but we'll have to tell him tonight. And here's a health to the lady for being so wise."

We drank it rapturously.

"She's a paying guest," said Berry. "That's what she is. I feel quite different already. My gorge is falling and my spleen is fast assuming proportions less inconvenient to its distinguished company."

Perdita smiled.

"If I'm bright tonight, you must thank your very good wine." She touched her glass. "Did the nuns leave this behind them? It's terribly rare."

"The custom of the house," said Berry. "Tomorrow is the chatelaine's birthday. In less than twenty-four hours my hag will be sixty-nine."

"Common man," said Daphne. "Last year I was twenty-seven, so now I am twenty-six. Entirely between ourselves, the Bilberry register will tell you I'm thirty-two."

Perdita lifted her glass.

"I'm so glad to be here," she said gently, and left it there.

The diviner compassed the flower bed, rod in hand. We watched him guiltily. After a little, he set a foot on the mould... And then he was full in the bed and was wiping the sweat from his face.

"There's water here," he said shortly. "Abundant water...at twenty to twenty-one feet."

Berry took the bull by the horns.

"We congratulate you," he said quietly. "You're perfectly right."

Frowning a little, the other stepped out of the bed. "Trying me out, eh? I might have known. There's plenty of sceptics about."

"We should like to beg your pardon," said Berry. "But it's fair to ourselves to tell you that two years ago we were very badly let down."

The diviner nodded abruptly.

"Plenty of them about, too." He pushed back his hat and tapped with his foot upon the ground. "There's a fine spring here." He laughed. "Good enough for a village, but not for a place like this."

The procession reformed: but we followed no longer as critics, but in humble respect for a talent we could not deny. So far as I was concerned, the man was a proven wizard – and that was that. The gardeners who brought up the rear were deeply impressed. Only the Knave showed indifference – or, rather, a faint surprise that we should honour a stranger whom he had rejected the moment he saw his face. The dog can hardly be blamed. The fellow was most unattractive, and so were his ways. Manners may not make magic, for all I know.

We left the walled kitchen-garden to enter the orchard beyond...

Strolling by Perdita's side, I found it strange that Nature should have chosen for her prophet a practical, business man. About the diviner there was nothing at all of the earth. That the country bored him was plain. He belonged to the town. With his precious gift, the fields should have been his office, the open sky his windows, the brooks his books. But the man was a man of business and his rod was a fountain pen.

I murmured my feelings to Perdita.

"The shepherd's complaint," she replied. "You must live and let live, Lycidas – though you may have been born out of time."

"There spoke Amaryllis," said I. "Supposing – "

The diviner's voice cut me short.

"There's a spring hereabouts. A good one. It mayn't be where you want it. I can't help that."

"It's quite all right here," said Berry. "Isn't it, Thorn?"

"A good head of water here, sir, would do us uncommonly well."

The diviner seemed to cast to and fro. After a little he straddled and pointed between his feet.

"Have you got a peg?" he demanded.

Thorn came forward and pressed a peg into the soil.

"At twenty-five feet," said the other. "Perhaps twenty-four."

"No rock?" said Berry.

"Rock be damned. You're lucky. I've found you a master spring. It's waste of time going on. You've got what everyone wants."

"I'm greatly obliged," said Berry. "Come back to the house. I guess you can do with a drink."

"I guess I can," said the other, and mopped his face.

Berry and I did the honours, and that in the library. At first we had to work hard, but under the touch of liquor our guest relaxed. This to our great relief. If what he told us was true – and we had no doubt that it was – the fellow had done us a service worth very much more than his fee. We were appropriately grateful. To have our advances rejected was most discouraging.

"I notice," said I, "that you don't work with a twig."

Sitting on the arm of a sofa, the diviner shook his head.

"I can: but I don't have to. If a man can really find, he can find with a bit of old iron. I've done it with wire – more than once. But some things are better than others. It all depends how you're made." He took a soft case from his coat. "I've three rods here. They're all of them specially built." He slid one out of its sheath and put the others away. "Now that's one that I use…"

With his words I saw the rod move and the sentence died on his lips.

"Good lord, more water?" said Berry.

Frowning slightly, the dowser got to his feet.

"Looks like it," he said abruptly. "What's beneath here?"

"Wine cellars," said I. "But they're as dry as a bone."

Rod in hand, the other nodded.

"It's a long way down," he said slowly. "You've nothing to fear." He put the rod away and picked up his cheque. "And now I'll be off," he added. "If you've time to burn, I haven't – and that's a fact."

His ill humour was back in full force. The slightest use of his talent seemed to lay bare his nerves.

In an awkward silence, we walked with him to his car. There we thanked him again and he asked us the way to Brooch. As his two-seater stormed down the drive –

"Well, I'm glad that's over," said Berry. "He may be a giddy wizard – I think he is – but of all the offensive…"

"Exactly," said I. "But I don't believe the man's normal."

"Yes, he is," said Berry. "As normal as you and I. He's a Communist – that's his trouble. One of the red-hot type…that wants to bring to ruin all homes like ours. And we employ and shelter twenty-two souls."

My sister leaned out of the oriel above our heads.

"My dears, what a birthday present! A master spring. What does that mean exactly?"

"I imagine," said I, "that it means a very rich source."

"And you do believe in him, Berry?"

"If I didn't, my sweet, he'd have gone twenty minutes ago – with a master flea in each ear."

"Poor man," said Daphne. "Perhaps he's a master spleen."

Three days had gone by, and the new well was nine feet deep. So much Jonah reported, measuring tape in hand. The hour was sundown, and we had but just come home, to rush to the scene of the labour which was to confirm or deny the report the diviner had made.

"Outrageous," said Berry. "They haven't done three feet today."

"It's been very hot," said Daphne.

"It's not skilled labour," said Berry, "and they've got five men on the job. Any fool can dig a hole in the ground."

Jonah looked up.

"He's perfectly right. We could dig it faster ourselves. If we put in four hours tomorrow..."

"I'm game," said I.

"That's the style," said Berry heartily. "I only wish I could help."

"Don't be a fool," said Jonah. "We must have three."

"Why can't you help?" said Jill.

"I've got to see the dentist," said Berry. "Heaven knows – "

"Have you got an appointment?" said Daphne.

My brother-in-law swallowed.

"Polteney always sees me – "

In a burst of indignant derision the rest of the sentence was lost.

"All right, all right," said Berry. "I'll put it off. After all, what is thrush?" He took up a pickaxe and weighed it – with starting eyes. "I think I'd better work at the top."

"Half-hour shifts," said Jonah. "We shan't want very much on."

"We'd better work barefoot," said Berry. "Then when we slice our feet off, we shan't have any boots to be cut away."

"Any fool," said I, "can dig a hole in the ground."

"With reasonable tools," said Berry. "That pickaxe – "

"It's the weight that does it," said Jonah. "You'll see what I mean when you've swung it for a quarter of an hour."

As soon as Berry could speak –

"We'd better not," he said shortly. "We shall only offend the men. When they find we've been doing their work – Yes, Falcon?"

I turned to see the butler two paces away.

"I came to say, sir, the men went off early today. It's the foreman's silver wedding. But they're going to make it up, sir, on Saturday afternoon."

"God bless them," said Berry with emotion. "God bless their simple souls."

"They were very anxious, sir, that you shouldn't think them indifferent to your desires. They're very grateful for the beer, sir."

"Tell them," said Berry warmly, "I'm more than satisfied."

"Very good, sir. And, if you please, sir, the wine has come."

"The wine?" said Berry. "What wine?"

The butler moistened his lips.

"I believe it, sir, to be claret. Sixty dozen were delivered this afternoon."

"Sixty dozen?" screamed Berry. "But who's been being funny?"

"There you are, sir," cried Falcon. "I was sure there was some mistake. Again and again I insisted that you would never have ordered – "

"Seven hundred and twenty bottles?"

"And all of them loose, sir. And not a label between them… It took two hours and more to get them into the bins."

Berry put a hand to his head.

"Stand back," he faltered. "Stand back and give me air."

"But where did they come from?" said Daphne.

"From some warehouse in London, madam. I'd have telephoned if I could, but they're not in the book."

"Well, it's their look-out," said I. "When they render the bill, we can tell them to take it away."

"That's all very well," said Berry. "Supposing I'm right, and somebody is being funny – ordering stuff in our name... We shall know tomorrow morning, but I don't want five tons of guano and a hundred and fifty bedsteads in weathered oak."

"For heaven's sake," breathed Perdita. "Is that sort of thing ever done?"

"I regret to say," said Berry, "it sometimes is. The Fairies of Castle Charing met it last year. They spent a week in Paris. When they got home they could hardly get into the drive. Four full-size billiard tables, seventy baby-carriages, over two miles of stair-carpet, eleven kitchen-ranges and twenty tons of the very best fish manure."

"Let's shut the gates," said Daphne, faintly. "If you think there's the slightest chance – "

"It's all right, my dear," said Berry. "They can't get very far as long as we're here. I'll give up Polteney tomorrow and spend the day on the steps."

In fact, he was spared this penance. At seven o'clock the next morning the men returned for the wine and took it away. The lorries were laden and gone before we were down.

It was Sunday afternoon; and Perdita Boyte and I were sitting at ease on the turf at the head of the well. The others were gone to tea at a neighbouring house.

The orchard was comfortable, breathing the honest leisure of other days. So far from ruffling its calm, the sound of a distant car deposed to its possession of a peace which the world of today cannot give. The silence was rich and golden, laced with the hum of insects and, now and again, with the delicate flutter of wings.

A little shaft of sunlight was thrusting between the leaves to glorify Perdita's hair. This was uncalled-for. Her beauty was vivid enough. At her feet the Knave lay couched, with his eyes on my face.

My lady opened a mouth which prose could never describe.

"Why does this spot attract you?"

"At the moment," said I, "I am here because you are here."

Perdita laid herself back and regarded the sky.

"If I were out of the country, you'd be sitting beside this well."

"I believe that," said I, "to be true. But I don't know why."

"Try and think," said Perdita, quietly.

Averting my gaze from the lady, I did as she said. After a little while –

"It's rather involved," I said feebly. "First, I've always had a weakness for fairy-tales. You know. There was once a youth who set out to seek his fortune. And he met a wise man by the way. And the wise man told him to dig at a certain place and that when he had dug so deep he would discover the treasure that there lay hid... Then, to come back to earth, the treasure itself is perfection – a lively thread of silver, a virgin source, that since the world began rolling has picked its way from the hills... And then again, the well is so very old. It's figured from the beginning – in the Bible, in Aesop's Fables, in Virgil and Nursery Rhyme. Men have always digged wells, and the simple ritual's the same as it was in Abraham's day. It is a natural labour – rendering unto Nature the things that are hers, for, once the well has been dug, it's as much a part of Nature as cockcrow itself."

A bright, brown eye found mine.

" 'Sermons in stones,' " said Perdita, sitting up. "My dear, you're incorrigible. You're the finest costumier I know. You could dress up a fried-fish stall or an Epstein bust. And 'Solomon in all his glory was not arrayed like one of these.' "

"Who eggs me on?" said I. "Who picks over the junk of ages and points to some faded relic I never found lovely before?"

"That's right. Dress me up, showman."

"I'm afraid I shall have to undress you – to go with the well. All the best nymphs went bare-legged, with a veil draped into a tunic and one of their shoulders free."

"Idylls while you wait," said Perdita. "Go on."

"I've done," said I. "You've got the shape and the skin and the right-sized stars in your eyes: you've got the eager air and the mouth which the dawn gets up on purpose to see: your hair would go straight into a shepherd's song, and as for your finger-tips..." I picked them up gently enough. "I'm afraid they're dangerous. If a god was passing when you waved your hand to a bird, I'm sure he'd come and ask for a drink. You'd have to give it him, of course. In your cupped palms, too. You know, I'm getting quite jealous."

Perdita began to shake with laughter.

"It's all very fine to laugh," I said severely. "There's the poor shepherd, clean off his feed and dreaming of the lights in your hair, trying to find a rhyme for 'provocative,' and all the time you're giving a god a...drink."

Perdita lowered her eyes.

"I daresay, if the shepherd asked nicely..."

The Knave, most discreet of sentinels lifted his lovely head – and I saw the servant coming, before he saw us.

He was plainly looking for me, so I raised my voice.

"I'm here, if you want me, William."

The man came bustling with a salver on which was reposing a card.

Chief Inspector R Wilson
CID
Scotland Yard

I passed it to Perdita, frowning, and got to my feet.

"All right, William," I said. "Show him into the library."

"Very good, sir."

As he left the orchard –

"But this is thrilling," said Perdita. "What can he want?"

I put out my hands for hers and drew her up to her feet.

"Come and see," said I. "I've not the faintest idea. But I wish the others were here."

My desire was granted forthwith.

As we left the stable yard, I saw the flash of the Rolls at the mouth of the entrance-drive.

Chief Inspector Wilson compelled respect. If his manner was masterful, his sense of duty stood out, while the way in which he stated his case would have done credit to any barrister.

He addressed himself to Berry, as being the obvious head of the eager court.

"I'm sorry to rush you like this, sir, but before I'm through you'll see that it isn't my fault." He glanced at the six pairs of eyes which were fast on his face. "I mean to speak openly. I'm sure that everyone here will keep what I say to themselves."

"I promise you that," said Berry, as a murmur of assurance went round.

The Inspector inclined his head.

"I've called to see you," he said, "about some wine… On Thursday last, I believe, some wine was delivered here…several hundred bottles, whilst you were out for the day."

"That's perfectly right," said Berry. "It was taken away the next morning at eight o'clock."

"Quite so," said the Inspector. "Mistakes do sometimes occur. I don't know if you saw the invoice, but *Rouse and Rouse* was the name, of *Commercial Road*."

My brother-in-law nodded.

"In fact," said Inspector Wilson, "there's no such firm. There *was* – five years ago: that explains the printed bill-head: but there isn't now."

We could only stare.

"Please get hold of this," he continued. "The delivery of that wine was not a mistake... And now may I see the butler?"

In a silence big with emotion, I rose and stepped to the bell...

After perhaps thirty seconds, the butler entered the room.

"Falcon," said Berry, "Chief Inspector Wilson would like to ask you some questions about that wine."

"Very good, sir," said Falcon, wide-eyed.

He turned to Inspector Wilson and moistened his lips.

The other looked up from a bulging pocketbook. "Tell me this, Mr Falcon. How many men brought the wine?"

The butler considered.

"There were five or six," he said. "I can't be exactly sure."

"And how many fetched it away?"

"The same as brought it," said Falcon. "I think there were six, but there may have been only five."

"Would you know them again?"

"I think so. Not all, perhaps. You see, my hands were full. The cellar's not very well lit, and what with counting the bottles and trying to – "

"Is that one?" said the Inspector, producing a photograph.

"That's right," said Falcon, at once.

"And that?"

Another photograph passed.

"Yes, that's another," said Falcon.

"Thank you," said the Inspector. "That's all I want."

Thus abruptly dismissed, Falcon took his reluctant leave. As the door closed behind him –

"I'd like to see the cellar," said Wilson, "almost at once. But before you take me down, I'll tell you what we shall find. That cellar has got an air-hole."

"That's perfectly true," said Berry. "There's a grating some three feet square – which gives to a slot in the ground like a miniature well."

"I never knew that," said Daphne.

"It's behind the lilacs," said Berry, "close to the stable yard." He returned to Inspector Wilson. "If you're thinking of entry, that grating could never be forced. It *can* be opened – from within. But I'll swear it's never been touched for fifty years."

"It's open now," said the other. "That's why I'm here."

The sensation this statement provoked expressed itself in a silence which is commonly coupled with death. The six of us sat spellbound, not seeming to breathe.

After a little, the Inspector continued quietly.

"You remember the butler said there were five or six men. Well, there his memory's perfect. Six men delivered that wine, and five went away. Five men came for the wine, and six went away. One man was down in that cellar all Thursday night. His job was to open that grating." He raised his eyebrows and sighed. "It's been done before."

"Well, I'm damned," said Berry, and spoke for us all.

"Now, I'm not a magician," said Wilson. "I couldn't tell you all this, if I hadn't been told. I've been told by an informant. I hold no brief for such men, but they earn their bread. This one's sitting at Cannon Row now, *afraid to go out*. But that's by the way. I've been after this gang for months, and, by your leave, I'm going to get them tonight."

"Tonight?" cried everyone.

The Inspector nodded.

"If my informant is right, they're coming tonight."

Berry sat back in his chair and folded his arms.

"What do we do?" he said.

The Inspector smiled.

"I suppose it's asking too much that you should do nothing at all. To be honest, sir, that's what I'd like. I've five men two miles off and I'm going to bring them along as soon as it's dark.

Sit up and watch, if you must – but if I'm to get home tonight, you must give that grating a miss. Try and forget about it – and all that side of the house. You see, that's the mouth of the trap... My men will be down in the cellar before they come. The door, of course, will be locked, and I'd rather you kept the key." He jerked his head at the Knave. "You must keep that dog quiet at all costs. I'd like him shut up in some room at the other end of the house."

"I was just going to say," said Berry, "it's going to be more of a matter for ears than eyes. I shall sit by the cellar door and listen in."

My sister shuddered.

"I shall go to bed early," she said. "And, as the Inspector asks, I shall try to forget. What do they want, Inspector?"

"Jewels and silver, madam." He hesitated. "You've got some notable bracelets, I understand."

Daphne covered her eyes.

"I believe every thief in Europe knows about them."

The Inspector shrugged his shoulders.

"These things get round," he said shortly, and rose to his feet. "And now may I see the cellars? After that, the outside of the grating: and then if you'd show me a place I can park the cars – just off the road, somewhere, as near the house as you can." He glanced at his watch. "As I said before, I'm sorry to rush you like this: but it's only a short six hours since the news came in."

"You've had to shift," said Berry. "And Sunday, too."

The other nodded ruefully.

"I was going to the Zoo," he said simply, "with my little girl."

Our visit to the cellars confirmed the informant's report. The grating had been unfastened, and its hinges were thick with grease. I swung it open myself without any sound.

Half an hour later we bade the Inspector goodbye...till the following day.

With a foot on the step of his car, he spoke his last word.

"You won't forget that dog, sir? If he were to go and give tongue…"

He broke off and shrugged his shoulders.

The Knave looked him full in the eyes and lifted his lip.

An hour had gone by, and Perdita, Berry and I were strolling beside the sunk fence, discussing the enterprise of the house-breaker of today.

"I confess," said my brother-in-law, "to a certain admiration for those about to be jugged. Sixty dozen of claret would gammon a herd of bloodhounds, let alone honest men."

"The very three that I wanted," said Jonah's voice. "Daphne's too nervous, and it wouldn't be good for Jill," and with that, he took my arm and fell into step.

"I wish to God," said Berry, "you wouldn't do things like that. Coming up from behind without warning. I'm ready to scream if anyone blows his nose."

My cousin ignored the protest.

"Keep on walking, please, and listen to me. I've been on to the Assistant Commissioner – at his private house. I wanted to ask about Wilson… He says he's an excellent man – *but he happens to be in Paris. No doubt at all about that. They had a talk this morning over the telephone.*"

"Good God," said Berry, weakly, and Perdita gripped my arm.

Jonah continued firmly.

"We have just received an impostor. Be sure of that. A wolf in sheepdog's clothing – paving his way. He's coming tonight all right, *but he and his men are the gang.*"

I put a hand to my head.

"But why – I don't understand…"

"It is confusing," said Jonah, "but I think I can give you a lead. Wasn't it Thursday night that the Knave barked twice?"

"Of course," I cried. "I'd forgotten. I got up and went downstairs."

"That's right," said Jonah. "I heard you. We were both of us half asleep. The Knave must have heard the fellow at work on the grating below. But, what is much more to the point, *the fellow at work heard the Knave*. Next day he says to his pals, 'The grating's open all right, but the dog's going to give us away.' So 'Wilson' comes down – under orders to clear the coast. I must say he did it well. Not only the dog but *all of us* out of the way. And simply by telling a tale the truth of which we could confirm. It's 'the confidence trick' once again, in a different guise."

My cousin's brilliant deduction left me dumb.

"I give you best," said Berry. "How did you know?"

"I didn't," said Jonah, frankly. "But one thing he said made me think. *I'd rather you kept the key* – of the cellar door. To me, those words rang false. They didn't seem to belong to Scotland Yard." He broke off there, to look at the western sky. "It won't be dark for two hours, and I've half a plan in my head. I wish we could cut dinner out, but I don't want Jill or Daphne to get ideas. And this is where you come in. It's up to you to get them out of the way – women and children upstairs by a quarter to ten."

"I beg your pardon," said Perdita.

"I didn't say 'maidens'," said Jonah. "I hope you'll come in on this. I was going to ask you if you'd take charge of the Knave. And now I must go. If I'm late for dinner, don't wait. I'll tell you all I've arranged at a quarter to ten. Meanwhile please do your best to find the answer to this? *What is 'Wilson' after?* I'd give a good deal to know."

"Jewels and silver," I said. "He told us himself."

"And warned us," said Jonah, swiftly. "Asked us to keep the key of the cellar door... I don't think that answer's right."

"It's a ruse," said Berry, and wiped the sweat from his face. "They mean to come in all right, but not by the cellar at all."

"I don't think that's right," said my cousin. "If they don't mean to use the grating, why did Wilson request that the dog should be put on the other side of the house?"

Perdita put in her oar.

"But if both those answers are bad, you get a third which is worse – that what they want's in the cellar."

"Which is absurd," said Jonah. "I quite agree. Burglars like their liquor as much as anyone else, but they don't go to lengths like these for a little Napoleon brandy and six or seven dozen of pink champagne. Never mind. Think it over. We ought to be able, between us, to do the sum."

With that, he was gone.

We watched him reach the terrace and enter the house.

"I'm quite sorry for 'Wilson'," said Berry. "He's going to get the shock of his life. When Jonah takes off his coat it's time to go home."

This was most true.

My cousin, Jonathan Mansel, is a man of action as swift and, if need be, as deadly as any machine gun that ever was brought into play.

A track runs into a wood which rises beside our meadows a short three hundred yards from the orchard gate. From my perch on the bough of an oak commanding the track I could, by day, have seen the roof of the stables against the blue of the sky. But it was no longer day. Night had fallen some twenty-five minutes ago.

My orders were clear. To signal 'Wilson's' arrival: to signal the strength of his gang: to signal whether or no the cars were left unattended when 'Wilson' set out for the house. All this, of course, with my torch. If the cars were left to themselves, Perdita and the Knave would join me, to watch while I opened the bonnets and cut the high-tension leads. And then we were to join Berry, who was lying within the orchard, close to the well. As for Jonah…

And there I heard the pulse of an engine.

A car – two cars had slowed down, on the road at the mouth of the track.

After, perhaps, thirty seconds I heard them begin to back...

Then I saw the glow of a tail-light – and made my report.

Two men were already afoot. Not till both cars had stopped did the others alight. Six in all I counted, and sent my news.

Things of some sort were taken out of the cars, but the lights were out now and I could not see what they were. The engines, of course, had been stopped, and since no words were spoken, the dark figures moving in darkness were worse than sinister. I saw them cluster below me, just clear of the leading car.

And then one opened his mouth – and I nearly fell out of my tree...

It was not 'Wilson' who spoke, but another, whose voice I knew.

As in a dream, I heard him issue some orders and tell off some man, called Jennet, to stay with the cars. His tone was as bitter as ever, his manner of speaking as short, and when he had done and was gone, I was not at all surprised when Jennet described him in terms which I dare not set down.

It was the diviner, indeed.

Bad masters make bad servants, and though, of course, I dared not lay hands on the cars, I was able to beat a retreat without any fuss, for Jennet, instead of patrolling, as he had been ordered to do, took his seat on one of the steps and lighted a cigarette.

I entered the meadows and followed the paling along. After perhaps forty paces, the Knave loomed out of the shadows, to put his paws on my chest.

"No luck?" breathed Perdita Boyte.

"Not at the moment," said I, and told her my news.

"Oh, my dear," twittered Perdita, "what does it mean?"

"I'm damned if I know," said I. "Can't you work it out?"

"I can make it rather harder by telling you this. D'you remember I asked you a question this afternoon? *Why does this spot attract you?* We were sitting by the head of the well... You gave me – so pretty an answer that I forgot altogether to give you mine." I found a small hand and held it close to my heart. "You see, Boy, it's not only you. That spot attracts us all. Ever since he told you to dig there – after all I'm only a guest, but it's never been out of my mind."

"Well, why's that?" said I, feebly.

The small hand caught hold of my coat.

"Call me a fool, if you like, but I think it's because that man's willed us...been willing us ever since Monday to think of that well. That he's got one strange power we know. Well, I think he's got another. And I think he's been using that to keep our minds on that well."

"But why should he do so, my beauty?"

The hand slipped away and up to the troubled temples which I could hardly see.

"I can't imagine," wailed Perdita. "And there you are. I told you I'd make it worse. But now that he's back here – in charge..."

"Let's go and put it to Berry. I must get in touch with Jonah about those cars."

Jonah and Berry were sitting on a log in the orchard, conversing in even tones.

"Come and sit down," said the former. "Our friends are deeply engaged. The cellar was their objective, as 'Wilson' said. They seem to be taking the floor up: and as flags are not like linoleum, we've plenty of time. Then again the work would go faster if they weren't so painfully anxious to make no noise."

"Did you recognize their leader?" said I.

" 'Wilson' was the first of the string."

"He's not in command."

"Who then?"

"Our friend, the dowser," said I. "There's no mistaking his voice."

"Go on," said Berry, incredulously.

"I am ready," said Jonah, quietly, "to believe anything. Understanding's another matter. I frankly admit I'm a long way out of my depth. But very soon now we shall know. They may as well get the stuff out – whatever it is."

"Perdita says – "

"Stop," hissed Berry. "Stop. I've got an idea. When he showed us rods, that wallah...*and one of them moved. In the library, Boy, that morning. He asked what was underneath, and you said the cellars were dry*."

"Of course," I heard myself saying. "Of course...of course."

I remembered perfectly – now. But I had forgotten the matter, as though it had never been.

Jonah was speaking.

"Tell me exactly what happened."

Berry told him, from first to last.

"All the same," he concluded, "it only explains his presence – the dowser's, I mean. We want to know what he's after. And he's not come here to uncover some secret spring."

"What does Perdita think?" said Jonah.

Perdita tried in vain to steady her voice.

"It all f-fits in," she stammered. "He made them forget that bit in the library. And he tried to make them forget by keeping their minds on the well – all our minds, in case they'd told us..."

"I've no doubt you're right," said Jonah. "This dowser's no ordinary man."

"What on earth d'you mean?" said Berry.

"This," said Jonah. "Water is not all that a really good dowser can find. He can detect the presence of minerals – under the earth. Gold and silver, for instance..." I found myself trembling with excitement. "When you saw his rod move that morning, you thought there was water below: but the dowser knew better: *he knew there was precious metal down in the cellars beneath*...he came Thursday night, to make sure – to find the exact place and the depth...and tonight he's come to take his findings away."

An hour and a half crept by.

Perdita, Berry and I sat upon the log in the orchard, conversing by fits and starts but always with bated breath, while the Knave stood beside us like a statue, conscious of the presence of evil which for some strange reason he was not allowed to declare.

About his business, Jonah moved to and fro, visiting the servants he had posted, reporting progress to us or listening himself to the sounds which rose from the cellar's depths.

Jennet had been 'disposed of' and was sitting, gagged and bound, in one of the cars. These had not been disabled – my cousin had changed his plan.

An hour and a half.

Time seemed to be standing still: excitement begot an impatience which sent us half out of our minds: desire rebelled against reason again and again.

"Lifting flagstones," moaned Berry. "They don't know how to work. I'd have moved a mountain by now. And I know I'd sell my soul to be doing the labour myself."

Perdita put it in a nutshell.

"It's like when you've been given a present – and somebody else unpacks it: and you have to watch them fumbling, undoing the string."

"I know," said Jonah, "I know. But when six desperate men play into your hands, it's very much better to let them. The great idea is to avoid unpleasantness."

"I hardly think," said Berry, "that 'the great idea' will mature. I mean, I can't help feeling that on their way back to Town, no one of the six will really be at his best."

With his words came the flash of a torch.

"They're off," said Jonah. "Still as death, if you please, until I come back."

I went down on one knee. With my arm about the Knave's shoulders, I held his head to my chest. After, perhaps, two minutes I felt his ears twitch…

And then I heard the men passing – two men, breathing hard as they went, as men who are anxious to hasten, while carrying weight.

Another two minutes went by.

And then, well out in the meadows, a light leaped up.

I saw figures moving against it, and one was standing still with his hands in the air...

"Oh, I'm sorry for them," said Perdita, and burst into tears.

I gave the Knave to Berry and picked her up in my arms.

"Rough justice," I whispered. "Not fit for a maiden's eyes. When Jonah comes back, I'm going to take you to bed."

"Couldn't you...give them...just something? I mean...poor men."

For the first time for seven days my brain seemed to leap to life.

"If they've found what I think they have, I'll give them five hundred pounds."

"Oh, you darling," breathed Perdita. A warm arm slid round my neck. "What – what do you think they've found?"

"Darlings to you." I kissed her. "*The Abbey plate.*"

And that is very nearly the end of my tale.

A glance at the first-fruits showed that my conjecture was good: the plate had been buried, and lest it should be disinterred, the nuns had spread the report that it had been taken to France.

I took Perdita back to the house and wrote out a cheque. Then I returned to the orchard, where Berry was sitting in darkness, addressing the Knave.

"From your point of view, old fellow, it's been an utter wash-out from first to last. No hue, no cry, no dust-up, no biters bit. And what have we got to show for it? A lot of rotten utensils which we shall never use. Look at that alms-dish, for instance. No self-respecting dog would drink out of that. What if it is solid gold? You'd very much rather it was enamelled steel...

"What's happened?" I said.

"History," said Berry, "has just repeated itself. Two more left the cellar, laden, and were relieved of their booty in the midst of yon dewy meads. There's only the dowser left now. When the others fail to return, I suppose he'll emerge."

"Who's in charge of the cars?"

"Fitch and Carson," said Berry. "They're going to deport the wicked as soon as Satan arrives. To Break Heart Heath, I believe – an appropriate spot. Jonah will follow and bring them home in the Rolls. He's really a perfect producer… I wish we could show a light. There's a monstrance here with a ruby as big as an eye. It can't be real, can it?"

"I'll be back in five minutes," said I, and ran for the cars…

'Chief Inspector Wilson' stared at the cheque.

Pay Mr Jennet or Order
Five hundred pounds.

"Is this a have?" he demanded.

"No," said I, "it's a present – from a very charming lady. You've done us extremely well, and she didn't like the idea of your going empty away." I showed it to each of the others: then I returned to 'Wilson,' folded it up and slipped it into his pocket and out of sight. "There are five of you here," I said, "and, as you saw, it's made out for five hundred pounds. In a way, the inference is obvious. On the other hand, there's your leader – he'll soon be here. I haven't spoken to him, and I'll leave it to you to decide how much he should have."

The five replied as one man. So far as I heard, each put it a different way, but each spoke straight from the heart – with a steady, blasphemous vigour that did me good. I have no wish to seem harsh, but we had done the dowser no ill, while he had abused his position with all his might.

I did not watch his translation…

At three o'clock that morning we stood in the dining-room. Windows and doors were fast, and the lights were full on. The table was crowded – crammed with the Abbey plate. Chalices, platters and flagons – sacred vessels and caskets for which I can find no name...there was not one of silver, but all were of gold.

But the beauty was not all to the board.

On my right stood Daphne, her glorious hair unbound, turning her jade-green dressing-gown into some goddess' robe: Jill stood between Berry and Jonah on the opposite side of the oak – a King's daughter in blue and silver, with her pretty hands in her pockets, appraising her father's hoard. On my right stood Perdita Boyte, swathed to the throat in old rose, a nymph awaiting her call – to meet the dayspring upon some mountain lawn. Curious in spite of himself, the Knave moved about the table, nosing the fusty collection we seemed so much to revere.

"All these years," murmured Daphne, "and nobody knew."

"What ever," said Berry, "what ever will Christie's say?"

"You're not going to sell it?" cried Jill.

"Yes, we are, sweetheart," said Jonah: "in self-defence."

Perdita breathed in my ear.

"Did they seem comforted, Boy?"

"Stopped crying at once," I whispered. "If their hands had been free, they'd have put their arms round my neck."

"Oh, I didn't" – indignantly.

I tucked her arm under mine.

"I know," said I. "Neither did I."

5

How Perdita Bought a Staircase, and Berry Put on Raiment that was Not His

"When I was a child," said Berry, "I was invariably sick after eating boiled mutton."

"Thank you very much," said Daphne. "And if you have any other similar reminiscences, perhaps you'll postpone them until we have finished lunch."

"If I must, I must," said her husband. "Only don't forget to ask me. I always feel that the pretty ways of childhood are too much ignored. Which reminds me. Tomorrow I must revisit scenes which I dignified in swaddling clothes. I can't say I remember the occasion, but I have always understood that it was at Thistledown that, my cot having disappeared, I was put to sleep in Queen Elizabeth's bed. And they all came up after dinner to see the child a foot long in a gold and crimson four-poster some ten feet square."

"How sweet," said Perdita Boyte.

"More," said Berry. "It was prophetic. For such as had eyes to see, my great predecessor's stomacher – the pearl one – had already fallen upon my t-tender trunk. I confess I can't swear in Latin, but the imperious personality is there. I sometimes wish it wasn't, you know. Repression is bad for the health. Yet what can I do? If I were to let it appear, those I love would be fighting to wash my feet."

With that, he raised his tankard and Daphne discharged a roll.

To duck in the act of drinking can always be done – at a price...

As Berry recovered his breath –

"We were talking of Thistledown," said I, swiftly.

"Couldn't we all go?" said Jill. "And take our lunch?"

"What could be better?" said Berry, wiping his face. "The park was always pleasant, and I rather imagine we shan't get another chance."

"Are you going to sell?" said Daphne.

"I suppose so. But I think I should see it once more before I sign it away." He turned to Perdita. "One hundred and fifty acres...beautiful acres of England...and I'm offered two thousand pounds. But what can I do? When everything's paid, it brings in about four and six. Four shillings and sixpence a year. Well, two thousand pounds in the hand is better than that. But I've got to say 'Yes' or 'No' within forty-eight hours."

"Why such haste?" said Daphne.

"I cannot imagine," said Berry. "That's why I'm going to take a look at the place."

"And the house and all?" said Perdita.

"No house," said Berry. "The house was burned to the ground twenty years ago. And never rebuilt. Still, the park's the same. I'd like to have it myself."

Perdita knitted her brows.

"But isn't it yours? I mean, if you're going to sell it..."

"I hold it as sole trustee for a boy at school. Poor little chap. But for the War, he'd be spending his holidays there – with the jolliest father and mother you ever saw."

"The Thistledown Curse," said Jonah, and left it there.

"Looks like it," said Berry. "You can't get away from that." He turned to Perdita. "Never cross a gypsy, my dear – a genuine

Roman, I mean. Old Sir John Raby did – about forty years back. Turned her out of the park, or something – I don't quite know what it was. And the lady cursed him and his house – to his face, in front of his grooms." He broke off and shrugged his shoulders. "From that day nothing went right. Wife, eldest son, and fortune – he lost them all. His second son, Colin, succeeded, he was the best in the world. He seemed to be pulling things round till the house was burnt. He was at the front at the time, and, because he'd too much to think of, he'd let the policy lapse. He was killed in 1918, and his wife gave birth to the boy and then followed him out. And now the boy's at Harrow, and all he's got in the world is a short two hundred a year and a hundred and fifty acres which nobody wants – except for this Mr Puncheon: and he can't want them much, if he's only willing to go to two thousand pounds."

"Poor child," said Perdita quickly. "And when he leaves school – what then?"

"I can't imagine," said Berry. "I sold out to put him at Harrow. I think I was right. After all, he's the eighth Baronet. But life can be very hard for a titled orphan who's less than two hundred a year."

"It might be worse," said Jill. "He mightn't have you for trustee."

"I don't actually rob him," said Berry, "if that's what you mean."

"No," said Daphne, "she doesn't. She means that you do your duty, but that your interpretation of 'duty' – "

"This discussion," said Berry, hastily, "will now cease. Where were we? Oh, I know – Thistledown. Well, shall we all lunch there tomorrow? It's sixty odd miles away, but a pretty run."

"By Salisbury," said Daphne. "Splendid. I want some silk for a cushion, and I think I can get it there." She turned to Jill. "We must take a piece of that cretonne, to match it with. Will you tell Dacre to put a length in the car?"

"Is that my favourite?" said Berry. "The one that looks as if somebody's trodden in something and then walked all over the place?"

As was only to be expected, the simile provoked great indignation.

"It's really shameful," said Daphne. "You never open your mouth without saying some filthy thing."

"That statement," said her husband, "savours of exaggeration – a failing which, as I have frequently indicated, tends to subvert the dignity of speech. Never mind. In this case I'm not to blame. You present to me something bestial, and I describe it as such."

"But it isn't bestial," shrieked Jill. "It's one of the smartest designs that – "

"If you mean it has atmosphere, I'll give you that. It is also subtle and effective – in a singularly loathsome way. It passes direct into the bloodstream, like some odourless poison gas. It does no more than suggest: but the cunning suggestion it makes would put a ghoul off its food."

"Of course," said Daphne, "you're making me feel quite ill."

"It isn't me," said Berry. "It's the cretonne that's doing that. The bare recollection of its burden is more than enough. Sluglike, it leaves behind it a trail of slime: as a result, the digestive organs are startled, like sheep that have smelt a goat – I mean a wolf. They huddle together, quaking – "

"I do wish you'd be quiet," said Daphne. "I tell you, I don't feel well."

"Of course you don't," said her husband. "I feel very funny, myself. And that's just talking about it... But you never can trust these futurist conceptions. I had my suspicions the moment I heard its name."

"It had no name," said Jill.

"This one had," said Berry. "I specially asked."

"What was it called?"

Before we could intervene –

"*Boiled Mutton*," said Berry. "Give Miss Mansel some water, Falcon. She's going to choke."

The Rolls was stealing through Salisbury when Perdita caught my arm.

"Oh, look, Boy. Isn't that priceless?"

I could not look, for the light-hearted traffic was thick: but I berthed the car where I could and prepared to descend.

"They won't let you stop here," said Berry…

"I opened Perdita's door.

We shan't be a minute," I said. "If the police intervene, just drive her round to the Close. Jonah's there, for a monkey. Daphne won't choose her silk under half an hour."

"Well, why don't you drive to the Close? Why should I have the onus of…"

With Perdita laughing beside me, I hastened the way we had come.

"And now – what was priceless?" I said.

"You'll see in a minute. I'm terribly glad you stopped."

And so was I – when I saw it. I would not have missed it for worlds. A miniature staircase of oak, for use in a library. That it had been designed by a master was very plain. Its handsome lines and the elegance of its proportions made it a work of art. The jut of the little 'pulpit,' its exquisite balustrade, the purity of the columns which held it up – these things stood out against its background, a curtain of cream-coloured rep. And, what was more, the dark wood was beautifully carved. Banisters, columns and base had been wrought with a delicate flourish that charmed the eye. With it all, it was made for use. I never remember a piece that looked at once so dainty and so substantial.

When I turned to Miss Perdita Boyte, the lady was gone. After a moment, I followed her into the shop… This was unattended. A voice from its depths declared that its keeper was occupied with a telephone call.

"...ten minutes ago. I tried to get on from there, but your line was engaged... Quite so... On the copy I had, it wasn't coloured as yours, and of course, as I said in my letter... Exactly. You might almost call it the key. It controls the situation. For one thing only, to bring the services round... More like seven thousand. And what about the main road?... Yes, I know. Well, it's all right now. The document's signed... This afternoon, then. Goodbye."

We heard the receiver replaced, and after a moment, a nice-looking man appeared. His eyes were steady and gentle, and iron-grey hair distinguished his clean cut face.

"Good morning," said Perdita, quickly. "That little staircase you've got..."

Amusement flashed into and out of the other's eyes. Then –

"May I call my partner?" he said. "He'll deal with this better than I." He lifted his voice. "Norm, where are you? You're keeping a customer waiting." He turned again to Perdita. "Won't you sit down?"

An older man came bustling from the back of the shop. As he approached, the other picked up a hat.

"If I may, I'll leave you to him. You'll be safe in his hands," and, with that, he smiled and bowed and walked out of the shop.

Some twenty-five seconds later, Perdita purchased the staircase for twenty-five pounds.

Then she drew an odd cheque from her bag and began to dictate the address –

"*Mrs Pleydell, While Ladies, Hampshire*. That's – "

"Perdita," I cried.

"Be quiet. It's my birthday present. Besides, it was made for White Ladies, and that ladder you've got isn't safe." She returned to the shopkeeper. "Could you possibly send it today? If it could be there this evening..."

"I think I can do it, madam. My van's going down to Southampton this afternoon." He hesitated. "I'm glad it's to go to White Ladies. It came from a house like that."

"Where did it come from?" said I.

"Thistledown, sir. I had it in my workshop at the time of the fire. It had very clumsy castors, and I was taking them off and generally cleaning it up. And then I was asked if I'd take it in settlement of my bill." He smiled. "I've often tried to sell it, but though it's very pretty, it's made for use. And it wouldn't look right outside of a library."

Perdita's face was glowing.

"Isn't that glorious?" she said. Before I could answer, she had returned to the man. "You know your partner said that I should be safe in your hands."

The other stared.

"My partner, madam?"

Perdita nodded.

"The one who called you and then went out of the shop."

Norm put a hand to his head.

"That wasn't my partner," he said. "That was Lord Prentice, that was – the head of the armament firm. He's down this way on business. I've known his lordship for years."

We withdrew in some confusion – on Perdita's part.

"And I took him for a tradesman," she wailed.

"And he was quick enough to cover up your mistake. He didn't want you to be embarrassed, so don't go and spoil the good work. Besides, he is a tradesman – of a rather distinguished kind."

But Perdita nursed her error and would not be comforted.

By way of changing the subject –

"The Rolls has gone," said I. "We must walk to the Close. And what about your sweetness? Am I to mention – "

"Of course you're not," cried Miss Boyte. "I want it to be a surprise."

We reached the Close to find the cars side by side and Berry and Jonah discussing the failings of women with crooked smiles.

"We haven't been long," said Perdita.

"Dear heart," said Berry, "though I find no fault in you, I deplore the company you keep. Consider the facts. That pin-toed leper was driving: rightly or wrongly, he was in charge of the car. It was, therefore, for me to go with you – to minister to your fancies and anticipate your desires. So far from enjoying that lawful privilege, I have, by his misconduct, been subjected to the foulest insults at the hands of a policeman, less qualified to control traffic than to groom goats in hell, and to the perspiratory inconvenience of manoeuvring a chassis, which I have always maintained was unnecessarily long, between vehicles, the drivers of which were devoid of the faculty of consideration, and round corners which could be comfortably circumvented by a goat-chaise."

"But I heard you – "

"Beloved," said Berry, hastily, "such strictures as an innate sense of decency dictated were not being passed upon you. If I may believe this blear-eyed but otherwise inoffensive representative of my sex, he has for three quarters of an hour awaited the return of a harpy who promised that she would be back before five minutes had passed."

"Add Jill to Daphne," said I, "and you ought to know what to expect."

"It's the old Eve," said Berry, and shook his head

"I don't mind his being kept waiting: in fact, it's good for his soul: but suppose I'd driven them over – I nearly did." As though appalled by this hypothesis, he sat back and mopped his face. "And what could I have done? Nothing – except sit still, while the tide of indignity rose, the seething but impotent victim of a lack of principle so vicious as to be almost Cretian. And now, shall we go? I don't suppose they'll be long and, in any event, we have the luncheon with us. Besides, if they saw me here, they might be afraid to come back."

With his words the delinquents appeared.

As they drew near, I perceived that all was not well, for Daphne's brows were knitted and a wistful look was hanging in Jill's grey eyes.

Then the Knave went bounding to greet them and set them smiling again.

My sister lifted her voice.

"All four of you here. How nice."

"And Berry's driving," cried Jill. "I'm going to sit beside him. When he gets tied up in the traffic, he makes me die."

She pitched a length of cretonne into the car, took the seat beside Berry and set her cheek to his sleeve.

A husband addressed his wife.

"I trust," he said grimly, "that your quest has been crowned with success: that the silk you set out to purchase some fifty minutes ago – "

"Oh, it wasn't too bad," said Daphne. "Not what we wanted, you know, and in any event it's gone. I suppose I must have dropped it. We did look back, but you know what the pavements are like on market day. And now do let us get on. I hate having lunch too late; it throws everything out."

An hour and a quarter later we berthed the cars in a lane which ran from the main highway.

The spot was notable, for it had the look of a cloister which man had long ago founded and nature had brought to perfection in many years. On one side a six-feet bank was supporting a hazel wood – arras above a dado, vivid, cool and fragrant, starred here and there with flowers: the other side lay open except for a row of beeches along the edge of the turf: and, above, the boughs had woven a living roof – a maze of choirs for singing birds to sweeten, airy and yet so stout that the sunlight had sunk to a glimmer by the time it had pierced the leaves. Between the natural pillars appeared a peaceful prospect, fit for the eyes of such as have long forsworn the vanity of the world. Meadows, studded with trees, sloped to a pleasant valley which broadened into a chessboard of well-kept fields: to the left, the ground fell sharply, to hide the middle distance except for the gay, green tops of a line of elms: to the right, a sash of woodland sloped with the park and made a handsome bulwark against the winter wind. Of such was Thistledown...

Jonah glanced at the lane.

"Perfect for us," he said. "But isn't this way ever used? I mean, nothing can pass here, can it? We are 'occupying' the lane."

"I rejoice to inform you," said Berry, "that here, at least, I can put my car where I like. *And no one born of woman can say me nay* – not even a policeman by Epstein, with a hand like a bunch of bananas and the way of an anthropoid ape. This is a private road, and as Thistledown stands in my name, no one can so much as use it, if I like to order them off. As for making me give place..."

We alighted without more ado and set about the business of making ready to lunch.

The chuckle of a neighbouring rill suggested a means of cooling what drinks we had, and, whilst Jonah attended to this, I lugged the luncheon baskets into the shade of some chestnuts which seemed to be taking counsel a little way off.

Averse to such menial duties, Berry took his seat on the turf and declared the points of the landscape for such as had ears to hear.

"The property ends at that fence. It's not a very good shape – about four times as long as it's broad, and there's too much slope about it. It's a frontage of half a mile to the Salisbury road: I used to think that was of value, but it seems I was wrong. The house stood down in that dip, where you see the heads of the elms. And a glorious sight it was – a memorial of cream and old rose, with, I think, the loveliest chimneys I ever saw. But there you are. Take away the jewel, and you see what the setting is worth."

Whatever its market value, it made us a dining-room that was fit for a king: and when, perhaps half an hour later, we gathered about the cloth which the girls had spread, the luxury of our condition compelled our gratitude. Earth, air and sky were giving us of their best: commanding handsome country, yet sheltered from wind and sun, we had to ourselves the smiling neighbourhood: food and liquor were before us: and the *tout ensemble* had the air of one of those hunting banquets that live in the tapestries.

"We should do this more often," said Daphne. "Lunch out of doors like this is really ideal."

"And who brought you here?" said her husband. "Whose was the lovely instinct that led you to – "

Here the Knave smiled into his eyes and then licked the piece of chicken adorning his fork.

"There's a skunk," said Berry. "There's an unprincipled – "

"It isn't his fault," bubbled Jill. "The silly fools forgot to put in his lunch."

"They didn't?" – indignantly.

"Yes, they did. We'll have to make him up some out of the scraps."

"Poor dog," said Berry, compassionately, and gave him the morsel which he had made bold to denote. "All the same, er – go to Daphne, old fellow." The Knave laid a paw on his arm and let out a bark. "Yes, I know. It's a rotten shame. I'm very sorry about it. If I had my way… This *ragout's* extraordinarily good. Why can't we have dishes like this when we're sitting at home?"

"What *ragout*?" said Daphne.

"Well, I don't know what you'd call it. It's made with savoury rice."

"Let me see it. I never ordered – "

"It's the Knave's lunch," shrieked Jill. "He's eating the – "

"Moses' shrub," screamed Berry, and covered his mouth.

Now since the Knave understood whatever was said, it was but natural that he should acclaim our discovery of the truth which meant much to him, which he had been doing his very best to expose. Be that as it may, the second sweep of his tail knocked Berry's glass of cool beer clean into his lap. And the glass was capacious and full.

The resultant confusion was awful.

With beer streaming down his legs, my brother-in-law stamped about the meadow, spitting grains of rice and roaring dismay. Weak with laughter, we pursued him, napkins in hand, while the Knave, unaware of his trespass, went backwards before his victim, barking a frantic approval of active revelry.

(My cousin said later that only the brush of a Boucher could ever have captured the scene: he suggested a title, *Silenus Routed by Nymphs*.)

With the return of coherence –

"Oh, very funny," said Berry. "Quite side-splitting. First, by the grossest negligence, I am allowed to consume a lot of filthy beastliness prepared for the belly of a dog."

"It's p-perfectly good," wailed Daphne. "The vet wrote down exactly – "

"Oh, I'm sure it was the best horse-flesh," said Berry. He swallowed, with starting eyes. "But I can't help feeling that this weather – "

"It – it w-wasn't horse-flesh," sobbed Jill. "*It was b-boiled mutton.*"

So soon as he could make himself heard –

"Thank you," said Berry, gravely. "In that case, as you surmise, we know where we are." He glanced at his watch. "To the best of my recollection – "

"B-be quiet," begged Daphne. "It can't do you any harm. It just happens to be called his food, but – "

"Yes, I know that bit. And what disgusting rites attended its concoction?" A gasp from Jill made him look round. "Good God, don't say he's having powders?"

With tears coursing down my cheeks –

"Only flowers of sulphur," I said.

"I see," said Berry, thoughtfully. "What a very beautiful name. Flowers of sulphur. It looks as if I was in for a busy time." He lowered his eyes. "Just consider those trousers, will you? Every bit about them that matters, steeped, stained, soaking and soon to stink."

"You must t-take them off," quavered Daphne.

"I propose to," replied her husband. "Almost at once. And other mysteries with them. What I want to know is why am I selected for these indignities? I came here in love and charity. In faith and hope I committed my body to your care. And here I am, corrupted within and without..."

My sister and I escorted him back to the lane.

Now to take off your trousers is easy: effectively to replace them is very hard – when you are in the depths of the country and your wardrobe is sixty miles off.

It was Jill who thought of the cretonne...

Under Perdita's supervision, I cleansed the stains from the cloth in the chuckling rill: then I found a bramble-bush and spread the trousers to dry in the blaze of the sun: then I rejoined the others – to find a transformation which had to be seen to be believed.

My pen cannot justly describe the picture which Berry made. So far as appeared, he was wearing nothing at all but socks, shoes and a *chiton*, as worn by the ancient Greeks – a shapeless tube of material, kilted about the knees and brooched upon either shoulder, to make one hole for the neck and two for the arms. The pattern of the cretonne, however, suggested leanings less orthodox... The whole effect was not so much arresting as frightening. The most daring of hikers would have withdrawn from the field. A post-futuristic ballet-master would have burst into tears. Even the Knave kept his distance, and, on being conjured to approach, retreated backwards, barking.

Since Berry can rise to an occasion more highly than anyone I know, the meal was memorable, while the exhibition dances with which, unasked, he rounded the entertainment would have made a more critical audience split its sides. It was half-past three before he decided to change.

"Not that I object to this kit. It's free and easy and cool, and, as I can't see the design, I've nothing to fear. But I feel that the world is unready for such an effect. People in Salisbury might stare, and the policeman I met this morning might seek to improve an acquaintance which I prefer to forget. So if somebody'd fetch my trousers… They ought to be dry by now."

Reflecting that all good things must come to an end, I rose to do his bidding without a word.

Two minutes later I had the shock of my life.

The bramble-bush was empty. The trousers were gone.

My report was received with hysterical consternation. The concern was genuine: the desire to laugh immoderately was irresistible: for a moment my hearers hovered between two stools. Then –

"Gone?" screamed Berry. "Gone? Oh, don't be obscene."

The stool of the sense of humour gave way beneath our weight.

Berry was on his hind legs.

"I demand," he barked, "the immediate restoration of the raiment committed to your charge. If it's lost, it's got to be found. If it's stolen, it's got to be recovered. I won't take any excuse. I let you convey it away in the full and sacred belief that it was to be handed back. That was the governing condition: I demand that it be fulfilled."

"I'm most frightfully sorry," I said. "But it isn't my fault. I can only think that – "

"I must decline," said Berry, "to discuss the matter. When my trousers have been restored, I will consider an appropriately worded apology for the delay. I don't suppose I shall accept it, but that is beside the point – which is that I refuse to contemplate a contingency which cannot occur." He regarded his watch. "Between now and a quarter past four I shall be glad to receive the apparel to which I have already referred. It has got to be produced – somehow. And that is my very last word. Within thirty-five minutes my modesty *must* be redeemed."

With that, he lay down on his back and closed his eyes.

Something had to be done.

After a hurried consultation, the Knave and I – with Perdita Boyte in support – set out on the hopeless quest, while Jonah took one of the Rolls, proposing to purchase some trousers in Salisbury Town. Daphne and Jill remained within Berry's call, ready to offer consolation as soon as the latter consented to swallow his nauseous draught. Carry it off as you will, to be short of a pair of trousers is to walk with Ignominy herself.

A quarter of an hour had gone by, and I was waist deep in bracken, savagely cursing the flies and hopelessly scanning surroundings which looked very honest and charming, but told me nothing at all, when a sudden outburst of barking came to my ears. This rose from beyond and below, and almost at once I heard Perdita calling the Knave. I, therefore, made for some bushes directly ahead, to find that, as I had thought, they were masking the head of some bluff. Lest this should be steep and sudden, I dared not thrust through: but I lay down and worked my way forward, passing beneath the bushes until I came to the brink...

I was looking into a sandpit. At the mouth of this were two dogs, confronting the Knave. In the pit was a gypsy encampment – a weather-beaten tent and a painted van, surrounded by vessels, tarpaulins and all the battered equipment which nomads use. A tripod bestrode a fireplace, made up of loose stones, and washing was hanging on a line which ran from the roof of the van to a neighbouring fir. On the top of the van – and so out of sight of all but the fowls of the air – were lying Berry's trousers, carefully spread to make the most of the sun.

A girl was standing, calling the dogs to order and watching the Knave: two children had suspended their play and behind the tent an elderly woman was sitting, with a battered book in her lap. Her demeanour was brutally furtive. She could not see, and, except from the edge of the cliff, she could not have been seen; but her head was cocked to one side, the better to hear.

Using the utmost caution, I withdrew by the way I had come, and, when I was back in the bracken, I hastened round and down to the mouth of the pit.

With a hand on the Knave's collar, Perdita was addressing the girl.

"He's very friendly: I don't think he'd start a row. Your dogs are watchdogs, of course: they were doing their job."

With her eyes upon me –

"You never know," said the other. "I am all alone."

Perdita turned to me.

"I expected you'd hear the flurry. Mercifully, her dogs are obedient and the Knave respected my voice."

"You spoke as one having authority."

"I did my best. Where were you?"

"Down by the water," I lied, and turned to the girl. "Will your grandmother tell our fortunes?" I took the loose change from my pocket and counted five shillings out. "At half-a-crown each...before the others come back?"

With her eyes on my palm –

"I am all alone," said the girl.

"If you say that again," said I, "I shall go and ask her myself."

The girl's eyes burned in her head. Then she turned on her heel, but before she had taken two paces, the other came forth.

There was no mistaking her race. She was a true-bred Roman. That she wore the kerchief and earrings was nothing at all. Her pride of carriage alone proclaimed her ancestry.

I lifted my hat.

"Good day," I said quietly.

The keen, grey eyes surveyed me – with a fearless, insolent stare.

"What do you want?"

"What I have lost," I said. I heard Perdita catch her breath. "And what one of your company found."

The gypsy stood still as death, with her eyes upon mine. Then she turned very slowly to stare at the head of the sandpit, where I had lain.

After a long look, she addressed the girl.

"Give him the clothes," she said. "He knows they are there."

In silence the girl obeyed.

Like any cat, she climbed a wheel of the van, and, standing upon the tyre, reached for the missing trousers and whipped them down.

As she gave them into my hand –

"Seeing's believing," said the other.

"Tell the lady's fortune," said I. "I don't have to see to believe."

She shook her head.

"Today belongs to the past. Your friend, whose clothes those are, will want to go to the police."

"I'll see he doesn't," said I. "You're comfortable here?"

"I live and let live."

"Do you?" said Perdita, straitly.

The gypsy started, and I know I stared at my lady with open mouth, for her tone was the tone of accusation. So Nathan said to David, 'Thou art the man.'

Each woman was looking the other full in the eyes, and I saw in a flash that they had joined issue on some matter, though what this could be I had not the faintest idea.

Perdita's gaze was level, and her beautiful face was grave: her air was quiet and steadfast, as the air of one who knows his contention just.

The gypsy's demeanour was curious. She could not drive the astonishment out of her eyes, and, while she seemed to be striving to make her face like a mask, she gave me the definite impression of one who knows in his heart that some accusation is true.

At length –

"You are quick and wise," she said slowly: "but you have not the gift. You use your eyes with your ears and you see the things you are shown as can very few. But you have not the gift."

"I don't pretend to it."

"You are of American blood: but your mother's mother was English. Think of her now."

"Very well."

The gypsy put a hand to her head.

"She was tall," she said, "and you have her ways and her name, but not her face. Her neck was longer than yours, and her eyes were blue. When her hair was white, it was thick as when it was gold. She wore one earring only, and she had a scar on her temple that came from the kick of a horse."

"You have the gift," said Perdita.

The other lifted her chin.

"Think of your past."

"Very well."

There was a pause, whilst I stood as good as spellbound, because the two were moving on ground which I could not tread.

Then the woman's face set and hardened before my eyes.

"I said *your* past," she said grimly. "What have you to do with these things?"

"They trouble me," said Perdita. "*I should like to think that Thistledown's penance was done*. The house of Raby has paid...very heavily."

"It is nothing to you."

"Yes it is," said Perdita, steadily. "It's represented today by one little, penniless child. Home, parents and fortune – he's lost them all."

"You know him?" – suspiciously.

"I have never so much as seen him. Till today I never was here."

The gypsy's eyes were like slits.

"Yet you know," she said.

"Of course I know. And it troubles me. It is time that the clouds – "

"No one can order the future. I can see, but I cannot ordain."

"You can bless or curse," said Perdita. "You broke our laws today: but, because we respect you, we shall not go to the police. In return, I ask you to pity a fatherless child."

The other lifted her head to stare at the sky. "My man was dying," she said. "I only asked that he might be suffered to give up the ghost in peace. But Raby laughed in my face. 'Then take him home,' he said. 'The rogue's and the vagabond's home is the open road." She sank her chin on her breast. "He cried with pain when we lifted him on to the horse..."

"I am very sorry. It was a rough age. I would not have done such a thing."

"You are all the same," spat the gypsy. "Every man's hand is against us, and ours is against every man. But we are too few to resist. Do you wonder that under oppression we bare our teeth?"

"No," said Perdita, quietly. "I do not judge you at all. I only ask you to pity a little child."

"That has the same blood in his veins."

Perdita shrugged her shoulders.

"That has paid...for forty years...for something he never did." I saw the other's brows draw into a frown. "As you hope for pity yourself – "

"Enough," said the gypsy in impatience. And then, as she turned away, "I wish you well."

"Wish the little boy well. I should like to remember you kindly – and all your race."

The woman stood still. Then she turned again, to stare into Perdita's eyes.

"And if I will not do it?" she said.

Perdita's voice was firm.

"We shall both remember today. I do not pretend to wisdom, but, as you have said, I can see the things I am shown."

There was a long silence, while the two, I think, saw nothing except one another's eyes.

Then at last the gypsy sighed, and a hand went up to her head.

"I am growing old. I would have blessed you," she said.

"Thank you," said Perdita, gently. And then, "Goodbye."

As though she had not heard her, the other turned on her heel and moved past the girl and the children, as she had come.

As she disappeared, I stooped and laid the silver upon the ground.

Then Perdita turned, and I followed her – out of the pit...

After a little, I ventured to touch her arm.

"How did you know, Perdita?"

"I didn't. I took a chance – and it came right off."

"But – "

"I've no power at all. I swear it. Oh, Boy, don't look at me so. There's nothing queer about me. If it comes to that – those trousers... How on earth did you know where they were?"

"I was up above and saw them from the head of the pit. But you – "

"No, no." She laid a slim hand on my arm. "Don't look like that. I can't bear it. I – I can't have you think I'm different to what I am."

Five minutes before, a Portia had demanded justice. And now a child was pleading – a child some twenty years old, with honesty leaning out of her anxious eyes and her lovely heart on her sleeve for a man to kneel to. The incarnation was so exquisite as to bring a lump to my throat.

"You're incomparable any way," I said unsteadily.

As though in understanding, her precious fingers tightened upon my arm…

After a minute or two –

"She'll do as you asked?" I ventured.

Perdita nodded thoughtfully.

"I think so. She's almost sure I've no power, but I don't think she'll run the risk of calling my bluff. You see, I'd got my facts straight and I laid the charge where it belonged. For what it's worth, I think she'll take off the curse. And, Boy, will you do something for me?"

"Yes."

"Don't ever tell the others. I'm glad you know, and if you hadn't been with me, I couldn't have done as I did. I leaned on you, all the time. But I'd rather they didn't know… If the little boy's luck should turn, you'll be sure to hear: and then you can write and tell me, and when you write and I read, we'll both remember today and how we stood together in the presence of something unearthly – a human being in touch with another world."

I dared not look at her, but, as I lifted my arm, her fingers left my sleeve and rose to my lips.

Our entrance might have been timed. As we were approaching the trees beneath which we had lunched, a car, which was not Jonah's, drew up behind the Rolls in the cloistered lane. Aroused by the pulse of its engine, Berry sat up, while Daphne and Jill, who were seated a little apart, suspended their conversation to see what the matter might be. No one of the three observed us, until the Knave put his nose to the nape of Jill's neck. And by that time the stage was held by somebody else.

A burst of indignation came floating out of the lane. Then a thick-set man in plus-fours flung out of the new-come car and lumbered on to the sward.

"What the hell does this mean?" he demanded.

Coolly Berry surveyed him.

"If you must know," he said, "it means that you can't go on. Your passage is obstructed, like Balaam's. If you had been riding an ass, I think it more than likely that – "

"Are you out of your mind?"

"I don't think so," said Berry. "Not that I haven't suffered enough to derange a sage. I suppose you haven't seen a pair of – "

"Get to hell out of this," raved the other, jerking his head.

My brother-in-law frowned.

"To converse," he observed, "it is unnecessary to be offensive. 'Please go away,' would be shorter, much better English, and, what is more, more polite."

With a manifest effort, the other controlled his voice.

"I'd have you know this is private property."

"So I believe," said Berry. "In fact, that is why I came. I find the country crowded in weather like this."

As soon as he could speak –

"Take your car and get out," roared the stranger. "Find some other place to rehearse your circus tricks. And think yourself damned lucky I don't have you jugged. Dressed up like a – "

"If we're to be personal," said Berry, "I may as well confess how much I dislike your suit. In fact, if I were you, I should change your upholsterer."

The red of the other's face began to change to violet before my eyes.

"Will you get out?" he raged.

"By what right," said Berry, slowly, "by what right do you order me off?"

"By what right d'you think? *I own it.*" An arm was savagely waved. "This is my land."

Berry fingered his chin.

"Is it indeed?" he said softly. "I'd no idea… Might I have your name?"

"Yes, sir. My name is Puncheon. And now perhaps you'll do as I say."

Berry raised his eyebrows.

"I don't think I shall," he said. "You see – "

"Don't think you will?" howled the other. He lugged out a watch and dabbed at the shining dial. "I'll give you two minutes to get that car out of my way."

"Don't be absurd," said Berry, and picked up a cigarette.

"*Absurd?*" screeched Puncheon.

"That was the word I used."

The fellow stamped to and fro, like a man possessed, while Berry, with studied nonchalance, reached for matches and lighted his cigarette.

The girls and the Knave and I might have been pure statuary. The thing was too good to be true. Puncheon had called the game and had dealt the cards, and Berry, who held a 'knock-out,' was going to raise the fellow into the stratosphere.

The latter was speaking thickly.

"D'you want to be summoned?" he said.

"Not particularly," said Berry. "Why?"

"Because you will be summoned, if you don't do as I say."

"What'll you bet me?" said Berry.

"Bet you?"

"Bet me. You see, you're foretelling the future and I believe that you're wrong. I don't think I shall be summoned. And I'm ready to back my opinion with fifty pounds."

"We'll see about that." Mr Puncheon produced a pencil. "I demand your name and address."

"Your demand is refused," said Berry, expelling a cloud of smoke.

"*What*?"

"You know," said Berry, reprovingly, "I can't help thinking you heard."

"D'you mean you refuse to give them?"

"That," said Berry, "is the construction to be placed upon my remark. If you found it obscure, I'm sorry. I always try to make myself plain."

The other mopped a plum-coloured face.

"I don't want to use force," he said darkly.

"That I can well believe."

Mr Puncheon swallowed.

"Will you move your car, or shall I?"

My brother-in-law closed his eyes.

"The answer," he said, "to the first part of the question is in the negative. With regard to the second, if you are capable of moving a car which weighs rather more than two tons, you are at liberty to do so. I shouldn't try to drive it, for that would be waste of time. You see, the switch is locked and I have the key."

Mr Puncheon was shaking his fist.

"You defy me, do you, you insolent – "

"I don't know about defiance. I've told you you have my permission to try your strength. Don't forget to take the brake off."

With a violence which was quite shocking, Mr Puncheon returned to a frontal attack.

"Are you going or not?"

"Well, I don't propose to spend the night here," said Berry, "if that's what you mean. I've no pyjamas, for one thing. Besides, I – "

"Very well then – I go for the police."

"I doubt it," said Berry, placidly.

"What d'you mean – 'doubt it?' "

My brother-in-law frowned.

"Either," he said, "you're not trying, or else the liaison between your ears and your brain leaves much to be desired. However, I'll try again. I am not satisfied that you will go to the police. You've said so, I know: but I do not believe that you will redeem your threat."

Shaking with passion, Mr Puncheon clawed at the air.

"I'll break you for this – I'll jug you – I'll hound you out of your job. If you think you can sit there and flout me, you're damned well wrong. At least your car's got a number – I'll trace you by that. I'll apply for a warrant tomorrow and have you laid by the heels."

"If you have been flouted," said Berry, "you've only yourself to thank. If you'd come and asked me politely to be allowed to go by – "

"Why the hell should I ask your permission?"

"Because in my opinion I have just as much right here as you."

"O-o-oh," drawled Mr Puncheon, as though scales had been flicked from his eyes. He laughed unpleasantly. "Socialism, eh? Free love, free drinks, free land, free everything. I might have known it. Unfortunately, my friend, I do not share your religion. And I can't help feeling – "

"I'm obliged," said Berry, stiffly. He rose to his feet. "I suppose you have some virtue – they say that no man is altogether vile. But perhaps you hide your light under the proverbial bushel, though I feel that a much smaller measure would be sufficiently large. Of course, I may be wrong, but, in any event, I think you'd do well to withdraw. I find your presence superfluous – I expect you know what that means. I don't like your looks or your manners and I have a definite feeling that we should be better apart. No doubt your car conforms to the law of the land and has a gear called 'reverse.' Be good enough to employ it – without delay."

The other appeared to have lost the power of speech. To judge from his countenance, amazement, wrath and indignation fought for his soul; but though he pointed a finger and wagged his head, the relief of expression was denied him and the strictures his reason demanded were never passed.

Berry continued mercilessly.

"And that letter you wrote me, Mr Puncheon – I'll answer it here and now. *Your offer for this estate is hereby refused.* Two thousand pounds isn't much, and Thistledown must be worth more to a man who can't wait two days for the right to call it his own."

The other was standing so still he might have been turned to stone. His eyes were wide and staring, his jaw had dropped, and his face which had been violet was growing pale. An emotion more compelling than anger had taken control.

"And now please go. As a magistrate, I happen to know the law, and if you – "

The slam of a door of a car cut the sentence in two. Then a nice-looking man stepped out of the shadowed lane and on to the turf.

He looked straight at us and took off his hat and smiled. Then he turned to Berry.

"Please forgive me," he said, "but I'm very much interested in a statement you made just now. If I understood it aright, you are the present owner of this estate."

"That's quite right," said Berry. "I hold it as sole trustee for Michael Willingdon Raby, of Harrow School."

"I'm much obliged," said Lord Prentice – and turned to look upon Puncheon with eyes of steel...

As the latter wilted before that merciless gaze, Lord Prentice's words of that morning leaped to my mind.

On the copy I had it wasn't coloured as yours... It controls the situation... More like seven thousand. The document's signed...

And now he was speaking again.

"It's a great mistake, Mr Puncheon, to sell to another something that is not yours. My company will hold you to your contract. *No matter what Thistledown costs you*, the deeds must be in our office one calendar month from today."

In the pregnant silence which followed, I watched the blood flow back into Mr Puncheon's face.

For a moment he seemed about to argue: then he turned on his heel and stamped to his car.

With violence he started her engine; with violence he put her in gear; then he turned to fight a fresh battle – and win, at my cousin's expense.

We had all forgotten Jonah. Mr Puncheon's outburst declared his silent return.

"Get back out of this," he bellowed. "I'd have you know that this is a private road… Don't bandy words with me, but do as I say… All right then, you dog, *I'll ram you…*"

We heard him let in his clutch…

My cousin is fond of his Rolls. To save her face, he had to back half a mile for all he was worth, with Puncheon, raving insult, in hot pursuit. To use his own words –

"The fellow had it all his own way. I could hear every word he said, but, though my ears were burning, I couldn't so much as reply. You see, he was facing me, but he set such a pace that I didn't dare look round for fear of leaving the road. You may have chastised him with whips, but he got a bit back with scorpions along that lane."

"Be of good cheer," said Berry, "we'll shove it down in the bill." He turned to Lord Prentice. "As a trustee it's my duty to do my very best for my *cestui que trust.*"

"I entirely agree."

My brother-in-law bowed.

"Please don't answer me, if you don't want to. I've no wish to spoil your deal, but – is Mr Puncheon good for ten thousand pounds?"

Lord Prentice laughed.

"The Press will tell you tomorrow, so I may as well tell you today." He pointed down at the chessboard of well-kept fields. "My company needed that land. We'd been all over England, searching and testing for nearly eighteen months, and, so far as we knew, that was the only stretch of country that was for sale and offered us what we want. It belonged to Mr Puncheon. Now how he found out, I don't know, but he learned that we *had* to have it – and put us up. He had us cold, of course… We offered him twenty thousand – all things considered, I think that was more than fair. But we're paying him sixty-five… One calendar month from today."

"Thank you very much," said Berry. "Twenty from sixty-five thousand is forty-five thousand pounds." He turned to smile at Daphne. "My dear, I can't help feeling that the Thistledown Curse is off."

Three hours and a half had gone by. We had all made friends with Lord Prentice, who proved a most amiable guest. When I was introduced, he almost certainly winked, but no other reference was made to Perdita's natural mistake in the furniture shop. He showed great interest in Thistledown's tragic past, and 'The Rape of the Trousers' afforded him infinite mirth. When we had carried him to Salisbury, he haled us into his lodging and shook us a prettier cocktail than many a man who was half his age could have mixed.

Berry had accepted the trousers which Jonah had bought. "Not that," he said, "I'm not thankful to have my own back, but among the most venerable of the traditions of Romany is a fine carelessness of the person, to the encouragement of sickness and lice – mysteries to which I have no urge to be admitted. When they've been to the cleaner's, of course…"

Finally, we had come home as the sky was flaunting a sunset worthy of Turner's brush.

In the hall stood the little staircase, dusky and gleaming in the light of a shaded lamp.

I saw my sister start and Jill put a hand to her head.

"But that's it," she cried. "That's it. And he said it was sold."

"It's some mistake," said Daphne. "Besides, I never mentioned my name."

Berry was regarding the label.

"It's addressed to you," he said, and stood back. "What a glorious piece."

"It's the one we saw," cried Jill. "We saw it in Salisbury this morning, just after we'd bought the silk. Of course we fell for it flat – it's made for the library. So we went straight into the shop. And then, to our horror, the man there said that he'd sold it five minutes before. And he'd had it for twenty years…"

"I could have wept," said Daphne. "We went out and stared and stared till we knew it by heart. I'd a wild idea of getting it copied… And then we knew it was hopeless and came away. We didn't tell you about it, because there seemed no sense in breaking your hearts. And now – here it is."

"But who on earth…"

Berry was looking hard at Perdita Boyte.

"Was that what was 'priceless' this morning? I'd meant to ask you, of course, but my luscious communion with the policeman put it clean out of my mind."

A child, in the shape of a maiden, looked suddenly shy.

"I was only the agent," she said. "It's 'A present from Thistledown.' "

6

How Berry Met His Match, and a Mule Lay Down with the Knave

Miniature in hand, Miss Boyte regarded my brother-in-law.

"It's really fantastic," she said. "Shave you and cut his hair, and you would be twins. A great-great-uncle, you said?"

"That's right," said Berry. "Bertram. I bear his name. He was a favourite of the Prince Regent and an inveterate gambler. One night, in his cups, he staked and lost a snuff-box which had been given to him by the future King. At least, that was what was said – and an enemy told the Prince. The latter was loth to believe it, but he sent for Bertram to Brighton, and when he appeared, he asked for a pinch of snuff. When Bertram proffered the snuff *in another box*, the Prince Regent turned on his heel, and, though later he begged for an audience, he never saw him again. The fashionable world renounced Bertram, and Bertram renounced the world. As soon as he could, he took orders, and from being a Regency Buck, he spent his life in the country, preaching the gospel and doing nothing but good. But he never forgot his disgrace. Rightly or wrongly, he resented it, and he left instructions that *Put not your trust in Princes* was to be cut upon his tomb. And so it was."

"I regret to say," said Jonah, "that I think he deserved what he got."

"I quite agree," said Berry. "But I think he was hardly used. He would never have done as he did, if he hadn't been tight: and that being so, the fellow who won the box should have handed it back. I mean, only a skunk would have kept it."

"I think," said Jill, "that it was a beastly shame. And only a cad would have gone and told the Prince."

"It looks like a put-up job," said Perdita Boyte. "What became of the box? Who won it?"

"That I don't know," said Berry. "And I don't believe Bertram knew, because if he had, he'd have gone to the fellow who won it and bought it back. But if, as I suggest, he was blind to the world when he lost it, then, of course, he'd nothing to go on. I imagine the first he knew was when he got up the next morning and found that the box was gone."

"It was rotten luck," said Daphne; "but it certainly turned a sinner into a saint. His name is still remembered at Ribbon, but his parish was wider than that."

"That's very true," said Berry. "What his sermons were like I don't know, but outside his church he made a tremendous hit. Probably because of his past, he had a weakness for the lawless, and many a rogue and a vagabond lost a good friend when he died. A famous highwayman, called Studd, who was finally hanged, bequeathed him the brace of pistols he always used. Bertram probably helped him once. Any way he was most insistent that 'the barkers should go to Buck Pleydell,' as the clerk in holy orders was always styled." He took his keys from his pocket and rose to his feet. "I've got them here, in that tallboy – Daphne won't have them out."

"They make me shudder," said his wife. "When all's said and done, Studd was a common robber who stuck at nothing at all. He confessed to seventeen murders before he was hanged. And most of those, I suppose, were done with these very arms. What I don't understand is how Bertram could ever have succoured a blackguard like that. I mean, he was a public enemy."

"That," said Berry, "is undeniable. Still, Studd must have had some reason for making his last bequest." He drew open a drawer. "And at any rate here they are. Murderous record or no, they're a handsome pair." He turned, with a fine horse pistol in either hand. "They were made by a gunsmith called Minty, of Bristol Town, and you'll find Studd's initials, *R S*, engraved upon each of the stocks."

Perdita Boyte took one and I received the other – to examine the elegant chasing with curious gaze and think of less fortunate eyes that had seen no more than the mouth – and a ruthless finger nursing the trigger below. Honest servants these, that had kept a rogue in his saddle for fifteen years.

Jonah looked over my shoulder.

"You know," he said, "it's a shame to keep them in a drawer. They ought to be on the wall, in a glass-fronted case. For one thing, they're very good looking: for another, they are a pair of historical documents. They were made by a famous gunsmith, used by a notorious highwayman, and left to a well-known priest. All that is hard fact. And if you like to draw on your fancy, they must have confronted – not killed – a good many well-known people, adorning the very world that Bertram used to adorn: for Studd used to work the home counties and, sometimes, London itself."

My sister shook her head.

"They're infamous relics," she said, "I'm glad to know we've got them, but I will not have them displayed. They've a cruel and pitiless record of blood and tears. Think of the widows and orphans those things have made."

Perdita shivered and handed her pistol back. As I made to do the same, my cousin stretched out his hand.

"One more look," he said, "before you hide them away."

Between us, we bungled the business, and the weapon fell with a crash to the polished floor.

A yelp of dismay from Berry ushered the diatribe we justly deserved.

"That's an heirloom, darlings. Not a sheep's head. A sheep's head is rounder than that – you blear-eyed, banana-fingered bugbears. You're only fit to scratch a hole in a swamp. Oh, my God, you've bust it. Fallen angels, you've broken a piece right off." He closed his eyes in distress. "Oh, why did I take them out before you were dead? In all their service – "

"Steady," said Jonah, stooping. "There's nothing broken at all. There's a secret slot in the butt, and the plug that concealed it's come out."

Feverishly examining the pistol, we found his estimate true.

A silver plug had sprung from the end of the stock, revealing a little socket sunk in the wood.

"There's a paper there," said Berry. "A pair of tweezers, someone. And, somebody else, a torch."

In great excitement the operation was done.

The torch illumined the socket, to show a morsel of paper, rolled into a little tube: this clung to the walls of the socket, as though reluctant to leave, but after a little persuasion the tweezers had their way.

"And now," said Berry, looking round.

With one consent, the five of us bade him proceed.

Carefully he smoothed out the paper. As he held it flat to the table, a child's umbrella might well have covered our heads.

The writing was ragged and dim, but still easy to read.

Bloodstock 43 Old Basing 8
15 toward O.B.
Burried thatt night.

For a moment there was dead silence.

Then Berry lifted his head.

"Buried that night," he said softly. "A pregnant phrase. I – I wonder if it's still there."

"Where?" said Jill.

"Forty-three miles from Bloodstock, plus fifteen paces for luck. Studd buried it close to the milestone and then wrote the mileage down."

"That's right," said Jonah. He tapped his teeth with his pipe. "Have we got any ordnance maps?"

"In the drawer of that table," said I. "But what would 'it' be?"

"I imagine, a nest-egg," said Berry. "A hat full of guineas, or something. For all we know, 'thatt night' was a bumper night, and Studd picked up a bit more than he needed for ready cash. So he 'banked' the surplus against a rainy day: but before that came, he was taken... It's happened before."

Perdita let out a cry.

"That's why he left Bertram the pistols. Bertram had shown him kindness, when everyone else was waiting to do him down: so Bertram should have his money – if anyone should."

"By Jove, she's right," cried Berry, and smacked the arm of his chair. "Why else leave 'the barkers' to a parson – the only man of those days who never went armed?"

Now that Berry had asked it, the pertinence of the question stood out as black against white. The robber's intention was clear. He could not have had much hope that Bertram would light on the secret the pistol hid; but there was a chance that he would, and, in any event, no one but Bertram *could* find it, when once the pistols were his. Though the good might reap no reward, the wicked were certainly doomed to go empty away. At least no vile turnkey or 'redbreast' would enjoy the balance that lay in their victim's 'bank.'

As we made these points to one another, the tide of excitement rose. Daphne and Jill were at the bookcase containing guide-books and maps: Perdita and Berry examined the other pistol, to be sure that another socket was not to be found in its stock: and Jonah and I considered the ordnance sheets.

It did not take long to discover that the mileage which Studd had given was out of date. According to the milestone he quoted, the distance between the two towns was fifty-one miles. The books and maps we consulted showed it to be forty-eight. The discrepancy seemed to be fatal. It showed that the road had been shortened since Studd had buried his gold: and that, of course, meant that the milestone which he had quoted had been removed. In fact, but for Jonah's refusal so soon to admit defeat, I think that before this blow we should have thrown in our hand. It was my keen-witted cousin that picked a way for us out of this hopeless pass.

"I want you to help me to place *The Dog-Faced Man*. That's the name of an inn we once lunched at – I should say about eight years ago. I doubt if I ever knew the name of the village it served, but I think it lay west of Old Basing... I'll tell you why I want this. I remember *The Dog-Faced Man* – I can see it now. It was once a posting-house. Which means that the road it stands by was once a coaching road. You see what I'm getting at..."

The smoking flax burst into flame.

Half an hour later, perhaps, we found that the village of Coven boasted a 'Dog-Faced Man.' And Coven lay west of Old Basing by seven miles. *And Bloodstock lay south-west of Coven by forty-four.*

The old coach-road had fallen from its estate – at least, the twelve miles which survived were little more than a lane, while the other thirty-nine had long ago been lost in a main highway. Coven, in a word, had been bypassed, and the bypass was shorter than the coach-road by just three miles.

All this we discovered later: for in searching for Coven, we found what we wanted to see.

My cousin, driving his Rolls, had properly taken the lead, and I was a mile behind him, expecting to join him again at *The Dog-Faced Man*. But we met before that.

At a quarter to twelve on a lovely August morning I stole round a fairy bend, to see his car at rest by the side of the way and himself and Jill and Daphne standing upon the turf which edged the road as a ribbon for half a mile.

"Oh, I can't believe it," said Berry, and Perdita smothered a cry.

To be honest, the hopes we had harboured had been but faint. It is an age of progress, and when cars began to come in, the gentle face of England began to change. Straighten a curve of a road, and half a hundred milestones will be bearing a false report. And because that is not to be thought of, the liars are taken away. Reason forbade us to think that with all the manifold chances of modern life the milestone that Studd had quoted should not have been put in the wrong. But it was so. Leaning a little, dressed in tight, grey-green lichen – that venerable livery peculiar to 'the constant service of the antique world,' the old fellow offered his news to such as passed by. Blurred by a hundred winters, the legend could still be read:

BLOODSTOCK
43
OLD BASING
8

As we alighted, I saw Jonah pacing the turf...

Before we could exchange our excitement –

"That's right," said Berry. "Go on. Give the whole blasted thing away before we've begun. If anyone's watching – "

"Don't be absurd," said Daphne. "Milestones are meant to be read."

"They're not meant to be slobbered over," said her husband. "They're not meant to be leered at and – Look out. Here's somebody coming. What did I say?"

The cyclist that had been approaching passed slowly by, whilst we all did our best to dissemble and Berry loudly declared that "the map must be wrong." The effect was marred by a wail of laughter from Jill: it remained for the Knave to destroy it – by overtaking the stranger at thirty-five miles an hour, gaping upon him like any bull of Basan and protesting against his intrusion with a volley of malevolent barks. The hurricane of invective with which we discouraged his zeal must have convinced the cyclist that we wished to disown such behaviour with all our might, but the incident sobered us all, for it showed that the Knave had perceived that we were about some business the nature of which we had no desire to disclose.

In an uneasy silence Jonah leaned over a gate that gave to a field to peer down the back of the hedgerow before which the milestone stood, while the Knave, wide-eyed with abashment, lay down on the turf with his muzzle between his paws.

"Quite so," said Berry, grimly. "And now, having done enough damage, we'd better be gone. Lunch at *The Dog-Faced Man* was what we arranged. But I won't go near the place unless it is understood that a certain subject is barred. If the faintest idea gets round of what's at the back of our minds – well, we may as well leave the country. I'll lay that Jonah agrees."

My cousin nodded.

"Can't be too careful," he said, producing a pipe. "But it's going to take some lifting, this box of bricks."

"What d'you mean?" said Daphne.

Jonah shrugged his shoulders.

"As you've just seen, this road is a thoroughfare. You can't keep people at bay or order them off. And, once you've begun, you can't disguise your labour… You can stop, of course – if somebody rounds that bend. But unless they're feeble-minded, they'll wait until you go on. And if you don't go on, *they will*. They've just as much right as you have to, er, practise landscape-gardening by the side of the King's highway."

There was an uneasy silence.

Then Daphne spoke for us all.

"I can wait for my lunch," she said. "Let's go straight home. At least, we can talk as we go."

"All right," said Berry. "Only, as we're here, we may as well locate the vicarage. It's almost certainly at Coven, but we'd better make sure."

"The vicarage?" said his wife. "Why on earth do we want to know where the vicarage is?"

"In case we're successful," said Berry. "The vicar's the proper person to administer what we find."

"But it's ours," shrieked Daphne. "The man meant Bertram to have it, and Bertram's right has now descended to us."

"For shame," said Berry. He raised his eyes to heaven and wagged his head. "Think of the widows and orphans to whom it never belonged. Think of the – "

"Rot," said Daphne. "The man – "

" – was a common robber," said Berry. "And I think it more than likely that when he'd sunk his, er, surplus, he went to *The Dog-Faced Man* and had a large blood and tears."

"I was talking of – "

"Some infamous relics," said Berry, "if I remember aright. Which a man meant Bertram to have and have now descended to us. If we add to the grisly collection, am I to be allowed to display the ones which we have?"

My sister swallowed.

"I don't see what that's got to do with it. If – "

"Then," said Berry, "we'll take the vicar's advice. If he says – "

"Oh, I suppose if you want to turn the library into a Chamber of Horrors..."

"That's a good girl," said Berry, and entered the nearest car. "On the way back we'll stop at *The Case is Altered* and drink the testator's health."

"Then you'll drink it alone," said his wife. "If there's anything going, we may just as well have it as anyone else. But I don't pretend I'm grateful. It wasn't the brute's to give."

"Quite right," said Berry, "quite right. Besides, the question of gratitude may not arise. I mean, it mayn't be what we think.

All sorts of things are b-buried. Sometimes they go so far as to bury the dead."

I helped my sister into the other car.

Three days and a half had gone by when I brought the Rolls to rest in front of *The Dog-Faced Man*.

Outside the inn, in the shade of some whispering limes, was standing a well-worn car to which was attached a trailer, no longer smart. The two carried camping equipment of every kind – I knew: I had helped to load them five hours before.

My cousin strolled out of the inn – according to plan.

"At last," he said. He turned to call to his sister. "Jill, they're here. Come along." He returned to us. "Your advance-guard has done very well. We've found an excellent field a mile away. I fixed things up with the owner an hour ago."

Jill and the Knave came flying out of the inn.

"Daphne darling, it's priceless. Wait till you see. He was awfully sticky at first – the owner, I mean. But Jonah talked farming with him and after a quarter of an hour he showed us a map of his land and said we could go where we liked."

"How – how marvellous of him," said Daphne, and meant what she said.

Ten minutes later I slowed down behind the trailer just short of the five-barred gate which gave to a field we knew. Here everyone alighted except my cousin and me. The gate was opened by Berry, and Jonah drove into the field: and then, my way being clear, I proceeded to place the Rolls. The turf by the side of the road made an excellent berth. I brought the great car to rest *with her nose in line with a milestone some seventeen paces ahead*. All this, according to plan. It was now but five o'clock and the daylight was broad, and the turf was conveniently smooth: but had it been dark and had there been a pit a yard square two paces in front of the Rolls, her headlights, when dipped, would have illumined the hole, and, what is as much to the point, if the car were advanced three paces, the petty excavation would have been lost to view. In a word, the stage was set.

That our preparations were laboured, I do not pretend to deny: but they had not been made without reason, for one cast-iron condition was ruling the enterprise. *Neither whilst it was being done nor after it had been done must we be so much as suspected of what we proposed to do.* We could not afford exposure. For one thing only, what we were going to do was against the law.

These things being so, it goes, I think, without saying that we could not make our attempt except under cover of night. Now, though we might hide our labour, we could not conceal our presence in such a neighbourhood. Hence the camping equipment. Once the two tents were up, no one would give two thoughts to the simple-minded strangers who had "managed to get old Belcher to let them camp in his field." So far, so good: but the work which we were to do had got to be done by the side of the King's highway. And the King's highway is open to all and sundry, by night as by day. The work would take time. Fifteen paces, Studd said. But what was the length of his paces? And had he walked perfectly straight by the edge of the road? Add to this that we could not work without light. And a light can be seen in the country a long way off…

The camp would account for our presence: the Rolls, with her headlamps dipped, would afford us a furtive light: and if the alarm was given, we had but to drive her forward to cover the hole we had dug.

As I entered the good-looking meadow –

"But we must have water," cried Daphne. "I'm dying to wash my hands."

"I know," said Berry. "So'm I. But I'm going to tread it under and wipe them upon the grass."

"Don't be a fool," said his wife. "I'm not going to go without water until we get home. Besides, we've got to wash up."

"There's a stream," said Jonah, pointing, "the other side of that ridge." He produced two canvas buckets. "Would you rather fetch the water or put up a tent?"

"That isn't grammar," said Berry. "No man born of woman can put up a tent. I'll subscribe to its erection, if that's what you mean. But I'm not going to drag my nails out, clawing sailcloth about against its will. Besides, we must spare ourselves. We didn't come here to make our abode in this field."

"We've got to pretend that we did. So the tents have got to go up and the water has got to be fetched."

With his eyes on the buckets –

"About this water," said Berry, thoughtfully.

"Why don't we make a chain? A chain of people, I mean – like they do at a fire?"

"From here to the stream?" said I.

"That's right," said Berry. "I know we're only six: but if we spread out – "

"Which end of the chain," said Daphne, "are you proposing to be?"

My brother-in-law swallowed.

"Well, we ought to draw lots," he said. "That's the fairest way. But I don't mind. If I can walk so far, I'll – I'll take the other end."

"All right," said Jonah. "You go on with the buckets. As you'll have the farthest to go, we'll give you ten minutes' start."

"But we all start together," cried Berry. "That's the whole point of the thing. Then Number One falls out – at the head of this field: Number Two at the top of the ridge: and so on. It's the only way to fetch water."

"But what's the sense of us all going?" said Jill.

"Well, it saves time for one thing," said Berry. "We get the water much quicker. Number Six fills the buckets and gives them to Number Five. Number Five runs with them to Number Four. Number Four runs to Number Three. And so on."

"But we don't get the water quicker, because when it arrives we're not here."

"I'm not going to argue with you," said Berry. "If you can't see – Besides, Number Six will be here. I mean, Number One."

"No, he won't," said Jill. "Nobody'll be here. You said – "

"But he *must* be here," screamed Berry. "How can the water arrive except by his hand? Number Six arrives with the water."

"Well, I call that silly," said Jill. "If Number Six – "

"I mean Number One," snapped Berry. "How the devil could Six be here? He's down at the stream."

"Well, you said it," said Jill, indignantly. "You said – "

"What if I did?" raved Berry. "Ignorant obstruction like this is enough to make anybody say anything. I understand you want water. God knows why, but you do. Very well. I teach you the way to get it. I lay before you the way in which water is got. In which water has been got for millions of years. It's the first labour-saving device the world ever saw. More. I – "

"But you said it saved time," said Jill.

"So it does."

"Well, I can't see it," said Jill. "There's six of us going to get it instead of one, and we shan't have it any quicker because we shan't be here when it comes."

"But we *shall* be here," raved Berry. "Almost at once. And there'll be the water waiting. We'll have rushed the whole thing through in one-sixth of the time. Less than that, really: for Numbers Five and Six can wash in the stream."

"Well, what about Number Four? He won't be able to wash for ages."

"Yes he will. Four can take some soap with him and wash on the way. And so can Three. And so can Two and One, for the matter of that."

"Then what's the good of getting it?" said Jill.

"There isn't any," yelled Berry. "There never was. Not the faintest odour of welfare. It's a waste of time and labour and an insult to common sense."

"It is – *your* way," said Jill. "Fancy running about with a lot of dirty water. And I don't believe they've always done it like that. Why don't you go and get it, as Daphne said? Your way, you'd have been Number Six, so what's the difference?"

There is a *naïveté* which is more deadly than any wit.

So soon as he could speak –

"Show me a tent," said Berry, violently. "Show me some pegs and a maul." Savagely he flung off his coat. "Especially a maul – and I'll show you how to pretend. I'm going to *pretend* to set up a monument. You know. A thing like Stonehenge."

"Well, don't overdo it," said his wife. "It's got to come down tomorrow."

Berry laughed hysterically.

"Wait till I'm through," he said, "and you'll think that we're here for years."

With a snarl, he fell upon some canvas, and, after two efforts to lift it, began to drag it incontinently towards the hedge...

Perdita picked up a bucket and looked at me.

"Shall we make a chain?" she said shyly.

Two minutes later I handed her over the fence at the head of the field...

It was as we surmounted the ridge that Perdita caught her breath and stood suddenly still.

"I don't believe it," she said. "If we go any nearer, I'm sure it'll fade away."

The scene before us might well have been painted or sung. It was like a piece of Old English – a page from The Book of Proverbs, so simple and yet as matchless as one of Shakespeare's songs.

A meadow went sloping down to the stream we sought. On the farther side of this, the rising ground was laid with a quilt of leafage, perhaps some sixty feet thick. Oak and ash and chestnut – all manner of magnificent trees, massed in inimitable disorder, made such a hanging garden as Babylon never knew, and the tops of those that stood highest were fretting with delicate green the blue of a flawless sky. Sunk like a jewel in the greenwood, set like a jewel on the silver sash of water, was an old, half-timbered mill.

Rose-red from footings to chimneys, the ancient seemed to welcome the smile of the evening sun. This laid bare a detail which filled the eye, and, even from where we stood, we could mark the good brick-nogging that was framed by the grey, old oak, the gentle sag of the roof, which is but the stoop of a man that is full of years, and the lead of the lattices keeping the aged panes. And something else we could see. Neighbouring the wall of the mill, the water-wheel hung upon its spindle over the race – a very comfortable monster, like Bottom's sucking dove. For me, it painted the lily, not only calling back Time as one having authority, but relating the business of Nature to the work of men's hands. And the wheel was running...the fine old fellow was at work. His felloes were dark and glistening, all the beauty of lively water flowed or dripped or leaped from his flashing fans, and the sunshine played upon the flourish, making a magic beyond the reach of art.

Perdita clasped two hands that would have added a verse to Solomon's Song.

"Oh, please may I have it? It is the very loveliest toy that I've ever seen."

Wishing very much it was mine –

"No toy," said I, "but a fable – the stuff the old England was made of...the England that Goldsmith knew."

Perdita nodded thoughtfully. Then she set a hand on my shoulder, keeping her eyes on the mill.

"England," she said, "is really a picture book. It's old now, and some of its pages are missing and many of those that are left are torn and spoiled. But there are such a lot that are just as they always were. And this is the little vignette that goes on the title page." She lifted a glowing face. "Am I lucky or not to have seen it?"

"Honours are even," said I. "It's seen a lot of fine ladies in all its days, but it's had to wait till now for an Eve with the way of a maid and the heart of a child."

"I'm afraid that's not true. Don't move." Her beautiful face approached mine. "I'm regarding myself in your eye, and I don't think so fine a fellow would fall for a lady like me."

"When you say 'so fine a fellow' " –

"I mean the mill."

"Never mind," said I. "Don't move. I'm considering the bow of your mouth. I believe – "

Perdita danced out of range and blew me a kiss.

"It's not the same," I said sadly. "And I needn't have given you warning of my approach."

"I know. But that's why I like you. You – Oh, I don't know. Most men regard women as game, to be trapped or caught. But you always encourage my freedom – like a man that is glad to let live. And now let's go down to the water and be Numbers Five and Six."

As we passed over the meadow –

"You know," said I, "you haven't got it quite right. I admit I'm not a satyr. But Plato's theories have never appealed to me. I'm glad to let live – as you put it: but I have a definite weakness for living myself."

Miss Boyte took my arm and laid a cheek to my sleeve.

"You are stupid, aren't you?" she said. "That's just what makes it so nice."

As soon as I could speak –

"You wicked girl," I said. I put an arm about her and held her up to my heart. "You wicked – Now I shan't eat a carp on St Anthony's day. Oh, and put up your mouth, will you? I want to…straighten my tie in one of your eyes."

With her face in my coat –

"Not before the mill," bubbled Perdita. "Besides, there might be somebody looking."

"Hush," said I. "Number Six is waiting – to give them to Number Five."

Seated upon a loose cushion that came from the Rolls, his back against the milestone, his right foot shoeless and resting upon a carefully folded rug, my brother-in-law greeted our appearance by raising his eyes to heaven and demanding a cigarette.

As I felt for my case –

"Lame for life," he said shortly. "That's what I am. I want to go home, but they say they can't spare the Rolls."

"But how did it happen?" said Perdita.

Berry sat up.

"The history," he said, "will hardly go into words. You may or may not remember that I offered to erect a pavilion – a work of supererogation, which, no doubt for that reason, found favour in the sight of those I love. On my offer being accepted, I humbly desired to be furnished with the appropriate tools. You can't make ropes without sand – or whatever they use. These were not forthcoming. Instead of the maul and pegs which I had a right to expect, one was given a blacksmith's hammer, and a lot of iron nails – harsh and bestial equipment, which, if we may believe the old masters, has figured in other martyrdoms. But it is, as you know, my practice to accept without comment such trials or disabilities as a jealous Fate may appoint. I, therefore, offered up a short prayer and fell to work. Was I permitted to labour as man has always laboured, working out his own salvation in the sweat of his trunk? I was not. From the instant that I began to put into action my design, my beloved consort saw fit not only to disparage my methods – thereby exposing the running sores of ignorance with which her mind is diseased – but actually to vomit instruction the nature and quality of which would have been most justly resented by an infant of tender years. The result was inevitable. Trembling with indignation and thirsty only to bring to an end a tribulation which I in no wise deserved, I failed to invest with the requisite degree of accuracy the elegant parabola my hammer was about to describe; and the blow which had been intended not only to relieve my emotions but to blot out the bullnosed bung which I had already missed twice, fell instead upon the toe or toe-cap of the Russia-leather 'Oxford' in which this foot was enshrined." As though the reminiscence were repugnant, he shuddered violently. "One might have hoped, one might, without presumption, have supposed that a *contretemps* so hideous would have commanded concern, if not dismay. One would have been wrong. The act of self-immolation was greeted with yells of mirth. Like those of the early Christians, my screams were drowned in an obscene derision which, till then, I had always believed to be the prerogative of the abnormal baboon. So far from – Oh, St Vitus' Trot! Look what's escaped."

It was with a shock that, following Berry's gaze, I perceived the approach of a pageant which justified his remark.

A small caravan, painted to resemble a doll's house in red and white, had been fitted with shafts, instead of the trailer bar: between these a mule was strolling with the nonchalance of his kind. The equipage was preceded by a man of perhaps thirty-five. He was wearing an apple-green beret, a pair of blood-red shorts and a sleeveless vest, no one of which became him in any way. A permanent grin illumined his wide-eyed face, and he looked up and down and about, as one who is pleased with life and delighted with all he sees. He was tripping, rather than walking, as though in ecstasy, and had he indeed been some prisoner, lately enlarged, he could hardly have revelled more plainly in his estate. By the side of the van was plodding another soul: but, though his attire was as wanton as that which his fellow wore, his demeanour was that of a man who would welcome death. For the most part he hung his head, but now and again he would lift it to glance at the van and the mule, after which he would cover his face as though he had seen some vision too dreadful for him to bear. Indeed, I felt sorry for him, for he plainly loathed his adventure with all his might and the relish of his companion must have inflamed his despair.

Carefully veiling our interest, we waited for the three to go by, proposing perhaps to direct them and certainly to give them good day. Of such is Life... It never occurred to us that the tents which Jonah had set up were declaring a fellowship which if anyone pleased to invoke we could not deny.

The leader of the procession ripped the scales from our eyes.

Raising his headgear to Perdita, he pranced to Berry's side with an outstretched hand.

"Well met, brother," he brayed. "What of the pitch?"

The three of us gazed upon him, dumb with dismay. Our fond preparation, recoiling upon itself, seemed likely to bring to ruin the hopes we held. The frightening fool before us was proposing to rest by our side, to establish a post of surveillance, *to spend the night within earshot of all we did.* We were ready for interruption: the supervision, however, of such a man was something with which we were not prepared to cope.

Dazedly Berry made answer.

"What pitch?" he said, shaking hands.

"Why your pitch," said the other, beaming. He pointed to the tops of the tents. "The blithesome spot you have selected for your repose."

There was a frightful silence. Then –

"Oh, it's not too bad," said Berry, faintly. "Not – not at all what we'd hoped though. Too – too many bumblebees."

"Bumblebees?" cried the other.

"Bumblebees," said Berry. "Great, big, blundering brutes." He pointed to his foot. "I've been stung already."

"But bumblebees don't sting."

"These do," said Berry, firmly. "That's what's so awful about it. Then again the water's too far."

"That's all right," said the other. "We've got a tank."

"Oh, is it?" said Berry. "I mean, have you? That's, er, very convenient, isn't it?" He got to his feet and wiped the sweat from his brow. "I hope you've plenty of carbolic. There's a terrible smell of drains."

"Drains?" said the other, starting.

"That's right," said Berry. "Drains. I'm inclined to think it's a sewage farm." The other was snuffing the air. "It comes and goes, you know. The stench, I mean. A moment ago it was enough to knock you down."

"It can't be the drains," said the stranger. "And any way it's no odds. As long as you can smell it, it's quite all right. It's the smell you can't smell that matters."

"That's what I'm afraid of," said Berry; stooping to put on his shoe. "You see, you can't smell it now."

"Then it doesn't matter, does it?" said the other, gleefully.

"Well, you can't have it both ways," said Berry. "If it doesn't matter when you can, then it does matter when you can't, doesn't it?"

"Doesn't what?" said the other.

"Smell," said Berry. "I mean, matter."

"Well, what if it does?" said the stranger.

In a silence big with emotion Perdita made her escape and Berry fastened his lace with all his might. As he straightened his back –

"The unprintable answer," he said, "is the biggest, burliest bumblebee that ever buzzed – and many of them."

"Now don't you worry," said the other, clapping him on the back. "If you don't think about them, you'll be as right as rain. And you can't move now: you've got your tents up and all."

"Oh, no," said Berry, shakily. "We – we're going to stick it somehow, just for one night. But what with that and the snakes…"

"What snakes?"

"I don't know what make they are," said Berry, gloomily. "I've only seen six so far. But they're black and red, and they make a gurgling noise."

The other shuddered. Then he turned to the caravan, which had come to rest on the opposite side of the road.

"D'you hear that, Harold? This gentleman's seen six snakes."

From his seat on the step of the van –

"Only six?" said Harold, miserably.

His fellow returned to Berry.

"That's the best of a van," he said. "Once in a van, you're safe. But I'm sure you'll be all right. You must try not to think about them. Is this your first night out?"

"Oh, no," said Berry. "We – we're really just finishing, you know. That's what's so – so unfortunate. I mean – now take last night. Only last night we had a peach of a – of a...pitch. That's right. Pitch. More like the Garden of Eden than anything else."

"Was it?" said the other excitedly.

"Oh, scrumptious," said Berry. "Everything you could want. Field like a bowling green, a lovely rill of water, absolute privacy – "

"Harold, the map," said the other. "We'll mark this down."

As Harold rose to his feet –

"You don't want a map," said Berry. "It's only just up the road."

"Only just up the road? Then why on earth – "

"Ah, now you're asking," said Berry. "Because our car's broken down. There's that pearl of Arcady only ten minutes from here – just the other side of Coven, and Coven's four minutes' walk – with a farmer to do your cooking...and there's another thing. This fellow's a tartar – the fellow who owns this field. He wouldn't have had us, you know, if we hadn't broken down."

"My friend," was the genial answer, "you have a lot to learn. 'Use first and ask afterwards' is the – "

"That's just what we did," said Berry. "And he came down in a fury to turn us out. We – we managed to bring him round, but he's coming back in an hour to assess the damage we've done."

"But what have you done?"

"Marked the grass," said Berry. "It costs us eighteen pence each time we sit down."

"You're not going to pay it, are you?"

"He's going to seize the tents if we don't. I tell you, the man's not safe. And what with the smell of snakes – I mean, drains, and the drakes – snakes and the bumblebees…"

The other threw out his chest.

"Let Eden wait," he declared. He found and wrung Berry's hand. "Be of good cheer, my brother, I'm going to see you through. Come all malevolent farmers, I'll put them where they belong." He turned to his wretched companion. "Lead on, Harold," he commanded. "We spend the night with our friends."

With that, he skipped to his van, laying hands upon it, laughing and cheering – and pushing, like a clown in some circus, before the mule itself had decided to take the strain.

As the doll's house lurched through the gateway into our field –

"Well, I'm damned," said Berry. "He may be a full-marks fool, but he's made me ashamed of myself. Goodwill like that must be honoured – at any cost. We must help them to settle down, and then they must come and dine. A bottle of Clicquot'll do old Harold good."

Before five minutes had passed, the reason for Harold's depression was clear as day. A 'weaker vessel' born, it was his misfortune to find himself allied with a man who combined a distracting energy not only with the instinct of managing direction but with a blasting incompetence which had to be seen to be believed. Indeed, I shall never understand how the three had contrived to get as far as they had, for they had been twelve days on the road, yet all were alive and well.

To pitch their camp was the simplest thing in the world. They had only to choose their site, bring the mule to a standstill, let down the sprags or props which were waiting beneath the van and lead the mule from the shafts. This, however, they proved unable to do – thanks, of course, to Horace: for that was the leader's name. By his excited direction, the mule was released before the sprags were let down, and the doll's house, which had but two wheels, immediately tilted back after the manner of a tumbril which is made to discharge its load. Everything loose within it fell to the lower end, and it settled down to the crash of breaking vessels and the frantic convulsions of the water within its tank. Before we could interfere, Horace, laughing like a madman, had actually entered the van – I suppose to assess the damage which had been done: ill-advisedly moving forward, he more than restored the balance the van had lost, and, after the way of a see-saw, the doll's house flung suddenly forward, to come to rest on its shafts. By this manoeuvre, of course, its contents were rudely transferred from aft to fore and Horace was thrown against the window through which in his efforts to rise he immediately put his foot. Though we cried to him to lie still, he preferred to pick himself up and make for the door. Since this lay behind the axle, before he could gain the threshold the van once more tilted back, thereby returning its contents to their original site and, of course, pitching Horace headlong against its end. It only remained for him to make his way to the middle and balance the thing: and this he did almost at once, whereupon, because of the slope, the doll's house ran violently backwards and came to rest in a hedge some seven yards off. In no way disconcerted, Horace emerged full of orders and laughing to beat the band and forgetting in his excitement that he had seen fit to open the tap of the tank. Why he should have done so, I cannot conceive, but since no one but he was aware of what he had done, before we had salved it the doll's house was fairly awash, while the tank, of course, was as empty as when it was new. As for the mule, by Horace's insistent direction, Harold had let the beast go without removing the harness upon its back, and when we had time to look round, we saw it languidly rolling, as bare as the day it was born, while its gear was distributed about the meadow as though it had been flung away to forward some headlong flight.

I set down these curious facts, not at all in malice, but simply because they are true, and I must most frankly confess that, observing their creation, I never laughed so much in my life.

What was, perhaps, the gem of the harlequinade was the instant understanding between the mule and the Knave. That the two agreed together there can be no doubt, for, before they took any action, they nosed one another kindly and considered each other's points in evident amity. And then they began to play. To see them chase one another would have made the sternest ascetic split his sides. Even poor Harold laughed till the tears ran down his face, and when Horace, perceiving the frolic and assuming that the two were in earnest and ought to be stopped, ran violently after them both, pursuing their utmost abandon with all his might, to be himself pursued as one who had no business to interfere – then we lifted up thankful hearts that we had made the acquaintance of such a man.

If we were glad of them, at least we gave them no cause to regret their encounter with us. Had we not been there to point the way to the water and, indeed, to give them to eat, I cannot think what they would have done. Their van was untenable: proposing to live upon the country, they had no food: their bedding was drenched, their crockery broken in pieces – and Horace floundered in the ruin, shaking with laughter, dilating in all honesty upon the joys of camping and continually dispensing counsel of almost incredible futility.

With such a personality present, we had almost abandoned hope of doing that night the business we came to do, but such was the entertainment with which we had been regaled that we were more than resigned to the prospect of trying again. However, our luck was in. By trying to fob the two off, Berry had hoisted us all with his own petard: his decision to show them attention retrieved the situation beyond belief.

At eight o'clock that night the two sat down with us to a decent meal: by half past nine Horace had fallen asleep with his glass in his hand, while Harold had grown so heavy that he could hardly talk. They were by no means drunk, but since they were physically exhausted by the miles they had walked and the many tricks they had played, the wine had acted like a drug upon senses which were only too eager to take their rest.

By ten o'clock our guests were wrapped in our rugs and were lying in one of our tents. Their condition closely resembled that of the blessed dead. So far as they were concerned, the coast was clear.

More than three hours had gone by, when Berry straightened his back and wiped the sweat from his eyes.

"I give it up," he said hoarsely. "The stuff's not here."

"Oh, we needn't stop yet," said Daphne. "It's only just one."

"Yes, I know that bit," said her husband. "I know that we *can* go on till a quarter past two. If we then reverse our procedure and work like so many fiends, we'll get our hole filled up as the dawn comes in. Well, the answer is that I'd rather die in my bed. I mean, face the poisonous facts. Are you going to argue that Studd ever laboured like this? 'Buried that night' were his words. D'you mean to tell me that after a spot of High Toby he rode to this place and dug a thing like a shell-hole some four feet deep?"

Looking upon our labour, I felt the force of his words. We had certainly worked like mad; but, had I not helped to make it, I never would have believed that such an excavation could have been made in three hours. Eight feet by three feet six by four, it would have swallowed a sofa of an enormous size: and Studd had buried a bag the size of his head. I found it hard to believe that our margin of error was insufficiently wide.

We had not been interrupted. The girls and the Knave, between them, were keeping watch, and were ready to flash a warning from either bend of the road. And my sister sat in the

Rolls, ready to take such a signal, drive the car slowly forward and put out her lights.

"Ten minutes' rest," said Jonah, and glanced at his watch. "And then we'll have one more go." He looked at my sister. "Will you relieve Perdita, dear? It's over her time."

As my sister sped up the road –

"Let's have the lights out," said Berry. "The sight of that hole makes me tired." He laid himself down on the turf. "Enough to make a cat laugh, isn't it? Fancy giving up a good night's rest to displace about three tons of earth and then shove it back where it was. Talk about futility. And I was laughing at Horace – three crowded hours ago."

"Some one has said," said Jonah, "that unless you have sweated or shivered, you'll never meet with success. I think it was Juvenal."

"I see," said Berry, thoughtfully. "In that case I've qualified for about three million pounds. I've larded the earth tonight. The wonder is the damned place isn't a swamp. Are you going to put those lights out? Or do you derive satisfaction from the almost immediate future that trough presents?"

As Perdita glided up to take her seat in the Rolls –

"I was waiting for the lady," I said, and put out the lights.

"This is heartbreaking," she said. "And I'm sure it's there."

"If it is, he was sozzled," said Berry, "and couldn't walk straight. We've nearly got down to the water under the earth."

"When we start again," said Jonah, "we can go on for half an hour: and then we must turn and come back."

"Oh, give me strength," said Berry, fervently.

"The burning question is – which way do we go?"

After a little silence –

"I think it should be wider," said I. "We've got enough length."

"I entirely agree," said Jonah. "But if we make it wider, we cannot advance the Rolls."

"I know that," said I. "Let's risk it."

"I'm terribly tempted," said Jonah, "I must confess. But if anyone did come along... I mean, you know, we should look such blasted fools. You can't explain a chasm like this."

"You could to Horace," said Berry. "You'd only have to tell him you'd dropped your stud."

"Ah, Horace – yes," said Jonah. "But the next to come by may be a shade less artless. We'll hardly strike two such giants in a summer's day."

In the silence which followed I closed my eyes and tried to forget my state. My hands were raw, my back and my knees were aching as though their bones were diseased, every stitch upon me was soaked and my face was smeared and my arms were plastered with dirt. The thought that all this was for nothing was hardly bearable.

At length –

"One minute to go," said Jonah. "Perdita, give us some light."

As the darkness fled, I dragged myself to my feet. Then I heard a footfall behind me and started about.

Before I could think –

"Oh, I'm so ashamed, Captain Pleydell," said Harold's voice.

"When I found myself in your tent, I had a dreadful feeling that you would be sitting up. I turned to Horace, but..."

The sentence faltered and died. The sight of the yawning chasm had murdered speech.

Berry had the youth by the arm.

"It's all right, Harold. But tell me. Is Horace awake?"

"No, no. I couldn't wake him. I – "

"Thank God for that. Can we rely upon you to hold your tongue?"

"Of course, sir. I'm awfully sorry. I never dreamed – "

"Why should you?" said Berry. "I can hardly believe it myself. Never mind. Just listen to me. By daybreak today that hole you see there will be gone. No sign of it will remain. The turf will show no traces of having been touched. May I have your solemn word that you will keep to yourself what you've seen tonight?"

"You can, indeed," cried Harold, earnestly. "I'm only so sorry – "

"Good enough, my lad," said Berry. "And now I'll tell you the truth."

And so he did, whilst I helped Jonah to loosen another twelve inches of turf.

Harold listened – with widening eyes.

When Berry had done –

"But how – how very romantic," he stammered. "I mean – after all these years…"

"It is, isn't it?" said Berry, swallowing. "It'd be still more romantic if we could have found the stuff: but it's nice to think that we've, er, mucked about a bit where it used to be."

"You're not going to give up, are you? Oh, don't. Let me bear a hand."

"By all manner of means," said Berry. "But it's very nearly time to start filling this cranny in."

Harold stared at the hole: then his eyes travelled to the milestone.

"Fifteen paces," he murmured. "Of course, if he didn't walk straight… I – I wonder why he made the distance so long. I mean, it seems unnecessary, doesn't it?"

Apart from the point he had made, the way in which he spoke was suggestive of more to come, and Jonah and I stopped working to watch his face.

"As a matter of fact," said Berry, "Studd said 'fifteen.' He didn't use the word 'paces,' but what else can he have meant? He'd have had no measuring line – the whole thing was improvised."

Again Harold measured the distance from milestone to trench.

"It's such a long way," he said slowly. "That's what gets me. It leaves so much room for error – especially by night. Of course you're right – he'd have had no measuring line, but" – he hesitated – "it's great impertinence on my part…"

"Go on, old fellow," said Jonah. "We'll say if we think you're wrong."

"Well, don't you think, perhaps – I mean, as a highwayman, he'd certainly have ridden a lot."

"Spent his life in the saddle," said I. "No doubt about that."

"That's what I mean," said Harold, eagerly. "So he must have been very...horsy. You know. Almost like a groom."

"Go on," said everyone.

"Well, when he said 'fifteen,' *d'you think he might have meant 'hands'* – the measure you use when you're telling a horse's height? I mean, it would be very easy – for Studd, I mean: and fifteen by four is sixty. That makes five feet. And that's much nearer the milestone..."

His eyes ablaze with excitement, his voice tailed on. Jonah was down on his knees, with one hand against the milestone and his palms side by side on the turf.

"Harold," said Berry, with emotion, "I give you best. You're right, of course. I know it. Whether the stuff's there or not, we all of us know you're right." He laid a hand on his shoulder. "You're the *deus ex machina,* Harold – the god that rolls up in the car to put everything straight. And I have the honour to thank you for turning a hideous failure into what I'm ready to bet will be a yelling success."

Twenty minutes later, fifteen handbreadths from the milestone, the spade I was using disclosed the remains of something that was not soil.

I do not know what it had been, for its many years of burial had corrupted it out of all knowledge and very near brought it to dust. I think, perhaps, it had been a wallet.

I gave my spade to my cousin and used my hands. When I touched it, the stuff gave way, and my hand went into a hollow – a slight, irregular crevice, which might have been the inside of what, when first it was there, was a stout, leather bag.

At once I felt some object, and, closing my fingers upon it, I drew it out.

It was flat and small and oblong – and made of gold.

In fact, it was an exquisite snuff-box.

When Perdita had wiped it, the Royal Arms of England, beautifully done in enamel, blazed at us from the lid. And within was engraved the cipher – of the man to whom it had been given, from whom it had been stolen away.

Seven days had gone by.

The doll's house stood in our meadows, the Knave was lying down with the mule in his own domain, and Horace and Harold were standing by the library table, regarding a box and two pistols with saucer eyes.

"And there you are," said Berry. "Studd stopped Great-great-uncle Bertram and robbed him of all he had. The money, no doubt, he spent, but he dared not dispose of the snuff-box because of the arms on the lid. So he buried it by the wayside. He never dug it up, and when he was about to be hanged, he tried to put matters right. He left his pistols to Bertram, and hidden in one of those was a note of the place. He hoped he'd find it, of course. He never did, but, er, one of his scions did. And he went to the place and, thanks to, er, divine intervention, he found the box. So after many years, poor Bertram's honour was cleared. He'd never staked the snuff-box at all. It had been taken off him by Studd."

"And yet he was hanged for it," said Horace. "You know, he ought to have spoken. Then they could have gone to the place and dug the pistols up."

As soon as he could speak –

"I never thought of that," said Berry, uncertainly.

Harold began to shake with laughter.

7

How Jill Enjoyed Herself, and Len and Winnie were Made to Waste Valuable Time

Berry lighted a fresh cigar, tossed the match into the river and then lay back on the rug we had spread on the turf.

"This," he said, "was the site of the pediluvium."

A sweet-smelling ghost beside me lifted her voice.

"I'm almost afraid," she said, "to ask what that was."

"Where the monks washed their feet," said Berry. "Once a week we used to do what we could. And when we were through, the water was sold to the faithful at fourpence a pint."

Jill's voice lightened the darkness.

"You are disgusting," she said.

"Not at all," said Berry. "If it did them no good, at least it did them no harm, and out of the proceeds we erected a private brewery which had to be smelt to be believed. The abbot declared it open by flooring a quart at one draught."

"Abbots didn't drink beer," said Jill.

"I beg your pardon," said Berry: "I never drank anything else. During my, er, supremacy the community was also enriched by the provision of a fried-fish-pond, two shocking squints and an elegant bear garden where the monks could rough-house. All traces of these have, I regret to see, disappeared."

There had been no cool of the day, but with nightfall a slant of air had stolen up from the sea, moving on the face of the river that used to serve the abbey whose bones it keeps. No relics are better cared for. As jewels upon a cushion, the rags and tatters of glory, the broken pieces of magnificence are presented upon a fair lawn – smooth as a bowling-green, stuck here and there with flowers. A strip of pavement speaks for the chapter-house: an exquisite row of arches tells of 'the studious cloister' it once adorned: a lonely pulpit remembers the lector's voice: odd columns, steps that lead nowhere, a window without a wall and doorways that have survived the courts they shut show forth The Preacher's sentence, 'All is vanity.'

We had, really, no right to be there. At dusk the precincts are closed to the public view. But the spot had found favour in our eyes, and when we were ousted at sundown, we made up our minds to come back. Daphne and Jonah were gone – to dine alone at White Ladies and answer some telephone call, but the girls and Berry and I had supped at the village inn. We had then returned to the abbey and, berthing the Rolls in the shadows, had clambered, none too easily, over a wall…

Deserving nothing at all, we had our reward.

A crescent moon was commending another world, where ruins, lawns and water made up a stately pleasance fit for the ease of kings. Here were no tears. The past was not dead, but sleeping: and the present was too rare to be true. Reality was transfigured before us. All the world became a stage, the scenery of which was enchanted.

"Is the Rolls' bonnet locked?" said Berry, out of the blue.

"It is," said I. "Why d'you ask?"

"I wondered," said Berry. "That's all."

Perdita lifted her voice.

"I know why he asked," she said. "Because of those men who were having a meal at *The Drum*."

"I won't deny it," said Berry. "I may be wrong, but I found them unattractive, and I think they'd look very well in a prison yard."

"I entirely agree," said I. "As ugly a couple of toughs as ever I saw. More than ugly. Evil. But people who own a sports Lowland don't go about stealing cars."

"I know," said Berry, "I know. But neither do wallahs like that come down to a place like this to study the pretty secrets of country life. And they took a marked interest in us, as no doubt you saw."

"They did," said Perdita Boyte. "And I cannot think why – unless they're bent on some crime and they have an idea that our presence may cramp their style."

"I trust that it won't," said Berry. "I should simply hate to obstruct two gentry like that."

I saw Jill glance over her shoulder.

"If they knew we were here," I said quickly, "I think their suspicions would fade. I can hardly conceive a locality less suited to the activities of a crook."

But Berry did better still.

"There was once," he announced, "a King, whose looking-glass told him the truth. One day his councillors suggested that the principal town of the kingdom should be bypassed without delay. The King listened to their proposals.

"Then –

" 'Half a minute,' he said, and whipped upstairs to the bathroom, to have a word with his glass.

"The latter heard him out. Then –

" 'Your crown's not straight,' it said shortly.

" 'Damn my crown,' said the King. 'What about this bypass business?'

" 'That's all right,' said the glass. 'Only take it round by the south.'

" 'South?' cried the King. 'But they've planned to take it round by the north.'

" 'So would you,' said the glass, '*if you'd bought all the land on that side*. Of course, if you want to present them with half a million pounds...'

"As soon as he could speak –

" 'The dirty dogs,' said the King. 'The – '

" 'Now don't be hasty,' said the glass. 'Besides, people who live in glass houses shouldn't throw bricks.'

" 'Are you suggesting,' said the King, 'that I have ever – '

" 'I was looking ahead,' said the glass, darkly. 'Have you any idea what they're asking for Bramble Bush?'

"There was a pregnant silence. The estate of Bramble Bush had been in the market for years. What was more to the point, it lay south of the principal town.

" 'Oh, and while you're here,' said the glass, 'you've got some egg on your – '

"But the King was gone.

"Two days later Bramble Bush passed to the crown, and, twenty-four hours after that, the King informed his council that the bypass must go to the south of the principal town.

" 'You can't do that,' said everyone.

" 'What d'you mean – can't?' said the King.

" 'Well, it's not convenient, for one thing,' said Privy Seal.

" 'Yes, it is,' said the King. 'Most convenient. If you take it through Bramble Bush – '

" 'Can't do that,' said Green Cloth. 'The owner of Bramble Bush will never give us his land.'

" 'Of course he won't,' said the King: 'but everyone knows he'll sell it. Bramble Bush has been in the market for years.'

" 'And why?' said Green Cloth. '*Because Buy Bramble Bush, buy trouble* is the motto of the house.'

" 'Go on,' said the King, paling.

" 'Fact,' said Gold Stick, shortly. 'As trustees of the kingdom's welfare, we can hardly fly in the face of – '

" 'Half a minute,' said the King, rising, and ran upstairs to his glass.

" 'You're a good one,' he said. 'What about this motto?'

" 'What motto?' said the glass.

" '*Buy Bramble Bush, buy trouble*,' said the King. 'And I've bought the blasted place.'

" 'In that case,' observed the glass, 'the mischief is done. I told you not to be hasty. And I'll tell you another thing – you'll have to cut out that port. Your nose is getting all gnarled.'

"With a frightful effort, the King controlled his voice.

" 'One thing at a time,' he said thickly. 'What about Bramble Bush?'

" 'Well, you can't go back,' said the glass, 'so you'd better go on. Tell them to lock up their motto and lose the key.'

"The King returned to the council-room.

" 'I decline,' he said, 'to pander to superstition. The bypass will proceed – to the south. Let the plans be prepared and submitted in two days' time.'

"Half an hour later his solicitor rang him up.

" 'I say,' he said, 'do you want to sell Bramble Bush?'

" 'I might,' said the King. 'Who to?'

" 'I'm told it's a syndicate,' said the solicitor. 'Anyway I can get you a profit of fifty thousand pounds.'

" 'Good enough,' said the King. 'Accept the offer at once. And don't you take any cheques. The money must be in my bank by tomorrow night.'

" 'Consider it done,' said the lawyer. 'I suppose you don't want to buy land to the north of the principal town?'

"The King's heart leaped like a trout.

" 'I might,' he said, 'provided it wasn't too dear.'

"Two days later the King informed his council that he had changed his mind.

" 'To use,' he declared, 'the beautiful words of Gold Stick – words, my friends, with which I am sure you concur – as trustees of the kingdom's welfare, we must not fly in the face of writing upon the wall. *Buy Bramble Bush, buy trouble* may or may not be true: but if we were to purchase it out of the public funds and if thereafter misfortune were to fall upon my people, we should never forgive ourselves. In a word, my friends, I was wrong – and you were right. The bypass must be made to the north, and the land had better be purchased without delay.'

"So the King made a profit of a quarter of a million pounds, most of which, because he was kindly, he gave to the poor, while the councillors lost a packet – as they deserved. And the motto which Green Cloth had coined became a proverb, and the looking-glass was given a golden frame. But that wasn't much good, for, only a fortnight later, it made itself so offensive about a little melon the King had left on his ears that he tore it down and had it cast into a well. And there you may see it shining, if ever you look down a well on a sunny day.

"Now that's one of the tales I used to tell the monks after Benedictine. It's not surprising they worshipped me. I used to have to have a new habit once a month."

"Why?" said Jill.

Berry waved his cigar.

"Veneration," he said simply. "They kissed the hem so much, they wore it away."

Here the Knave rose up where he was and let out a growl.

His eyes were upon the river, the half of which was in darkness because of the pride of chestnuts which neighboured the opposite bank: but though we watched and listened, we neither saw nor heard any sign of life, and after a full two minutes the dog dismissed the matter and laid himself down on the sward.

"Water rat," said Berry, yawning. "And, much as I hate to remind you, if we're to be home by midnight I think we ought to be gone."

As we made our way past the ruins, a hand came to rest on my shoulder and Perdita breathed in my ear.

"That wasn't a water rat."

I tucked a slim arm beneath mine and lowered my head.

"I know," I said. "I think it was the dip of a paddle. But what if it was? The river is open to all."

"I know. But there's something wrong. Don't think I'm afraid. I'm not. But there's something that's really wicked abroad tonight."

"There's a witch abroad," said I, "if that's what you mean – with the scent of flowers in her hair and the breath of the dawn on her lips."

"Don't be stupid. I mean what I say."

"So do I," said I. "You're dangerous enough by day: but by night you seduce the senses – and that's the truth."

Miss Boyte withdrew her arm.

"Will you be serious?" she said.

"I am being serious," I said. "Come all the Powers of Darkness, and I'll commend your charm."

"I can't do more than warn you. You know that when I sense something – "

With a sudden movement, I picked her up in my arms.

"I know you're wise," I said. "I know you've a curious sense that we haven't got. And you know that I honour it blindly – I will tonight. But what you don't know is that you are so lovely and natural that when you confide in a man he can think of nothing at all but his *confidante*. It'll pass, of course. I'll pull myself together before we get to the Rolls. But it's…rather fun to let the world slip for a moment…especially if, as you say, there's trouble ahead."

A child laid her head against mine.

"Don't I know that it is?" she said softly. "And now put me down, there's a dear. Remember, we've got Jill with us. And I give you my word I'll be glad when we're under way."

Her saying brought me up with a jerk. If Perdita Boyte was excelling each mortal thing, my cousin was 'such stuff as dreams are made on' – a very delicate texture, to be used with infinite care…

Three minutes later I lifted the Rolls from the shadows into the moonlit mystery that stood for the Bloodstock road.

That we were being followed was perfectly clear. When we had entered the Rolls, I had neither seen nor heard any other car: but we had not been moving two minutes before a car had appeared, going the way we were going, a drive and a chip behind. Moving much faster than we, it had closed to a hundred paces or thereabouts: and there, at that distance, it stayed. Had it maintained the speed at which it approached, it must, of course, have passed us almost at once.

All this my mirror had told me, for the driver behind me was keeping his headlights dimmed.

When I made him free of my news, Berry, sitting beside me, smothered an oath.

"And the girls and all," he growled. "What the ruby hell does it mean?"

"To be perfectly honest," said I, "I haven't the faintest idea."

"Assume it's those wallahs we saw – well, what in the world's their game? Robbery's out of the question. The stuff the girls are wearing wouldn't make twenty pounds."

"I can only suppose," said I, "that they are mistaking us for somebody else. Do you connect them at all with the water rat?"

"I would if I could, but I can't. You can't connect two things with a chain of missing links. That sound was the dip of a paddle – I'll lay to that: and I have an idea that someone was holding water under the opposite bank. They may have been there to watch us: or they may have stayed in the shadows because they didn't want to be seen: then again they may have been lovers… I'm damned if I know what to think."

"Shall I have a dart," said I, "at shaking these fellows off?"

"Why not?" said my brother-in-law.

I put down my foot.

However, our luck was out, for the bend ahead was hiding a level-crossing whose gates were shut.

Before these a car was waiting, and as I drew up in its wake, I saw that its doors were open and uniformed police were standing on either side.

"Hullo," said Berry, "a hold-up. That's what it is. The police are using the crossing to stop all cars. Now how will our friends like this? Are they going to submit to inspection? Or as soon as they see the police, will they do a bunk?"

"Here they are," said I. "And it is the Lowland all right. Show the police your card, and make a complaint."

With my words an inspector of police moved into my headlights' beam.

"Better still," said Berry, and raised his voice. "What's the trouble, Colyer?"

The inspector spun round on his heel and came up to the Rolls.

For a moment he peered at Berry.

Then –

"Oh, good evening, sir," he said. "I'm sorry to stop you like this, but as soon as we're through with that car we'll let you go. I needn't ask if you're carrying contraband goods."

My brother-in-law whistled.

"Smuggling, eh? So you've reason to think..."

"Very good reason, sir. Some – some highly valuable stuff has been landed tonight. And it's got to be stopped somehow. We've simply got to get it. The roads are closed round here for thirty-five miles."

"Then let me commend to your notice the gentry behind this car."

"Go on, sir," said the inspector. "What do you know?"

Swiftly Berry told him what had occurred.

The inspector fingered his chin.

"Too good to be true," he said. "They're the men we want – they're right at the top of the trade. But they'd never travel the stuff. And without it I can't do nothing. They'll laugh in my face, they will. And I'll have to let them go – two o' the wickedest blackguards as ever called for a Scotch." He pushed back his cap and wiped the sweat from his brow. "Still, I'll hold them here for a while, an' give you a pretty start. All the same, sir, if you'll forgive me, I don't think they're following you. If they're who I think they are, they're on big business tonight."

"I think you're wrong," said Berry, "but perhaps you're right. But give us ten minutes' start: we've a couple of ladies behind."

"I'll see to that, sir. Excuse me..."

A moment later the crossing gates were opened and we followed the car before us over the rails. As we regained the road, I heard the gates close behind us and settled myself in my seat. If the Lowland was properly tuned, she could move as fast as the Rolls: but with ten minutes' start...

As we swam through the scented air, Berry spoke over his shoulder, relating what had occurred and explaining that smuggling was rife on some of our coasts.

"But what do they smuggle?" cried Jill.

"Brandy and silk and – and all sorts of stuff on which the duty is high."

"What was it tonight?"

"I don't know at all. 'Highly valuable stuff,' he said. But it must be pretty precious to warrant precautions like that. Think of the police it takes to close every road running out for thirty miles round."

"If you hadn't known the inspector, I suppose they'd have searched the car?"

"Roughly," said Berry. "As a matter of fact, they wouldn't have bothered us much. You see, we're obviously honest: and they go by the look of the people as much as anything else."

"Still, it's just as well you knew him. They were searching the car in front, and when they let us through, they shut the gates in the face of the car behind. How did you happen to know him?"

"As a magistrate, my darling. I've often met him at Brooch."

With his words I had the shock of my life.

An unfamiliar vibration was running out of the steering into my wrists...

There could be no doubt about it. One of our tyres was flat.

As I brought the Rolls to rest, I considered our case. This was disquieting. We were still on the main highway, and the police and the level-crossing were six miles off. So, no doubt, was the Lowland: but the latter would be released in three minutes' time. And I found the puncture surprising. The tyre which was flat – the off hind – had done less than two hundred miles.

Berry and I worked in silence – with all our might, while Perdita stood beside us, holding the torch: but the darkness fought against us, hiding our tools and making our fingers fumble the simple task.

As I drew the wheel from its hub –

"Listen," I breathed. "We must not be caught *with you*. If you should hear them coming before we're through, whip into that wood with Jill and lie low till I call."

"All right."

I gave the wheel to Berry and rolled the spare into place...

It was as he was withdrawing the jack, whilst I was tightening the wheel cap with frantic blows, that I heard in the distance the drone of a coming car.

"Get in and switch on," I roared. "Get into the car."

Twice more I slammed the spanner. Then I flung the tools in the car and leaped for the driver's seat. As I let in the clutch, I saw the lights of the Lowland half a mile off. This in the driving-mirror – I had not dared look behind.

It was touch and go, for we had a standing start: but the other was going all out and coming up hand over fist.

I called on the Rolls: and even in that moment the way in which she responded lifted my heart. No thoroughbred could have done more. When I flicked her into top gear, the Lowland was forty yards off. And then she was thirty...twenty...making to pass.

And there she stayed – a short twelve paces in rear, to the right of the road. We were moving as fast as she, and she could not get by.

"I give you best," said Berry. "I thought we were done."

"I was just going to jam them," said I. "I can hold them now all right, and I think I can make a bit: but I can't get away."

"What the hell does it mean?" said Berry.

"I wish I knew. And we can't go on like this. For one thing, it isn't safe. I may have to give way any moment to save a smash."

"Where do we turn?"

"We can't – at this pace. We *should* at Maidenhair – in about four miles. If only we could, they'd be done: they don't know the roads as I do, and if they tried to keep up they'd break their necks."

"What then?" said my brother-in-law.

"We must hope for Bloodstock," I said. "I can't believe we'll make it, and, if we do, the place'll be fast asleep. But what can they do if we stop in the heart of the town?"

"That tyre – could they have done it?"

"Easy enough," said I, "if you know your job. They placed the nail after supper and left us to work it in."

By now we had gained a little – the hooded lights of the Lowland were sixty yards off. Such a lead, of course, was useless: and, as I had said to Berry, the pace was too hot to last. I determined to make a great effort to gain the room I must have if I was to slow for the corner at Maidenhair.

As a draper tears cloth, we ripped the veil of night for the next two miles. Broad and black and empty, the road was permitting a speed which embarrassed the wits. Our headlights glared upon a rise: before I could gauge the gradient, the Rolls was up. As I marked a wall on our left, a gust of murmur reported that we had passed it by. An avenue flung itself at us: before I had read the illusion, I was taking the bend beyond. For us there was no present: before we could think, the future became the past. Looking back, I fully believe that my eyes directed my hands without making use of my brain. Be that as it may, I never have moved so fast on the open road. But the Lowland was tuned for the track, and though I increased our lead, I could not gain what I needed if I was to turn to the right.

The corner was very sharp and the Rolls was a heavy car. If I was to bring her round, I must so much reduce my speed that the Lowland would be upon us before I could make the turn. She was ninety yards behind us – or so I judged: but ninety yards is not much – to a car which is moving at eighty-nine miles an hour.

I could not think what to do. And then, a mile from the turning, I had the idea.

As though the Rolls was flagging, I began to reduce my speed. With the tail of my eye I watched the Lowland approach. Nearer and nearer she came. A quarter of a mile from the corner she pulled out to pass. I let her come on. When her nose was abreast of my shoulder, I brought up my speed to hers. And there, for a moment, I held her. She was badly placed, of course, and strained every nerve to get by. Then I saw the Maidenhair signpost – and stamped on my brakes...

As the Lowland shot by the turning, I whipped into third, put the wheel hard over and let the Rolls go. The great car entered the by-road as though on the wings of the wind.

"I'm much obliged," said Berry. "The secret of success is surprise. But I wish you'd told me first. When I saw their snout beside us, I damned near died."

I switched to the left by a barn and put out my lights.

"I'm taking no risks," I said, and wiped the sweat from my face.

I confess I was as good as my word. The course I set was fantastic. Will o' the Wisp himself would have had his work cut out to follow the line I took. If this delayed our arrival by half an hour, at least we had put the Lowland out of the race. From the moment we left the main road, we saw her no more.

As I brought the Rolls to rest by our own front door, Jill's arms went about my neck, and I felt her lips brush my ear.

"Oh, Boy, it was lovely. I've never been so fast. That car was racing us, wasn't it? I suppose they think they beat us – unless they saw us turn off. Why didn't you come straight home?"

"I don't know," said I. "It – it seemed a shame to come in. And now you go up to bed. I'm going to put the Rolls away."

"All right. I did love it so."

"I'm so glad, sweetheart," I said.

Perdita was standing beside me, twisting her hands.

She seemed about to say something... And then she changed her mind and followed Jill into the hall.

I let in the clutch and drove round to the stableyard.

I put the Rolls in the coach house and shut the doors. Then I entered the harness-room to let myself into the yard. There I switched on the light to show me the latch. As my hand went out to this, some instinct made me look round.

Two pairs of eyes were regarding me quietly enough.

They belonged to our friends of the Lowland – the two 'unattractive wallahs' to whom I had given the slip forty minutes before.

Feeling rather dazed, I set my back to the door.

"Say it," said the taller, and his fellow began to laugh.

"There's a lot I could say," said I: "but I'll wait till you're under arrest."

"What for?" said the taller, whose name I learned later was 'Len.'

I had no answer ready. Had I been asked to do so, I could not have made a charge. I knew that their intentions were evil, but nothing more.

"Take your time," said Len, with his beady eyes upon mine.

With his words I heard a snuffle below me. The Knave had come to find me and had his nose to the sill.

"Seek Berry," I said, still looking Len in the face.

The latter frowned.

"English'll do," he said shortly. "What have we done?"

"Well, you've got across me, for one thing. And – "

"Now isn't that funny?" said Len. He jerked his head at the other, shaking with mirth. "If you were to ask Winnie here, he'd say that you'd got across me."

"Would he, indeed?" said I. "And how would he work that out?"

Len wrinkled a sinister brow.

"I'll give you two guesses," he said. "And here's a hint. When I show a squirt what I want – well, I don't like disobedience, and that's a fact."

"I'm like that, too," said I. "When I cold-shoulder a swine, I expect to be left alone."

Winnie was plucking his lip as the blood came surging into his fellow's face. As the latter lurched forward he set a hand on his arm. Len shook him off and came on.

I began to draw back my right arm…

And then I saw the pistol.

"Did you say 'swine'?" said Len, and thrust the mouth of his weapon beneath my belt.

White in the face, the unfortunate Winnie gave tongue.

"He isn't worth it, Len. Don't do him in."

At the risk of seeming ungrateful, I must confess my belief – that Winnie was thinking more of his safety than mine. Be that as it may, at that most critical moment, we all of us heard Berry coming – over the cobbled yard.

Before I could think –

"Breathe a word," hissed Len, "and I drill your guts."

All things considered, it seemed better to let Berry 'buy it' than lose my life.

We heard him come straight to the door.

Then –

"Boy," he said, "are you there?" and struck the oak with his fist.

At once Len drew the latch and opened the door: as it moved, this screened us both from the stableyard. As Berry stepped into the room, Len thrust me back with his left hand with all his might – thus slamming the door behind Berry and putting me back in my place. In that same moment he must have gone backwards himself, for I know he was well out of reach in the midst of the room: but his movement had been so swift that I never saw him make it, close as I was – and I think that that did him great credit, for he was a heavy man.

"Now isn't that nice?" said Berry.

Len looked him up and down.

"You gave it that name," he said shortly.

"Well, don't you think so? I mean you and your fish-faced friend with the bit of glass on his tie have been trying to bring this off for over an hour."

"Bring what off?"

"Forgive me," said Berry, "but I thought you desired our acquaintance. I mean, recent events were suggesting that that was at the back of your mind. And permit me to say that had we been by ourselves, you would have attained your ambition some twenty-five miles from here. But the ladies disliked your appearance – you know what women are. I argued with them, you know. I said I was perfectly sure that you couldn't be as vile as you looked. But I could do nothing with them." He took out a cigarette. "I don't mind a felon, myself, if he knows his place. And I'm told that you and your, er, familiar are right at the top of the tree. The police spoke most warmly about you."

"Very kind of them," said Len, grimly.

"They did indeed," said Berry. "I don't know your names, of course, but the moment I said 'a dirty, over-dressed Hebrew with beady eyes and a most engaging habit of sucking his teeth,' they got you at once. All the same, I wish..."

"Messrs Len and Winnie," said I, "my brother-in-law."

"Not the Pooh?" said Berry. "It can't be. He never had heart-disease."

"What's that?" said Winnie, starting.

"Well advanced," said Berry, "if you ask me. I should try and avoid excitement of any kind. I told the police that if they wanted to get you, they'd better look sharp."

Winnie turned an unearthly green.

"It's a lie," he mouthed. "It's a – "

His fellow rounded upon him.

"Cut it out," he spat, "you —."

"He can't," said Berry, mournfully. "An operation would be futile. The anaesthetic alone would – "

"*And* you."

Berry raised his eyebrows.

"I like to think," he said, "that you will reconsider the propriety of that remark. That you've gone a long way to meet me, I don't deny: but this interview was not of my seeking, and that I receive you at all argues a broad-mindedness on my part which many would consider quixotic or even undignified. Yes, I see the rod: but I don't think you'll let it off. You see, if you did – well, Colyer would know who'd done it. He was that nice inspector who spoke so warmly of you. 'Blackguards,' he said. 'Two of the wickedest blackguards that ever walked into a trap.' So he's got you taped, hasn't he? And what with the Press and the wireless – "

"Say that again."

My brother-in-law sighed.

"I do wish you'd listen," he said. "I hate repeating myself. Never mind. How far did you get?"

"Wot the police said."

"About the blackguards?" said Berry. "Two of the ugliest blackguards that ever walked out of a trap?"

" 'Out of' or 'into'?"

Berry put a hand to his head.

" 'Into,' I think. I'm not sure. It was one or the other, I know. Wait a minute. We'd been talking of flogging. Some prisoners, he said, never eat the day before they're to be flogged. No appetite, you know. Now I find that very peculiar. You can understand a man toying with his breakfast upon the morning itself, but – "

"Gawd 'elp," said Winnie, and wiped the sweat from his face.

Len cursed him savagely. Then he returned to Berry, who was lighting his cigarette.

"*Wot did he say?*" he demanded.

" 'Gawd 'elp,' " said Berry, staring. "I suppose it to be a prayer. All the same, I can't help feeling – "

"The busy," yelled Len. "*The busy*. Wot was it the *busy* said?"

My brother-in-law frowned.

"Is that a conundrum?" he said.

"It's a – question," raged Len.

"Then it's one I can't answer," said Berry. "The, er, species is new to me. Busy. Is it anything like the blow-fly?"

"Policeman," howled Len. "Inspector. The one that was talking to you."

"What, about the blackguards?" said Berry. "I thought we'd finished with that."

"Well, we haven't," blared Len. "Go on."

"I do wish you'd listen," said Berry. "I've told you twice." A hand went up to his brow. "It's gone out of my head now. I shall have to go back." As though to assist concentration, he closed his eyes. "The inspector asked what you looked like, and I asked him if he'd ever been to the Zoo."

"You can cut that bit," said Len, thickly.

Berry opened his eyes.

"There you are," he said. "You've spoiled it. It was all coming back, and you've torn it. I had the whole scene before me – and now it's gone." He shrugged his shoulders. "You request me to try to recapture – "

"I asked wot he said," – violently.

"And I'm trying to tell you," said Berry. "Please don't conceive that it's any pleasure to me. The whole thing's intensely odious. But though it means nothing to me, it appears to mean something to you. Out of pure courtesy, therefore – an instinct which in your case, as, indeed, in that of the warthog, appears to be lamentably undeveloped – I determined to accede to a request the inconvenience of which I am unable to estimate except in terms so bitter that I prefer to leave them to your stunted imagination. And now, for the last time, am I or am I not to endeavour to do as you wish?"

Len maintained a furious silence.

"Very well," said Berry, "I will. But if you interrupt me again, you can ask till your eyes come out and all you'll get will be small talk about cremation or what your father said when he saw you first."

With that, he set his back to the wall and, once more closing his eyes, appeared to devote himself to recalling the past.

After an appropriate silence he opened his lips.

"The inspector asked me to describe you, and I said that only your death masks could ever do that – and that even then everybody would say they were faked. And then I asked him if he'd ever been to the Zoo. That's right, and he said yes, he knew it quite well. And then I said, 'Well, forget it. If the animals saw these two coming, they'd eat their young.' " Len's face was working, and even Winnie produced an indignant stare. Berry proceeded relentlessly. " 'I've got them,' said the inspector. 'Outside Hell, there's only one pair like that. Is the fat one dressed up like a nigger on Saturday night?' 'That's right,' said I, 'and his ears are twice life-size, and the other's nose has spread all over his face. He's pale as cheese – that's his heart: but the other – well, what about a couple of oysters afloat in a bucket of blood?' 'They're the blackguards,' said Colyer." Despite himself, Len leaned forward. "Two of the lousiest blackguards that ever walked."

Berry opened his eyes and looked round.

"That's all," he said comfortably.

The explosion which followed this statement will hardly go into words. More black than red in the face, Len let himself go.

Spouting the most shocking imprecations, he denounced with hideous metaphor the whole of the human race, but more especially the police and my brother-in-law. The latter's future he painted in blood and foam, scouring the dregs of abuse to gain his effect, but when Winnie made bold to support him in his attack, he turned and rent him with a fury which had to be heard to be believed.

When at last he had made an end –

"Not bad," said Berry, coolly. "A shade too florid for me, but anyone could see what you meant. And what do we all do now? I can't ask you into the house, because the carpets are clean."

The apology was blasphemously received.

"Quite so," said Berry, "quite so. Never mind. Sit down on that chair, won't you? If the servants can't get it off, it can always be burnt. You see, we're at your disposal. I want you to remember this visit in case you should be prevented from coming again."

With an effort Len mastered his voice. "You've got me wrong," he said. "You're not on my visiting-list. I'm here because I'm here – and that's a good enough reason for dirt like you. And now I've seen what I came for, I guess I'll go. Pass over the keys of that Rolls. She'll do well enough to lift me to where I got out of my car."

His announcement took me aback, as well it might.

The man was evil-disposed. He had observed us at supper and had at that time determined to commit against us some trespass by force of arms. This he had purposed to do on the open road. To prevent our escape, he had tampered with one of our tyres. When this precaution had failed, he had risked his life in an effort to overtake us and stop us by the side of the way. Failing in this, he had actually driven to White Ladies, and, taking advantage of the fact that I had gone a roundabout way, had ensconced himself in the stables before we arrived. And now, after all this trouble, he was proposing to leave…

He had, of course, no intention of stealing the Rolls. Such a theft would have been suicidal. He might as well have walked to the nearest jail.

If I felt more bewildered than ever, I may, I think, be excused.

(Here, perhaps, I should say that he must have obtained our address from the papers we kept in the Rolls. These, no doubt, he perused, whilst we were taking our ease on the riverside.)

My brother-in-law nodded.

"I see," he said slowly. And then, "What's wrong with your car?"

"Nothing," said Len. "I guess you can swear to that."

Berry raised his eyebrows.

"It's a question of preference, is it? You like ours best."

Len turned his attention to me.

"Hand over those — keys. You'll find the car where I leave it – along the road."

"Yes, that's easy," said Berry. "That's easy. But how do we know? To be perfectly candid, that car is worth the best part of three thousand pounds, and I wouldn't trust either of you with a basket of rotten eggs. Besides, you came here on foot."

"An' I'm driving back," raved Len. "In the furniture van wot cost you three thousand pounds. And if that's too tough to chew, I guess you can swallow it whole."

"But how rude," said Berry. "Never mind. You'd much better walk. If you'd walked more in the past, you'd look less misshapen today."

Like some dreadful Bull of Basan, Len gaped upon me with his mouth. After a speechless moment –

"I'm waiting," he said shakily.

I leaned against the door and folded my arms.

"Winnie," said Len, "go through him and get those keys," and, with that, he levelled his pistol, to keep me still.

"Don't you, Winnie," said Berry. "If you do, I shall make it exciting – and that will be bad for your heart."

The unfortunate Winnie blenched.

"F-fetch him over to me," he stammered. "I can't do it there."

"You do as I tell you," howled Len, "you white-livered scum."

I saw the sweat break upon Winnie's repulsive brow.

" 'Ow can I – "

"You can't," said Berry. "You'd be between me and the gun. And that would be terribly exciting." A change came into his voice. "And another thing. From this time on you will take your orders from me.

"*What's that?*"

Len spat the words rather than said them.

"You, too," said Berry, coldly. "We've got you stuck, and you know it. As I told you five minutes ago, you dare not fire. If you did, you'd be laid by the heels within twenty-four hours. And you can't afford that. They're simply stamping to get you – on any charge. And 'attempted murder' would suit them down to the socks. In fact, you've only one card." I saw Len blink. "And it's Lombard Street to a lemon you've no idea what it is."

There was an eloquent silence.

Berry continued quietly.

"Because it suits my book, I'm going to show you this card: but before I do so, I'm going to clear the air. 'Clear' it, I say. Not 'clean' it. I can't do that. If they sank you two in a cesspool, they'd turn it sour."

"See here – "

"*Silence!*" barked Berry. "I let you state your case a moment ago. I let you foul my ears with your filthy tongue, and I never said one word until you were out of breath. And now it's my turn...

"I know who you are, you two: and I know your stinking trade. Ghouls feed upon the bodies of men: but at least they wait until the bodies are dead. But you feed upon the living – a very unpleasant thought. You meant to ply your poisonous trade tonight. *You meant to levy blackmail...*" Again I saw Len blink. "But now you're here and you've seen the shape of this place, you know that you're on a loser – and so you propose to withdraw.

"Well, that's all right for you, but what about us? What about the nail in our tyre? What about being chased for five miles on the open road? And then you've the blasted nerve to enter our premises. And when we catch you out, you pull out a gun... And I am a magistrate. I've only to sign a warrant – "

"Wot for?"

"Have you ever heard the phrase 'felonious intent'? Yes, I thought you had. It covers a lot of sins. Of course you could say that you only came here to chase moths. But I don't think the jury'd believe you: and once your record was known...

"And now I'll show you your card – the only card that you hold. *I do not want to alarm the ladies who dwell in this house.* You see, you two together are like a bad dream – a sort of hideous nightmare, which one does one's best to forget. Well, they had that dream at supper, because you were there in the room: but they've no idea it pursued them, and they must have no idea that it is within a stone's throw of where they are sitting now.

"Now they know that we left for the stables: unless we return very soon, I think they will come themselves to see if there's anything wrong. And since that must not happen, my brother-in-law and I are now going back to the house. In ten minutes' time, however, we shall make some excuse to return – to make sure you are gone. And I warn you that, when we come back, we shall carry a pistol apiece. What is more, knowing you to be armed, we shall take the obvious precaution of firing at sight. I, therefore, recommend you to make the most of this chance and go as you came." He glanced at his wrist. "It is now six minutes to one. If we find you here, my friends, at five minutes past, the balloon will go up with a bang. It goes without saying that that would be bad for Winnie: but I give you my word that it won't be too good for you."

With that, he opened the door, ushered me into the yard, slammed the door behind him and took my arm.

In silence, we crossed the yard, whilst I was still asking myself what the truth of the matter might be.

Berry had played a truly magnificent game – that fact stood out as mountains against the dawn. What bothered me was that I did not know the rules of the game. I could not understand what was really afoot. From what Colyer had said, I assumed that the two were smugglers: Berry, however, had laid a charge of blackmail. But why were they there, in the coach house? Why…

"Poor old fellow," said Berry. "You've had a hell of a time. You see, I knew where I was. *And I knew what cards they were holding*: and when you're playing poker – well, that's a deuce of a help."

"But I don't understand – "

"How should you? But for Jonah, I shouldn't be wise myself. And now step out. I'll talk as we go along."

"Where to?"

"To where they've left the Lowland. The last act's about to begin, and, if Jonah's had any luck, it's going to be pretty good."

I put a hand to my head.

"You spoke of blackmail."

"Hot air," said Berry. "I wanted to ease their minds. I daresay they do a bit, but it's not their trade."

"Which is…?"

"Dope," said Berry. "Distributing dope to addicts – and making a steady profit of four or five thousand per cent."

"Good God," said I. And then, "But why are they here?"

"D'you remember what Colyer said? 'They're the men we want, but they'd never travel the stuff.' Well, Colyer was perfectly right. They were not travelling the stuff. *We were travelling it for them. Whilst we were down by the river, they planted it in the Rolls.*"

With his words, the parts of the puzzle fell into place, and I saw the interpretation of what had befallen that night.

Perdita's intuition, the check at the level crossing, the chase to Maidenhair, the scene in the harness room – all that had happened slid suddenly into focus. Robbed of his whelps, Moloch had pursued us in person – to get his subsistence back. Berry was speaking again.

"By the Grace of God, our wily, if leprous, cousin was not abed. To be precise, he was still in the library: and before I'd been speaking one minute, he'd got it straight. 'Dope-mongers,' he said. 'They knew that the net was spread, so they let you carry it through. And they'll be here any minute, sure as a gun.' He fell on the telephone and asked for the county police. The idea was to get hold of Colyer – headquarters could telephone through to the signal box. He'd hardly put the call through, when the Knave came streaking in and got hold of my coat. 'They're here,' says Jonah. 'Boy's sent him. I'll lay they're out in the stables, holding him up.' Then he told me to go and gain time. 'Hold them in check for ten minutes – that's all I want. I've got to have a word with the police and then I must find the Lowland and put her out. Oh, and ring for William, will you? As for the wallahs, play with them all you know. And when you're through, walk out – they'll be only too thankful to see the back of your necks. But mind you forget the word *dope*. I should try and believe they're burglars – just for a quarter of an hour. And then come down to the gates: I'll try and have William there, to pick you up.' He's damned efficient, Jonah. He can set a sum while he's working another out. And as for making plans – why, he's got his cut and dried before most people's are sown."

Here the Knave leaned out of the shadows, with William behind.

The man was agog with excitement.

"Two hundred yards to the left, sir. They've left her in Three Horse Lane."

One minute later the four of us joined my cousin, who was lying behind a hedge perhaps twelve feet from the car.

When Berry had made his report –

"Splendid," he said. "And Colyer is under way. I think we must wait till he comes, but I've done my best to ensure that we shan't be dull. After all, their tails deserve twisting. The purveyor of dope is no saint. That good-looking car was purchased out of the money that men received for their souls."

We were not dull.

In fact, for the next twenty minutes, our one concern was lest we should be unable to smother our mirth. To say that we laughed till we cried conveys nothing at all. No music-hall turn was ever one half so diverting as that which Len and Winnie provided that summer night.

They reached the lane, blown and breathless – Winnie bearing a suitcase and going extremely lame. It seemed that his boots were tight, for, whilst Len climbed into the Lowland, he sat himself down on the step and proceeded to take them off, condemning the shop that had sold them in shocking terms and finally hurling them into the back of the car.

As he did so, his fellow let fly…

When he stopped for breath –

"An' wot's biting you?" said Winnie, caressing a frightful foot.

"Wot's going to bite you," snarled the other. "The starter's dead."

"Dead?" cried Winnie. "It can't be."

"I tell you it *is*," yelped Len. "I've damned near shoved me thumb through the instrument board. Get out the starting-handle – she'll 'ave to be swung."

"But I've got my boots off," screamed Winnie. The concise directions Len issued concerning his fellow's boots were quite unprintable, and, after a fearful scene, poor Winnie stood up to the tool-box, to search for the starting-handle he could not see. He was not, I think, accustomed to handling tools, for he plucked and dug and fumbled till Len was half out of his mind.

At length, however, his fingers encountered the handle he sought, but, in dragging it out, he brought the jack with it and this fell on to his foot.

His screech of pain would have made a statue start, and I know I hung on to the Knave, lest he should forget his orders and give our presence away: but, on learning his cause of complaint, Len only expressed his pleasure at what had occurred and then demanded that he should employ the handle in the way it was meant to be used.

"*Wot, swing her?*" howled Winnie. "Me swing her? Why, I don't know 'ow to stand up. My foot's a – jelly. I shan't be able to walk for – "

With a soul-shaking oath, the other bade him proceed...

Muttering hideously to himself, Winnie made his way round to the front of the car and, squatting down in the shadows, felt, I suppose, for the socket into which the handle should go.

After a while he stood up.

"There ain't no hole," he reported.

Len's reply was to hurl himself out of the car.

"Look out for my feet," snarled Winnie. "If you was to – "

"You bet," spat Len, viciously.

Mistrustful of this assurance, Winnie started aside from the *rendez-vous*: but he fouled a wing in the dark and, striving to recover his balance, stepped on to a stone...

"That's right," hissed Len. "Wake up the blasted world."

"I wish I could," mourned Winnie. "I'm ripe for an ambulance."

Len snapped its cap from the socket and thrust the starting-handle into the bowels of the car.

If the engine was heavy, at least it was more than warm, and after one or two efforts, he managed to swing the shaft. But my cousin had done his work well, and though we could hear her breathing, the engine refused to fire.

After two frantic minutes, Len wrung the sweat from his face and tore off his coat.

From his seat at the edge of the lane –

"You've overdrove her," said Winnie. "That's wot you've done. If you 'adn't – "

The impeachment was furiously received.

"An' see here," concluded Len. "I don't want no wise cracks from you. Wot do you know about cars? Shovin' a pram on rails is about your mark. 'Please teacher, there ain't no hole.' An' you 'ave the lip to talk about over-drivin'…"

With that, he returned to his labour, turning the shaft like a madman until he could turn it no more.

He was, indeed, so much exhausted that two or three moments elapsed before he could talk: but when he had recovered his breath, he dealt with the situation in terms which I dare not set down.

"Perhaps it's them Willies," said Winnie.

"Wot d'you mean – them Willies?"

"Well, perhaps they've done it on us. Turned off the jooce, or something, indulgin' their wicked spite."

"Ow could they?" snarled Len. "They didn't know where she was, an' they 'aven't 'ad time."

For all that, he stepped to the bonnet and opened one side. He peered and poked about, grunting and dashing the sweat from his eyes, but, because he had no torch, he could not see what he was doing or trying to do: in fact, if the truth were known, I think his action was that of a desperate man, who hopes against hope that by touching some rod or connection he may correct the fault which he cannot find. Be that as it may, in his efforts to see behind something, he laid the side of his head against the exhaust, which was still, of course, nearly red-hot, for the night was warm. The bellow he gave might well have been heard a mile off, and Berry swears that he jumped straight up in the air. I can vouch for the fact that he stamped all over the road, yelling most shocking imprecations and condemning to dreadful dooms the men that had built the car, and that when his companion ventured to ask what the matter might be, he turned and ran upon him – I fear, with the wicked intention of treading upon his feet. Perceiving his horrid design, Winnie fled screaming before him, and the two went down Three Horse Lane, polluting the night with a clamour which might have been rising from Hell.

I think we had all expected that this was the end of the masque, but, when they returned, it was clear that they had agreed together to make a joint endeavour to start the car. Winnie climbed gingerly into the driver's seat – no doubt to play with the throttle, while Len was turning the shaft.

Now the Lowland was equipped with twin post horns, fitted to the front of the car and ready to sound such a call as would waken the dead. As Len laid hold of the handle, the two let fly, making their master leap almost out of his skin and letting a blast of uproar that shook the night.

Len danced into the roadway, convulsed with rage.

"You clumsy wash-out," he roared. "Who told you to – "

"I never done it," wailed Winnie. "It give me no end of a start."

"In course you done it," blared Len. "Why can't you keep your fists to yourself?"

"But I never touched nothing," screamed Winnie. "It done it all on itself."

I must confess that I thought he was in the wrong and had happened to touch the switch without knowing what he did. His character, however, was almost instantly cleared, for, without any further warning, the horns began to blow – with a steady, constant fury which showed that some short circuit was doing its worst.

My cousin later denied that this was his work, so that I can only suppose that Fortune herself had decided to take a hand. She could hardly have played the two rogues a more disconcerting trick. Not only was the racket distracting, but its awful persistence gave it the air of a tocsin, advising all within range to arise and repair to its station with all convenient speed.

That the two were alive to this danger was very plain, for, though, of course, we could not hear one word that was said, their frenzy declared itself in the action they took. Instead of cutting the wires, they sought, like madmen, to silence the horns themselves, wrenching and slamming the metal with that unprofitable fury which only despair can provoke. Each of them dealt with one horn, but the twins were close together, and the violence displayed was so reckless that sooner or later someone was bound to be hurt. Of this contingency Winnie was plainly aware, and when Len, in his agony, clung like some ape to a head-lamp and sought to kick his trumpet into collapse, I think we all felt that Winnie was badly placed. Indeed, our fears were realized almost at once, for Winnie 'stopped one' with his elbow which would have disabled a horse. As a matter of fact, it broke the camel's back. For a moment the subordinate writhed: then he stepped back behind Len and swung to the jaw... His victim fell over the wing and into the road.

Electricity knows no law. For me, the jar of Len's fall just happened to break the short circuit which had been made. Be that as it may, in that moment the noise stopped dead – and we all of us heard, close at hand, the drone of another car.

As Len sat up, the police turned into the lane.

Seated on the lawn the next morning, my sister surveyed her husband with high contempt.

"Three o'clock," she declared. "That was the time you came up. Past three, really, because my wristwatch is slow. You ought to be ashamed of yourself."

"I am," said Berry, sinking into a chair. "I am covered with confusion."

"You don't look it."

"I am though," said Berry, selecting a cigarette. "Simply smothered with it. I don't know how to hold up my head."

There was an indignant silence.

Then –

"It's really indecent," said Daphne.

"Obscene," said Berry, "obscene. Has anyone got a match?"

"Breakfast at a quarter to twelve! You can't expect any servants to – "

"Well, that's your fault," said Berry. "If you'd let me lie, I should have arisen refreshed about half past nine."

"I only woke you to say that the barber was there. You always have him on Fridays. You haven't apologized yet for what you said."

"What did I say?" said Berry.

"You said he could put his scissors where Winnie kept her boots." Jonah and I began to shake with laughter. "Yes, I thought it was something vulgar. Of course there was nothing to do but to tell them to send him away."

"That's what I meant," said Berry. "But you didn't let me lie even then."

"Yes, I did," said Daphne. "I only got up."

"Only," said Berry. "Your idea of rising is to put it across the world. You seem to glory in uproar. That gurgling noise you make – "

"What gurgling noise?"

"Like a bath running out against time. I can't think how you do it."

"Well, it *is* the bath running out."

"No, it's worse than that," said Berry. "Never mind. Let's try and forget it. If you gave your mind to it, I expect you could think of some failing that I've got. Just look at that sky. You know, it reminds me of heaven."

The silence which succeeded his words was big with frightfulness.

My sister, however, decided to fight upon ground she knew.

"And I hear you had William up...at one o'clock in the morning...to bring some more ice."

Berry put a hand to his head.

"I don't think he minded," he said. "And he did very well."

"What d'you mean – did very well?"

"Well, he brought up the ice very well," said Berry, hastily. "Beautifully cold it was." He threw a frantic look round. "And I do wish you'd live and let live. I'm not at my best this morning."

"Whose fault is that?"

Looking ready to burst –

"Mine," said Berry, wildly. "For sitting up, carousing, when I ought to have been in bed."

"Well, you know it's true" – reproachfully.

There was another silence, which I very nearly disgraced.

Perdita lifted her voice.

"Talking of uproar, what was that funny noise? It woke me up – I think about half past one."

"It was Daphne snoring," said Berry. "It almost always means her stomach's upset."

"You wicked liar," said his wife.

Perdita turned to Jonah.

"Didn't you hear it?" she said.

My cousin wrinkled his brow.

"Now you mention it, I have an idea I did. A sort of high-pitched horn."

"That went on and on. That's right. What d'you think it was?"

Jonah shrugged his shoulders.

"Somebody being funny, as like as not."

Jill looked up from her business of brushing the Knave.

"He keeps on yawning," she said. "What time did you put him to bed?"

"I don't know exactly," I said. "When I went myself."

"Poor dog," said Jill. "D'you mean he was up till three?"

"Don't be silly," said I. "He enjoyed it."

"What?" said Jill, staring.

"Well, being with us," said I. "You – you know he likes company."

"It was very unkind" – severely. "You're a man and can please yourself. But how would you like to be kept from going to bed?"

Unwilling to trust my voice, I rose to my feet and sauntered into the house…

Five minutes later, perhaps, two beautiful hands came to rest on the back of my chair.

I laid back my head and looked up – to meet two eyes that made me forget the hands.

Perdita spoke very low.

"A prophet is not without honour, save in his own country."

"Thank you," I said.

"Entirely between you and me, did you put them where they belonged?"

"Berry and Jonah did. I only looked on."

The hands moved on to my shoulders.

"You'd done your bit. You saved Jill and me from the very unpleasant experience of being waylaid by beasts. We should not have forgotten it – ever. And whenever we remembered, the light would have left our eyes."

"You put it too high," said I.

"I don't think so. Never mind." The hands, which were very cool, came to rest on my lids. "But I saw Jill thank you last night, and – and I wouldn't like you to think that I wasn't grateful, too."

8

How Perdita Left White Ladies, and Berry Sat Down with a Lady Who Knew No Law

As Berry entered the room –

"It's in," cried Jill. "There's a photograph in *The Times*."

"What's in?" said my brother-in-law.

"The Abbey Plate. Listen. *By the great generosity of the family from whose cellars the superb collection was unearthed, the world will be able not only to enjoy a spectacle of the utmost magnificence but to contemplate for the first time* – "

"Thank you," said Berry, shakily. "I don't want to hear any more."

He turned to the sideboard, seized a carving knife and did a good-looking ham some grievous bodily harm. As he wrought, he spoke over his shoulder.

"Half a million sterling that stuff was worth – and we've as good as thrown it away."

"What rot," said Daphne. "You know it's only on loan."

"Loan," said her husband, contemptuously. "Loan. And who's going to ask for it back?" Plate in hand, he made his way to the table and took his seat. "It's labelled now – for ever, *Not to be touched*. If we were to breathe the word 'sale,' such a screech would go up to heaven as never was heard."

"Well, it would have been wicked," said Jill.

"Look here," said Berry. "You know as well as I do the fruitful counsel I gave – with which Jonah and Boy concurred, which you would not take. I said 'Have it valued at once, and offer it to the country at half its worth.' If we'd done that, we'd have got a houseful of bouquets and a quarter of a million pounds. As it is, we're down on the deal – *down*."

"Not – not very much," said Daphne.

"Ninety pounds," said Berry. "I had to give the servants a tenner apiece."

There was an uneasy silence, and Perdita moistened her lips.

"As a matter of fact," she said, "Boy gave the gang that found it five hundred pounds."

The effect of her announcement was that of a bursting-charge. The imperturbable Jonah started like a colt: my sister half-rose from her seat: Jill let out a gasp of dismay: and, his fork halfway to his mouth, Berry stared upon his informant as though she were not of this world.

At the third attempt –

"Are you being humorous?" he said.

"No," said I, "she isn't. It's – it's perfectly true."

Berry dropped his fork and clapped a hand to his head.

"Five – five hundred pounds?" he screamed.

I nodded.

"On the spur of the moment, you know. You see, I assumed we should sell it. I gave them a cheque."

"What those blasted – "

"He was right," said Jonah, quietly. " 'Thou shalt not muzzle the ox when he treadeth out the corn.' But I wish to God he'd told me. *I did exactly the same*."

The effect of this frightful confession was that of paralysis. The five of us sat as though frozen or suddenly turned into stone. For myself, I felt more than dazed. Ossa slapped down upon Pelion tends to submerge the wits.

So for perhaps ten seconds. Then, with a dreadful deliberation, Berry spread his napkin over his plate.

"You must forgive me," he said, "but the sight of food has become suddenly obnoxious to me. Not to say, revolting. It's nothing to worry about – I think perhaps I've a touch of bubonic plague. Never mind. Let's see where we stand. Let us cast up or vomit our accounts… Two minutes ago I believed we were ninety pounds down – a condition which, all things considered, most God-fearing people would find sufficiently disquieting. I now understand that certain – certain *pourboires* were given – not to the poor and needy, but to six treacherous gaol-birds, who did their best to deprive us of what was ours."

"But for them," said I, "we'd never have known it was there."

"In accordance with the best traditions, these alms were done in secret – with the unhappy, if natural, result that two *pourboires* were given, instead of one. And each *pourboire* amounted – not to five, or even fifty, but to five…hundred… pounds."

"Out of a quarter of a million," said Jonah. "Don't forget that. It's only one fifth per cent. Of course, like Boy, I assumed we were going to sell."

"And there I don't blame you," said Berry, violently. "All the same, one thousand pounds." He covered his face with his hands. "And you owe me thirty quid each. You can't get away from that."

Jonah and I sat silent, while Daphne and Jill with one voice compared Berry's sense of decency unfavourably with ours.

"Go on," raged Berry. "Go on. Slosh the sob stuff about. Look for the mote in my eye – with a lumberyard in your own. I'm to lose my money – I mustn't be paid a just debt, because two Wardour Street Caliphs – Oh, and what about you?"

"Me?" shrieked Daphne.

"Yes, you. They've only blued a thousand. But you've chucked a quarter of a million into the draught."

As though overcome with emotion, he snatched away his napkin and, putting his lips to his plate, seized his ham in his teeth and gnashed and worried it, growling, much as a lion or tiger grumbles over his meal.

Perdita and Jill, as was proper, dissolved into tears of mirth. But Daphne stood fast.

"I observe," she said, "that your appetite has returned."

Her husband regarded her, munching. "Even so," he declared, "shall the flesh of mine enemies be devoured. There shall not be left of them – And I'll tell you another thing. We've forgotten the goldsmith's bill."

There was another silence.

At length –

"How much will that be?" said Daphne.

"I should think about a hundred," said Berry, wiping his mouth.

"Didn't you get an estimate?"

"Of course I didn't. I thought we were going to sell. One doesn't squabble over a tenner when one's just about to receive a quarter of a million pounds."

"Well, you'll have to pay it," said Daphne. "That and the tips to the servants you'll have to pay. And Jill and I will help Boy and Jonah out."

"Why them and not me?" snarled Berry. "Why should their immorality be visited on my head? They elected to encourage felony – to put a premium upon wickedness and vice..."

"We gave," said Jonah, "a consolation prize. Unhappily, we gave it twice over, but that was because we had no time to consult. It wasn't particularly generous, because we both expected to get it back very shortly a hundredfold. As it turns out, we're not going to get it back: but that is our affair, and we're not going to take any help from Daphne and Jill. But we're going to accept your assistance to this extent – that you shall pay our shares of the tips and the goldsmith's bill."

"But I haven't offered it," screamed Berry.

"I know," said Jonah, "I know. But we're going to accept it just the same. We've had, er, a lot of expenses lately."

I took up the running with a rush.

"As a matter of fact," I said, "we're all in the same tureen. Each of us did what he did, believing that the stuff would be sold. If it had been sold, neither Jonah nor I would have spoken, and you'd have paid the tips and the goldsmith without a word."

"Perhaps," said Berry, "perhaps. But it hasn't been sold."

"So we're each of us down," I continued. "If you think we should pool our losses – "

"Strange as it may seem," said Berry, "that solution had not occurred to me. If you like to play with a skunk, you can burn your own clothes... As an act of grace and on the distinct understanding that this – this *Danse Macabre* is never again discussed, I will discharge the just debts of this frightening deal. Of course the whole thing's a nightmare: but let that go. We've made such fools of ourselves as never were seen. If you wrote it down, no one would ever believe it – it's mathematics gone mad. Take twelve hundred from half a million, and the answer's a stomach pump."

Here Falcon came in with the letters, that moment arrived.

Since there were none for me, I picked up *The Times*.

By the great generosity of the family...

With his hand to his heart, my brother-in-law was making a rattling noise.

"What on earth's the matter?" shrieked Daphne.

"*Angina pectoris*," said Berry. "Get me a cordial, someone. I shan't last long." He held up a bill. "I should like this buried with me. It'll soon be a deodand."

Standing about him we studied the fatal note.

MAJOR PLEYDELL *Dr. to*

BAUBLE AND LEVITY

Goldsmiths to HM the King.

Cleaning and polishing twenty-nine important pieces of fine Church Plate, unsetting, cleaning and resetting one

hundred and forty-seven precious and semi-precious stones, together with three weeks' insurance of the whole
£295-0-0

"I'm not surprised," said Jonah. "When you said it'd be a hundred, I thought you were putting it low. And then, of course, the insurance... We ought to have thought of that."

"I won't pay it," yelled Berry. "It's an obscene demand. I hereby refuse to contemplate it. I expunge its filth from my mind."

Weak with laughter, his wife laid her cheek against his.

"Oh, my dear, I'm so sorry. I really am. But you did ask for it, you know – not having an estimate."

"And you'll still be up," quavered Jill, "on Jonah and Boy. You'll only be down three – three hundred and eighty-five pounds."

"Less," said I. "They'll allow him five per cent discount, if he pays cash."

With a loud and shaking voice, my brother-in-law prophesied no good to any one of us, but evil.

Nine hours had gone by, and the pocket village of Quality offered us such as it had. This was the work of men's hands – so old, so simple and so exquisite as to seem not made but natural as the spread of an English oak.

A road runs round the roughly three-sided green – a quiet, well-kept road that leads to another world: beyond the road, on two sides, are gathered Quality's homes, each with its apron of garden, alight with flowers: on the third side a baby river has called for an old, stone bridge.

The houses are ancient and not at all alike: white walls and thatched roofs are neighboured by rose-red bricks and liveried tiles: half-timber faces cut stone: mullioned windows and dormers and fan-lights may all be seen at one glance: yet all agree together, because all are beautifully done. Of the gardens the same may be said: clipped yew and fine turf, worn brick paths and a riot of stocks, a mulberry ringed by a bench and roses clambering over a miniature porch disclose that orderly disorder the secret of which belongs to Nature herself.

The village green has been cared for for many years. Here and there a white post is still standing to show that once it was fenced against the rule of the road. But now it is a thing of such beauty that no one would ever offend its emerald pile. Not quite in the middle of the sward are the ancient stocks, sounding a trumpet-call to summon yesterday. Their oak is grey but as sound as the hour it was sawn, and, though they remember a justice which we call rough, the passage of Time has made them a reverend hatchment, announcing the dissolution of an antique world.

Behind the houses rises the quiet church tower, grey against the green of the chestnuts which stand beyond: to the left is a pride of elms to which rooks have repaired at sundown since James the First was king: and beyond are woodland and meadow and rolling park, whose lord is a jealous lord and will not sell an acre of all his heritage. So Quality has been saved – a shred of the stuff that English dreams are made of...some local habitations, gathered about a green.

Miss Perdita Boyte sat down on the velvet sward.

"Why," she said, "have you kept the good wine until now?"

"Because you are going," I said. "So that when you sail away, a picture of what you have left may be fresh in your mind."

"I've seen so many pictures, and I remember them all."

"Perhaps. But this is the source from which all the others have come. Close and manor and farm – they, one and all, descend from the village green. The heart of England is beating under this turf."

Perdita smiled very gently and patted the grass by her side.

As I took my seat –

"I've so much," she said, "such a great deal to thank you for."

"I don't see that," said I. "I had to make some return."

"What for?"

"The pictures I've seen," said I. "And I remember them all. A hand on my sleeve, with its delicate, pointed fingers and exquisite fingernails...a knee such as Actaeon died for – and found it cheap at the price... Eve herself looking out of your beautiful eyes...and a mouth that Psyche saw in the dew that Cupid brought her, cupped in his palms."

Perdita sighed.

"Your young men shall see visions," she said. With a gesture of helplessness she indicated the scene. "And now you've left me nothing to give in exchange for *this*."

"You wouldn't say that, if somebody set up a pierglass six paces away."

"What should I see, Paris?"

"A child," said I. "An eager, beautiful child – who knows her world but belongs to a Nursery Rhyme: for whom, when they see her coming, the gates of that pretty country will always lift up their heads: whose charm, like soft music, precedes her, wherever she goes."

"Oh, Boy, what an epitaph!"

"With my love," said I, and laid a hand to my heart...

For the short half hour that followed we two considered in detail the rare and unsullied virtue of Quality's gorgeous fee. Then the Rolls floated over the bridge to come to rest in the shade of a whispering lime.

Berry was at the wheel, with Jill by his side. After setting us down at cross roads, the two had driven to Warfare, where Berry must sign some papers which could not be sent by post. And now they were back – rather later than I had a right to expect.

The Knave leapt out of the car, chased an indignant blackbird into the thick of a yew and then came, panting, towards us, cheerful under rebuke.

Jill preceded Berry over the turf.

"Oh, Boy," she cried, "we've had the most awful time. As we were leaving Warfare, a woman backed into the Rolls."

"Good Lord," said I, starting up.

"It's all right. The bumper saved us. But she really was awful about it. She said – "

"It's a hideous satire," said Berry, "from first to last." He laid himself down on the sward and closed his eyes. "Swift might have done it justice – I can't think of anyone else. With illustrations by Hogarth… I suppose she was a woman: she'd a voice like a bugle-band and her upper parts were just about twice life-size."

"What exactly happened?" said Perdita.

Berry drew a deep breath.

"You won't believe me," he said, "but Jill will confirm what I say. About to emerge from Warfare, I found myself directly behind a mechanically-propelled vehicle which for some reason which I was unable to see had ceased to advance. I, therefore, stopped too, as did the lorry behind me and the hackney-coach or omnibus, apparently designed for the conveyance of eight elephants or a hundred and twenty men, a short two inches away from my offside wings. After a considerable delay – which was nonchalantly improved by one of the younger patrons of the omnibus by spitting such plum stones as he no longer required across the gulf between us into my lap – the driver of the car before me saw fit to recoil upon the Rolls. At once I sounded my horn… Retire myself I could not – the lorry was biting my neck. But the car before me came on. I continued to protest – frantically. Then the car ahead of me stopped, and its driver leaned out and looked round…

" 'Stop that noise,' she blared, 'and reverse your ridiculous car.'

"There are upon this earth some beings whom having seen one feels it would be imprudent to thwart. To be assaulted in public by a harridan of such dimensions would have been unsatisfactory. And violence sat in her face.

"I turned to the lorry driver and asked if he could give place. From his reply, which included two oaths I had never before encountered, I gathered that he was reluctant to do so. The man may be forgiven. I later perceived that he had behind him two trailers, laden with stone.

"As I returned to my bugbear, the threatened collision occurred, and, as if it had been waiting for that, the traffic jam was relieved and we all were free to proceed. But only for a moment or two. As I got to the side of the street, we were stopped again – this time with my nose abreast of the bugbear herself.

"Well, I got out to see the damage – which, happily, hadn't been done, and as I looked up from the bumper, the bugle-band voice rang out. Will you believe me? *That hell-cat ticked me off.* Said that by sounding my horn I had sought to impose upon her my 'vulgar will.' That she pitied my womenkind. That I was 'a tin-pot tyrant,' and that next time I wanted a lesson I'd only to let her know. When I tried to reply, she told me to hold my tongue, to go and 'bully my slaves,' or, better still, to hire a children's nurse to teach me how to behave... She broadcast these recommendations – screeched her rotten lies for the world to hear. And of course it did. A crowd began to collect. Everyone within earshot began to rush to the scene. And though nobody knew what had happened, everyone heard the monstrous suggestions she made. And then the traffic gave way and off she went... And as I got back in the car, the police came up and told me to 'move along.'...

"You know that's the kind of show that shortens one's life. It's brutal injustice gone mad. And what can I do? Nothing. Jill got her number, but what can I charge her with? In the old days she'd have been ducked for a common scold: but today she can scorch my soul for something I never did, and because there's no mark on my car..."

"Poor old fellow," said Jill. "You really behaved like a saint." She turned to us. "When he found she wouldn't listen, he bowed very gravely to her and then came back to me and began to tell me how Warfare got its name."

"One had," said Berry, "to try and carry it off. I mean, that was all that was left. And now let's dismiss the affair. I've not felt too good all day – since Bauble and Levity landed their kidney-punch."

Perdita lifted her voice.

"If Daphne were here, she'd drink to you with her eyes, and you'd feel refreshed. But she isn't here, and so we must – call for wine." She pointed across the lawn. "There's an inn there, *The Running Footman*, just out of sight. It looks like a woodcut – a tail-piece to some old volume of Georgian days. But I expect it's meant to be used… And Jill and I will wait here, if you're not too long."

As Berry got to his feet –

"My dear," he said, "you'll make a marvellous wife."

Perdita's judgment was good. To be stayed with a flagon was just what Berry required: the creature comfort ministered to his mind. For myself, it quenched a thirst which I was thankful to slake. And when we returned, the girls were unwilling to move. So we lay on the greensward, talking…and sipping another liquor, older and rarer than any the innkeepers sell. And Quality made a good host. Sip as we would, our cup was always full.

Even the Knave fell under the spell of the place. He moved about gently, proving the beautiful turf, raising his head and snuffing, as though the scented past was stealing upon the air. And once, when a cat came out of a garden gate, he watched her take to the road and then returned to a reverent study of the stocks. Perhaps, on Quality's green the lion would lie down with the lamb.

When we took our leave of the village, the sun was low, and I had to let the Rolls out, to make up the time we had fleeted, gathering rosebuds that bloomed when Herrick was young. We ripped the veil of evening for thirty sweet-smelling miles, while meadow, wood and hamlet flashed to our side – as though to bid farewell to the pretty stranger who loved them with all her heart. Perdita Boyte was to leave us the following day.

As we swept to the door of White Ladies, my cousin, Jonathan Mansel, appeared on the steps.

"Daphne says you've got to be quick. We've a guest – for one night only: a Miss Theresa Weigh. She was to have stayed at the Vicarage, but one of the children's gone sick and they can't take her in. Glanders, I think. No, mumps. She's mucking about, giving lectures – to such as have ears to hear. And she seems to be pretty hot stuff where pomps are concerned. We've got to have our cocktails upstairs."

There was a dreadful silence.

Then –

"Oh, give me strength," said Berry. "Twice in one eight-hour day! You know, it's rather hard."

"Twice?" said Jonah, frowning.

"Twice, as I live," said Berry. "What's this one like?"

"Striking," said Jonah, simply. "She's roughly twice life-size and – "

Four cries broke the sentence to bits.

"St Skunk and all devils," screamed Berry. "Don't say she's got a voice like a bugle-band."

"Almost exactly," said Jonah. "And now I should look alive. If anyone's late for dinner, she'll tell them where they get off."

Seated at Berry's right hand, Miss Weigh surveyed the table with an aggressive eye. Then, with a scowl, she turned her champagne glass down.

"Strong drink is raging," she said.

"Er, on occasion," said Berry, moving his glass out of range. "A desire, which I venture to maintain is laudable, to honour the sex which you adorn is responsible for the presence of these sinister beakers or goblets, for which I could otherwise offer no shadow of excuse."

Miss Weigh regarded him straitly.

"Explain yourself," she commanded.

Berry sat back in his chair.

"Unable," he said, "any longer to support the flagrant abomination of my company, despite my frantic entreaties, your beautiful *vis-à-vis* has determined to leave this house. In accepting this natural decision, I have conceived it to be my manifest duty on this, her last, night to do her the utmost honour I can. According, therefore, to a tradition so ancient as to compel respect, I have brought forth my rarest wine – not in a futile endeavour to make glad our hearts, which in view of her imminent departure would be impossible, but to pledge her charm and wisdom as best we may. It is, therefore, no vulgar carouse, but a seemly rite to which in all honour we mean this night to subscribe – the honest, if clumsy, homage of a man not yet sunk so low as to be unable to recognize virtue, to distinguish right from wrong, and to render to lovely woman the things that are hers."

Miss Weigh appeared to hesitate. Then, to her lasting credit, she once more reversed her glass.

"Not that I'm deceived," she announced. "Any excuse for an orgy will serve for you. But at least you're civil about it. Why couldn't you have been civil this afternoon?"

"Madam," said Berry gravely, "had you not been prevented by the instant roar of a traffic for which the streets of Warfare were never designed, you would have heard my humble endeavours to explain that my failure to accommodate you was dictated by no indecent impulse to resist your lawful desires, but by the bile or venom of the foul-mouthed carrion to whose charge the vehicle directly behind me had been unaccountably committed. The moment that I perceived that you were proposing to retire – an intention, I may say, which I had the honour to anticipate – I naturally determined to accord you such place as your manoeuvre might demand. Most unfortunately, however, the rude and incompetent boor to whom I have already referred had so placed his wain or waggon that I was utterly prevented from consulting your convenience, and, when I acquainted the reptile with my predicament, my words were received not only with the foulest contumely but with a disregard of the proprieties so shocking as to be almost impious. To advise you of a position which caused me much pain, I made bold to sound my horn, for, while I was well aware that such action might be mistaken for that of a bully or road-hog demanding way, it seemed to me still more important that you should not put in peril your elegant car – by counting upon an obedience which you had a right to expect, which I, through no fault of my own, was unable to bear. To my infinite confusion, madam, though not, I may say, to my surprise, you most naturally interpreted the somewhat peremptory note, not as the counsel of despair, which in fact it was, but as the impudent agent of an outlook which would, I submit, disgrace a blue-based baboon; and I suffered a disapproval which was most justly due, when in fact it was the toss-pot behind me – that black-throated son of Belial, whom we may shortly expect to be eaten of worms – that was, so to speak, the fountain of my dishonour."

With a suspicious sniff, Miss Weigh appeared to consider the value of Berry's reply, much as some god, by snuffing the rising smoke, might seek to appraise the ingredients of sacrifice done. Before she had finished, Jonah, beside her, made some polite remark, and Perdita fell upon Berry, demanding an oral itinerary – of which she had no need, which, if Berry pleased, would take some time to recite. All ears, as was only natural, Daphne, Jill and I made some pretence to converse, and to accept as normal the most embarrassing meal to which I have ever subscribed. Meanwhile the champagne was served…

Miss Weigh was addressing Berry with all her might.

"And what is your mission in life?"

"I – I don't think I've got one," said Berry. "I've waited for years, but I've never had a definite call. You know, that does happen sometimes," he added, plausibly.

"Never," said Miss Weigh, shortly. "Everyone has some mission, however vile they may be. Consult your conscience, sir.

If that's not dead, it will answer. If it is, I shall revive it. The revival of conscience is one of my missions in life."

The vision of Miss Weigh applying artificial respiration to Berry's soul was so awe-inspiring that we sat about the table like dummies, holding our breath.

After a frantic look round –

"M-meditation," said Berry, wildly. "That's right. Meditation. I often think I ought to have been a nun – I mean a monk. But it's too late now." '

"What do you mean – meditation?"

Never were five words so crammed with indignant scorn.

"Well, that's my call," said Berry, desperately. "My conscience tells me that that is my mission in life."

"Don't trifle with me, sir," said Miss Weigh.

"Madam," said Berry, gravely, "even if I had not the honour to be your host – a relation which automatically forbids impertinence – I am not, believe me, so – so verminous as to be unable to perceive the enormity of such an attention." Before Miss Weigh had recovered from this majestic broadside, he continued fluently. "At the same time I would beg you not to condemn out of hand the efforts of a definitely weaker vessel to raise himself and his fellows not to the peaks of self-discipline which you command, but at least above the level of the steaming midden of inefficiency upon which the lower animals are content to sprawl."

Miss Weigh drank some champagne.

"Fine words," she said. "Meditation is bosh – and you know it as well as I."

"But look at the lamas," cried Berry. "Look what they do… And all by meditation."

"Well, what do they do?" said Miss Weigh.

"They perceive the meaning of things. And that's where we fail. We take everything for granted – a hideous mistake. Take that glass of champagne, for instance."

"What about it?" said Miss Weigh.

"Well, it's more than that, really," said Berry. "A great deal more. Only you and I can't see it."

"This is beating the air," said Miss Weigh, testily.

"That's just what I said," said Berry. "My very words. And then I tried. I meditated upon some ordinary, commonplace thing. And after a while, you know, I began to see round. I saw that it wasn't what it seemed."

"What did it seem?" said Miss Weigh.

"A slop-pail," said Berry. "A common, vulgar – "

"And what was it really?"

"A human document," said Berry. "I can't put it more plainly than that. The secrets of meditation will never go into words."

"Yes, they will," said Miss Weigh, violently. " 'Drivel' and 'Balderdash.' "

My brother-in-law sighed.

"I don't blame you," he said. Miss Weigh choked. "Before the snails – scales fell from my eyes, I felt the same. I was even more outspoken. From my criticism of the mystery I omitted no circumstance of ribaldry, and epithets I blush to remember spurted like – like grapestones from my lips. And then one day, in prison, I – "

"In *what*?"

"Prison," said Berry. "You know. Captivity. Bondage. Well, I was sitting there in my cell, when – "

"What were you in prison for?"

"Felony," said Berry. "Never mind. I was sitting there in my cell, when – "

"Sir," said Miss Weigh, rising, "I have been most grossly deceived. I was given to understand that this was a respectable house. Had I entertained the faintest idea – "

My sister was on her feet.

"It was all a mistake," she said. "My husband – "

"Madam," said Miss Weigh, "I have heard that explanation before. But never before have I witnessed such a callous and brutal indifference to the stigma most people attach – "

"But I tell you – "

"Your husband, madam, has told me more than enough." My sister sat down. "Kindly order my car at once – and my things to be packed." Daphne nodded to Falcon, who left the room. "At Brooch, no doubt, I can find an honest hotel."

"*The Fountain*," said Berry, rising, "is irreproachable. If you mention my name – "

"I hope," said Miss Weigh, with great violence, "that I should be turned from their doors."

"I don't think you would," said Berry. "You see, if you'd let me explain – "

"I blame myself," said Miss Weigh. "The moment I saw you, I ought to have left the house. The impression I formed of you at Warfare was most unfavourable."

"Yes, I – I gathered that," said Berry, "from what you said at the time."

"Don't you dare," said Miss Weigh, "to answer me back. My mission has brought me in touch with the vilest of the vile, but not one of them has ever before presumed to abuse my confidence."

"In other words," said Berry, "they never had the pleasure of entertaining you."

"Such hospitality," said Miss Weigh, "is an insult. I do not sit down with social outcasts, however rich the table which, doubtless, their acquaintance with crime has enabled them to spread."

"Madam," said Berry, "you have the wrong sow by the ear. If you will permit my wife or me to explain – "

"Silence," said Miss Weigh.

My brother-in-law bowed.

"Whilst accepting your ruling," he said, "that a certain subject is barred, I trust you will allow me to regret your decision to leave this house, thus cutting short an acquaintance which, in spite of recent indications to the contrary, I shall always believe to have been big with promise."

"Sir?" gasped Miss Weigh.

"A very Canaan of the soul," continued my brother-in-law. "I represent the dregs of one sex, you the cream of another. Caliban and Ariel hob-nobbing... What tasty and succulent fruit might not so rare a relation have brought forth? I have, of course, learned of you. The garbage of my mind has been stirred: the cess-pool of my imagination has been troubled: and had I been able to develop the truths which, to the best of an ability so meagre as to be almost imperceptible, I was attempting to expose, I believe it to be within the bounds of possibility that you in your turn would have gone not altogether empty away. Since, however, you feel unable any longer to support the demands which a presence such as mine must inevitably make upon a nature as sensitive as yours, our pretty dreams must be abandoned, our sportive gambols upon the flowery fields of reason must be forgone. Be that as it may, I beg you to believe that age will not wither the, er, mental stimulus which I have derived from our communion, so unhappily about to be dissolved, and I venture to express the hope, but without much confidence, that while you have been within my gates such creature comforts as my establishment has been able to offer have been entirely to your convenience."

Bristling with indignation, Miss Weigh surveyed Berry, much as a goose might survey a presumptuous toad.

"I have yet to learn," she declared, "that it is incumbent upon me to acknowledge entertainment which only a brazen reprobate would have allowed me to accept. I do not consort with convicts. And such of those unfortunate beings as I have addressed have never dared to approach that unbridgeable gulf which an innate sense of decency tells them is fixed between repute and degradation."

In the silence which followed the butler re-entered the room.

I do not know what it was that made me look at him twice. His manner was faultless as ever, but – well, I have grown up with Falcon and I was immediately aware that he was the prey of an excitement which he could hardly suppress. I decided that, after all, this was natural enough. His master had been grossly insulted – by the stranger within his gates.

"The car is at the door, madam."

Miss Weigh bowed ponderously to Daphne, ostentatiously threw up her head, and turned on her heel.

I nodded to Berry and, as she made for the door, I fell in behind.

Dacre was standing in the hall, with a wrap in her hand. As she set it about Miss Weigh's shoulders, William swung open the great front door of the house.

Miss Weigh passed impressively out.

As I followed, I saw two cars.

By one stood Fitch, our chauffeur. By the other were standing three men, one of whom was an inspector of police.

As Miss Weigh was approaching her car, he stepped to her side.

"Theresa Weigh?" he said bluntly.

Miss Weigh looked him up and down.

"That," she said, "is my name."

"In that case I hold a warrant for your arrest. Dangerous driving and obstructing the police on the 25th of June last at Relish in the County of Wiltshire. A summons was applied for and issued which you 'ave consistently disobeyed. Consequently – "

"Stand back," said Miss Weigh. "I know nothing of man-made laws."

"I warn you that anything you say is liable to be taken down and used in evidence against you. Kindly enter that car: we've got your suitcase inside."

"You tin-pot tyrant," said Miss Weigh, "you – "

"Now don't take on," said the other. His two companions closed in. "It'll only make matters worse. If the Bench sits tomorrow, you'll only 'ave one night in jail. An' it isn't our fault, you know. If you 'adn't ignored – "

Miss Weigh struck him full in the face...

And there I turned my back on a scene which was bound to be sordid, which I shall always believe that Justice herself had set.

As may be believed, my news was received with a delirious enthusiasm which swiftly developed into an exuberant ecstasy of jubilation.

For two minutes we let ourselves go.

Perdita, Jill and Berry were performing a *pas de trois* which is not in the books: halfway between laughter and tears, my sister was hanging upon me, imploring me to repeat the deathless epilogue: and Jonah and I, bent double, were recalling the shortcomings of Relish to whose court he had gone as a witness six months before.

We fled to resume our seats, as the servants re-entered the room.

"The lady gone, Falcon?" said Berry.

"Yes, sir," said Falcon.

"And her – her escort."

He hesitated.

"I said I hadn't witnessed any – any fracas, but they wouldn't take 'no' from Fitch: and William had to help the inspector, so if they should call upon him, I'm afraid he can't hardly refuse."

"Help him?"

"Only afterwards, sir. He – he'd injured his nose, I believe. Not seriously, sir. And William brought him a sponge."

"I see. And the lady's car?"

"That has gone, sir. One of the, er, executive took it – so I believe."

"Sunk without trace," said Berry. "What a very beautiful thought." He pointed to the place at his side. "Er, remove those baubles, will you? And then let's have some champagne."

From that time on, the meal was a festival, and when the cloth had been drawn, my cousin, Jonathan Mansel, got to his feet.

"I give you Berry," he said, and lifted his glass. "God knows he has his faults, but I'm very sure you'll agree that his performance this evening was more than masterly. The music he faced was frightful: yet he never made one mistake, and for me he has added a really brilliant chapter to 'the way of a man with a maid.' "

When the acclamation had died, my brother-in-law rose to reply.

"We shall," he said, "remember today. It began with the disclosure of the repulsive fact that between us we are the poorer by fourteen hundred pounds – due partly to a generosity which I shall always consider to have been uncalled for, and partly to the unconscionable avarice of the fly-blown lepers in whom I had put my trust. It went on to the, er, rise and fall of that most remarkable woman, Theresa Weigh. As you know, she swam into my sphere this afternoon: and, though our communion at Warfare was not only one-sided but brief, I had barely recovered from the, er, energy of her attentions when I learned that a still higher honour was to be thrust upon me. As you saw, she is difficult to please. Indeed, I am prepared to submit that fellowship, as we understand the word, with a lady of her outlook and, er, design, to whom reason is the foulest intolerance and courtesy a bestial affront, could only be effectively achieved by a man of the capacity of Attila: but I am equally ready to believe that, if she was still alive at the end of twenty-four hours, their lively appreciation of each other's attributes would result in an *entente* of almost passionate cordiality." Here Jonah, playing butler, recharged his glass. "But that is, of course, by the way, for if she bade fair to disorder an existence which had done her no harm, we may comfort ourselves with the reflection that for the next few hours her own vile being will be itself disordered to an incredible extent.

Indeed, if we may believe Falcon, one of the officers of justice had been suffering from epistaxis or bleeding of the nose, and, while no one knows better than I that that organ delights to select the most inconvenient moments for its relief, in the present case I am frankly disposed to attribute its activity to the striking physique of the lady whom the officer in question had been commanded to arrest. If I am right, I fear that such battery will find but little favour in the eyes of the justiciaries before whom she must inevitably appear, and, should she adopt to them the somewhat critical attitude of which, from time to time, I was vouchsafed a glimpse, I think it more than likely that she will be compelled, owing to circumstances over which she has no control, to cancel her more immediate engagements. One might have been forgiven for thinking that these things had been sufficient unto this day, but I cannot forget that Perdita's place will be empty at this hour tomorrow night. It is appropriate that I should commend her, for by reason of my bitter portion I am particularly qualified to appraise her virtue."

"What bitter portion?" said Jill, suspiciously.

"Enough," said Berry, "that it has been alleviated. When I have trembled for the well-being of those who would presume to be my censors, when the sewers of ignorance have been opened and the soak-pits of execration emptied upon this venerable head – "

"When was all this?" said Daphne.

"It comes and goes," said her husband, hastily. "Perdita will know what I mean. As I was saying, at these unhappy moments I have been fortified as much by the consideration of her bodily charms as by the reflection that beyond the slough of incoherence in which the poor fools rout, there has been standing a darling with sympathy in her eyes for the prophet the baboons have bespattered – "

"I insist," said Daphne, "upon knowing to whom you refer."

"To the wicked," said Berry. "You know. The – "

"What wicked?"

"Now look here," said Berry. "I'm in the middle of proposing a precious toast. If – "

"You're not," said Jill. "You're simply calling us names."

"There you are," said Berry. "The lie direct. I seek to lay my homage at the beautiful feet of our guest, only to be b-bludgeoned with insult and – "

"That's a good one," said Daphne. "What about the 'bespattering baboons?' You ought to be ashamed of yourself."

"I must decline," said Berry, loftily, "to continue a discussion which would be ludicrous, if it were not indecent. Instead, let me give you the health of a beauty I shall always remember with all my heart if only for the startling contrast her excellence affords to that distressing atmosphere of imperfection which is, as you know, my cross – the gaseous propensity of three or four slow b – bellies."

With that, before we could stop him, he raised his glass, and, since we could scarcely decline to honour the toast, we were forced to subscribe to a suggestion which I shall always maintain was unnecessarily provocative.

But Nemesis was at hand. With a foresight, born of experience, Jonah had laid a lump of ice on his chair; and on Berry's resuming his seat, he sat down not only on this but in the small pool of ice-water which the length of his speech had enabled the berg to create.

The result may be imagined, but hardly described. With a yelp of dismay, our critic leapt into the air, palms clapped to the scene of the outrage, accusation looking out of his eyes.

"Yes?" said Jonah, encouragingly.

My brother-in-law drew himself up.

" 'There's a *vulgarity*,' " he said, " 'that *slakes* our ends, *Endue* them how we will.' "

For which we forgave him everything.

The next day, at a quarter past one, I handed Perdita over to Mrs Boyte. This, as was right, at Cock Feathers, where the two were to spend some days before they took ship.

After lunch we all strolled in the garden, rich with the clean-cut magic of immemorial yew and an ancient, emerald vesture which once was turf.

Then Mrs Boyte grew lazy and made excuse…

For a short half hour we sat at the foot of the sundial, remembering pretty things, with the world to ourselves. And then I glanced at my watch – and found it was time to be gone.

For the last time I looked at my lady – and felt refreshed.

Sitting sideways, as children do, one brown arm propping her up, her slim, silk stockings sheer sculpture against the cloth of the grass, she seemed to me to embody the maidenhood which belonged to the Golden Age. There was nothing common about her: from soft hair to delicate foot, she was exceptional. Her features, limbs and body did one another honour, because they were all so fine, and the eager spirit which dwelt in this lovely flesh, which leaped in the light of her eyes and the flash of her smile, declared her a true king's daughter, 'all glorious within'.

I took her right hand from her lap and put its palm to my lips.

"I'm sorry you're going," I said.

"I'm sorry to go."

I pointed to the nursery window.

"Don't forget you belong to all this. To the lawns and pavements, to the woods and meadows and 'hedgerow elms' of England, to manor and mill and hamlet, to mullion and rose-red chimney and lichened oak."

"They belong to me now," said a child. "I've got them here – in my heart."

I sighed.

"I must be going, my pretty maid."

"God go with you, sir, she said."

"I shall always remember my pretty maid."

"Thank you kindly, sir, she said."

I sighed again. Then I turned to the sundial, to see what legend it bore.

Perdita turned as I did. Together we read the words.

ALL IS VANITY

For a moment we regarded the saw. Then we turned, once more together, to read one another's eyes...

And what we saw written there was time-honoured wisdom before The Preacher was born.

I reached White Ladies again at half past six. Daphne and Jill were abroad, but the Knave made as much of me as a good dog can.

As I entered the hall, a whoop of hysterical joy rang out of the library.

Then –

"Say it again," roared Berry. "Keep on saying it over. It can't be true."

As I entered the room –

"I put seventy pounds," said Jonah, "upon this particular horse. And it's won, as I thought it would, at twenty to one. That's fourteen hundred quid – I did it to put us square. On Monday I'll give you a cheque for three hundred and eighty five pounds."

"God bless you," said Berry, fervently. "God bless your honest heart. But how on earth – "

"These things happen," said Jonah. "The moment I saw its name, I knew we were off. *Where There's A Will* – that's its name. And remembering that of the lady – the name of our recent guest..."

Berry began to laugh uncontrollably. Not choosing to ask to be shown what it seemed that I ought to be able to see for myself, I thought very hard indeed upon Perdita Boyte.

After perhaps two minutes, I remembered Theresa Weigh.

Dornford Yates

As Berry and I Were Saying

Reprinted four times in three months, this semi-autobiographical novel is a comic rendition of the author's hazardous experiences in France at the end of World War II. Darker and less frivolous than some of Yates' earlier books, he described it as 'really my own memoir put into the mouths of Berry and Boy', and at the time of publication it already had a nostalgic, period feel. A hit with the public and a 'scrapbook of the Edwardian age as it was seen by the upper-middle classes'.

Berry and Co.

A collection of short stories featuring 'Berry' Pleydell and his chaotic entourage established Dornford Yates' reputation as one of the best comic writers of his generation. The German caricatures in the book carried such a sting that when France was invaded in 1939 Yates, who was living near the Pyrenees, was put on the wanted list and had to flee.

Dornford Yates

Blind Corner

This is Yates' first thriller: a tautly plotted page-turner featuring the tense, crime-busting adventures of suave Richard Chandos. Chandos is thrown out of Oxford for 'beating up some Communists', and on return from vacation in Biarritz he witnesses a murder.

Teaming up at his London club with friend Jonathan Mansel, a stratagem is devised to catch the killer. The novel has equally compelling sequels: *Blood Royal, An Eye For a Tooth, Fire Below* and *Perishable Goods*.

Blood Royal

At his chivalrous, rakish best in a story of mistaken identity, kidnapping, and old-world romance, Richard Chandos takes us on a romp through Europe in the company of a host of unforgettable characters. This fine thriller can be read alone or as part of a series with *Blind Corner, An Eye For a Tooth, Fire Below* and *Perishable Goods*.

DORNFORD YATES

AN EYE FOR A TOOTH

On the way home from Germany after having captured Axel the Red's treasure, dapper Jonathan Mansel happens upon a corpse in the road, that of an Englishman. There ensues a gripping tale of adventure and vengeance of a rather gentlemanly kind. On publication this novel was such a hit that it was reprinted six times in its first year, and assured Yates' huge popularity. A classic Richard Chandos thriller, which can be read alone or as part of a series including *Blind Corner, Blood Royal, Fire Below* and *Perishable Goods*.

FIRE BELOW

Richard Chandos makes a welcome return in this classic adventure story. Suave and decadent, he leads his friends into forbidden territory to rescue a kidnapped (and very attractive) young widow. Yates gives us a highly dramatic, almost operatic, plot and unforgettably vivid characters.

A tale in the traditional mould, and a companion novel to *Blind Corner, Blood Royal, Perishable Goods* and *An Eye For a Tooth*.

OTHER TITLES BY DORNFORD YATES AVAILABLE DIRECT
FROM HOUSE OF STRATUS

Quantity		£	$(US)	$(CAN)	€
☐	ADÈLE AND CO.	6.99	11.50	15.99	11.50
☐	AS BERRY AND I WERE SAYING	6.99	11.50	15.99	11.50
☐	B-BERRY AND I LOOK BACK	6.99	11.50	15.99	11.50
☐	BERRY AND CO.	6.99	11.50	15.99	11.50
☐	THE BERRY SCENE	6.99	11.50	15.99	11.50
☐	BLIND CORNER	6.99	11.50	15.99	11.50
☐	BLOOD ROYAL	6.99	11.50	15.99	11.50
☐	THE BROTHER OF DAPHNE	6.99	11.50	15.99	11.50
☐	COST PRICE	6.99	11.50	15.99	11.50
☐	THE COURTS OF IDLENESS	6.99	11.50	15.99	11.50
☐	AN EYE FOR A TOOTH	6.99	11.50	15.99	11.50
☐	FIRE BELOW	6.99	11.50	15.99	11.50
☐	GALE WARNING	6.99	11.50	15.99	11.50
☐	THE HOUSE THAT BERRY BUILT	6.99	11.50	15.99	11.50
☐	JONAH AND CO.	6.99	11.50	15.99	11.50
☐	NE'ER DO WELL	6.99	11.50	15.99	11.50
☐	PERISHABLE GOODS	6.99	11.50	15.99	11.50
☐	RED IN THE MORNING	6.99	11.50	15.99	11.50
☐	SHE FELL AMONG THIEVES	6.99	11.50	15.99	11.50
☐	SHE PAINTED HER FACE	6.99	11.50	15.99	11.50

ALL HOUSE OF STRATUS BOOKS ARE AVAILABLE FROM GOOD BOOKSHOPS
OR DIRECT FROM THE PUBLISHER:

Internet: www.houseofstratus.com including author interviews, reviews, features.

Email: sales@houseofstratus.com please quote author, title and credit card details.

Hotline: UK ONLY: 0800 169 1780, please quote author, title and credit card details.
INTERNATIONAL: +44 (0) 20 7494 6400, please quote author, title and credit card details.

Send to: House of Stratus Sales Department
24c Old Burlington Street
London
W1X 1RL
UK

Please allow for postage costs charged per order plus an amount per book as set out in the tables below:

	£(Sterling)	$(US)	$(CAN)	€(Euros)
Cost per order				
UK	2.00	3.00	4.50	3.30
Europe	3.00	4.50	6.75	5.00
North America	3.00	4.50	6.75	5.00
Rest of World	3.00	4.50	6.75	5.00
Additional cost per book				
UK	0.50	0.75	1.15	0.85
Europe	1.00	1.50	2.30	1.70
North America	2.00	3.00	4.60	3.40
Rest of World	2.50	3.75	5.75	4.25

PLEASE SEND CHEQUE, POSTAL ORDER (STERLING ONLY), EUROCHEQUE, OR INTERNATIONAL MONEY ORDER (PLEASE CIRCLE METHOD OF PAYMENT YOU WISH TO USE)
MAKE PAYABLE TO: STRATUS HOLDINGS plc

Cost of book(s): ____________ Example: 3 x books at £6.99 each: £20.97
Cost of order: ____________ Example: £2.00 (Delivery to UK address)
Additional cost per book: ____________ Example: 3 x £0.50: £1.50
Order total including postage: ____________ Example: £24.47

Please tick currency you wish to use and add total amount of order:

☐ £ (Sterling) ☐ $ (US) ☐ $ (CAN) ☐ € (EUROS)

VISA, MASTERCARD, SWITCH, AMEX, SOLO, JCB:

☐☐☐☐☐☐☐☐☐☐☐☐☐☐☐☐☐☐☐☐

Issue number (Switch only):

☐☐☐

Start Date:

☐☐/☐☐

Expiry Date:

☐☐/☐☐

Signature: ____________

NAME: ____________

ADDRESS: ____________

____

POSTCODE: ____________

Please allow 28 days for delivery.

Prices subject to change without notice.
Please tick box if you do not wish to receive any additional information. ☐

House of Stratus publishes many other titles in this genre; please check our website (**www.houseofstratus.com**) for more details.